THE FOX FAMILY CRIME SYNDICATE

hate ME

SUMMER O'TOOLE

ISBN: 9798370867767
Imprint: Independently published

Cover and paperback formatting by Acacia, Ever After Cover Design
Ebook chapter art by Valerie, Turning Pages Designs
Editing by Saxony Gray, Editing by Gray
Proofreading by Rachel at DarkbyDesign

You can't run from Fate,
especially if your Fate likes the chase.

Author's note

This book is a dark romance. There are many scenes of graphic violence and sexual content. The hero of this book is not a good man. There are several scenes involving non/dub-con (for a complete list of content included, please visit SummerOtoole.com/content).

This book will not be for everyone, and please for the love of God, if you know me in real life, don't read. But if you do, remember this is a work of fiction.

Dark romance is an incredible, beautiful, gritty way of storytelling that people enjoy for many different reasons. Reading and writing about something does not mean you condone it in real life. If that were true, Stephen King should have been locked up long ago.

Please also note that this is not meant to accurately represent safe sex or kink.

Playlist

Keep an eye out for footnotes to pair specific scenes to the songs that inspired them. I'd recommend playing the suggested song on repeat until the end of the chapter or ornamental break.

You can listen to the full playlist at SummerOtoole.com/Playlists

Speakers - Acoustic Mixtape—Sam Hunt

Fed Up—Ghostmane

Pull That Trigger—Tommee Profitt, Fleurie

Run My Mouth—Ella Mai

ALPHA—Layto

Bottom of the River—Delta Rae

Something to Someone—Dermot Kennedy

Houndin—Layto

Lost It All—Jill Andrews

you broke me first—Tate McRae

Fine—Kyle Hume

Tears of Gold—Faouzia

Something in the Orange—Zach Bryan

Darkest Hour—Andrea Russett

Hurts So Good—Astrid S

Love Is a Bitch—Two Feet

Insane—Post Malone

Villain—Julia Wolf

Hurt Me—Låpsley

Pray for Me—The Weeknd, Kendrick Lamar

i feel everything—Amelia Moore

Next—Shaker

I Chose Violence—iamjakehill

Mount Everest—Labrinth

E-GIRLS ARE RUINING MY LIFE—CORPSE, Savage Ga$p

Chills – Dark Version—Mickey Valen, Joey Myron

Dandelions – slowed + reverb—Ruth B., slater

you should see me in a crown—Billie Eilish

Prologue

Finn

My fingers tap on the worn leather of the old steering wheel fighting the urge to reach out and touch hers. The cab of the truck is dark, the headlights lighting up the country road ahead of us. Ranch fence lines zoom past in the sideview, the occasional yellow sign warning of deer crossings.

Effie rolls down her window, and the fresh smell of pine rushes in.[1] My stomach flips seeing her dark brown hair whip around her face in the wind. I turn up the volume on the staticky radio playing old school country to cover the sound of the open window. And my beating heart.

It jumps like a skipping stone in my chest. Sharp, staccato hops that leave you anxious and waiting for the drop.

Effie and I had known each other for years. We're only a couple years apart, and our fathers run in the same circles. Those circles being the rich and dirty criminal underworld. But it wasn't until we graduated high school a few years ago that we really started spending time together as more than

---

1 *Speakers* – Acoustic Mixtape—Sam Hunt | SummerOtoole.com/playlists

two crime bosses' kids. I had my brothers of course, but there was something freeing about spending time with another person who knew what it was like to wake up in the middle of the night to gunshots and eat breakfast to the smell of bleach the next morning.

She understood that I didn't break the cashier's nose because I wanted to, but because he disrespected me, and as a Fox, I can't let that happen without consequences. I glance down at my bruised knuckles wrapped around the wheel now and can almost feel the sting of the ice she held on them after as she cursed our fathers and their damn egos.

As if reading my mind she turns to me from the passenger seat, "How's your hand feeling?"

I flex my swollen fingers and take my eyes off the two lane road just long enough to meet hers. We're passing one of the few streetlights and the rusty glow makes her mahogany eyes shimmer like amber. My throat tightens. "Fine."

I may be imagining it, but I think I see her frown slightly at my short answer. It's not fine. My knuckles feel like they were run over by a steam roller. But it's not like I'm gonna say that out loud.

I spot a sign for Bartlett Farms. "We're almost there."

Bartlett Farms is a small, family-run berry farm. They have fields of strawberries and long hedges of blueberries and some other stuff I can't remember. The large, white farm house that we see as we pull into the dirt drive has a wraparound porch faintly glowing with old-fashioned gas lamps. The couple who lives here now is in their seventies and the white paint is chipping and curling off the wood siding, but the porch steps are always swept clean, and the flower baskets neatly pruned.

The Bartletts are proud and honest people, which is probably why my father chose them. They don't know I'm coming tonight—no one does—so when the truck crawls past the house to the back, a light flicks on upstairs. They must recognize my truck, and the light turns off within a few seconds.

"This looks more like a place you'd take a girl to murder her, not on a date," Effie muses as she looks up at the dilapidated barn we've parked in front of. I think she says something else, but I can't hear over the blood thumping in my ears.

A date? Fuck.

I mean, I'm not complaining. I've had a thing for her since we were seven fucking years old. Back then of course, I just thought she was the most beautiful girl I'd ever seen and wanted to hold her hand. But now, I can't deny the number of times I've jacked off in the shower to the thought of her soft skin, graceful curves, and bone-warming smile.

I never considered she might think of me the same way.

And that thought makes anxiety roil in my stomach.

Because I want it to be true. I want it more than anything I can ever remember wanting in my life.

I lead us through the overgrown grass behind the barn to the woods. There's enough moonlight filtering through the leaves to guide our feet. Still, Effie's foot snags on a root and she flies forward. Instinctively, I reach out and grab her around the waist before she breaks her fucking neck.

Her body is warm and soft, and I immediately notice how her chest rises and falls with heavy breaths. Her pretty pink lips part and I am frozen to the spot as she looks up at me through her lashes.

I could lean down and kiss her right now. I could. But I don't. Instead I drop my arm and continue ahead, "Just a bit further."

The rest of the way, Effie walks behind me instead of at my side so she can follow in my exact steps. We arrive at the lake without any other near-accidents. The trees part, and the foliage thins from rooty brush to thin, wiry weeds. The silvery water ripples faintly with the night air feathering above it.

Effie eyes the wooden dock stretched out in front of us skeptically, "That thing looks one gust of wind from falling down."

"It will be worth it." I swallow down the rising lump of nerves in my throat and hold out my hand. "Promise." She sets her hand in mine and butterflies erupt in my stomach. *Fuck.*

We walk out to the end of the dock. It does creak ominously with our steps, and it would be my fucking luck if this old dock chooses tonight to crumble. "Look down," I tell her.

I don't need to look. I already know what's down there. Instead, I watch her. Her brows rise and a sweet smile tugs on her lips. "That's beautiful," she says, eyes still taking in the web of water lilies floating on top of the water.

Big white blooms dot the water, the moonlight making them look ethereal, especially with cricket songs humming in the air and the gentle breeze. Effie spins and catches me staring. I want to look away, pretend I wasn't memorizing every feature and line of her face. But she steps closer, so close our chests almost touch.

My hand trembles as I slowly reach out and tuck a strand of hair behind her ear. She bites her lip when my fingers graze the shell of her ear. Without thinking, I take my thumb and pull her lip out from under her teeth. The air is thick and heavy. Our breaths are weighty as we stay locked in deep eye contact.

I swallow hard as my thumb slides down to her chin and I tilt her head up. My other hand cups her cheek, and she lightly places her hands on my waist.

I've never been so nervous in my life.

She rises on her tiptoes and our lips almost—

A sharp ring pierces the air. My pocket buzzes with my vibrating phone and the hypnotic moment shatters. She steps back at the same time I pull away and dig into my jeans. I realize it isn't a phone call, but a slew of text messages coming in one after the other making the text alert tone continue pinging like a call. Missed call notifications also come in.

They keep popping up again and again and I realize the time stamps go back an hour. I usually don't get service out here. My brother's caller ID pops up on the screen, and I answer.

"Where the fuck are you, Finneas?" Cash growls as soon as I answer. "I've been trying to reach you for a fucking hour!" I can't put my finger on it, but there's something off about his tone. He's an angry person, yelling is his default, but there's something anguished about the way he snarls.

"I just got service. What's going on?" I ask and Effie looks up at me with worried brows. She knows that an urgent call like this from family isn't likely a request to buy milk on my way home.

"Dad's been arrested—"

"What for?" I holler back.

"They're saying he shot Governor Albright."

"*What?*" My blood chills. Albright has been a longtime ally.

"Get your ass home. Now." My bruised hand aches with how tightly I'm gripping my phone. "And Finn?"

"Yeah?"

"Get home safe. There's a war coming."

Chapter 1:

Arrivals

Present

I didn't think my father would say yes to the *Les Arnaqueuses* solely because they're an all-women crew. Even if they've pulled off some of the biggest heists in modern history—a Monet from the Louvre, a collection of Faberge eggs from a Russian oligarch, an entire *wall* from a building in Bristol with a Banksy original—I could go on.

But then again, he loves any reason to fuck with the Foxes. So when the infamous crew reached out to him about the Fox cache and wanting a local backer, he didn't hesitate. And if the rumors of the worth of the Fox cache are true…well, I suppose he figured the potential payout was worth the risk.

What did surprise me, however, was the fact he wanted *me* to be the liaison. My brothers were deep in dealings with the New York families, so I expected him to have Bruno, his bruiser of a Capo, take lead. But of course his misogynistic ass didn't think a man could work with women without fucking them, so that left me.

"This job is too important to risk because a whore can't keep her legs closed."

I'm sure he is just as unhappy about it as I am.

I understand I have a role to fill, a duty to family, but I always figured that would be marrying whoever my father decided was most beneficial for the family. He's kept me out of almost all operation details, and I'm fine with that. Not that I am fine with him pawning me off like a dowry of cows, but I'm resigned to know my place, my worth.

I hear the jet before I see it. Jonathon hands me a pair of neon orange earmuffs. He almost comically fulfills his role as my security by dressing identically to the Secret Service. Black suit and tie, starch white shirt, night-black sunglasses and an earpiece. The jet breaks through the clouds and its nose lines up with the runway's yellow lines. I slide on the earmuffs and laugh to myself when Jonathon just clenches his jaw and makes his back rigid instead of putting on a pair himself. *Men.*

The small jet is the only plane in sight in the whole private airport. My father no doubt used his considerable resources to make sure no one would be here when the crew arrived. I wonder what would happen if the Foxes knew *Les Arnaqueuses* were in town. Would they know they were coming after them? My mind involuntarily recalls a warm summer night and the glowing petals of water lilies under the moonlight.

I swallow the knot in my throat and remind myself that was a long time ago. As the plane rolls to a stop and lowers the steps, I try to replace the memories from when my heart sang, with memories from when my heart screamed. My favorite cousin unrecognizable from the beating he took. Watching from a window as another soldier was curb stomped, hearing the horrible crushing sound three stories up.

That is who the Foxes are. Brutal. Ruthless. Heartless.

And Finneas Fox is the worst of them.

The bloodshed only stopped when a delicate and brittle ceasefire was agreed upon before the two families eradicated each other. Mutually assured destruction or survival.

I hate what they did, but I hate what we did too. Framing Finn's father,

Aiden Fox, for the murder of the governor, driving him to kill himself in prison. All of it sickens me.

I wasn't cut out for this life. I'm cold but not ruthless. I'm cold because I was never shown the warmth of love, except for that one summer—*No, forget about that, that Finn no longer exists.*

A woman steps out, her blonde hair slicked back in a tight bun, her midriff visible between a tight, cropped tank and cargo pants cinched at the ankles. With one scan of her athletic build, I'm sure she knows twenty different ways to kill me with her bare hands.

My father meets her at the bottom of the steps, shaking her hand as men take the designer duffel bags from her hands and put them in the trunk of a limo waiting on the tarmac.

The rest of the women follow and once everyone has deplaned, Jonathan and I walk over to the group. "My daughter, Euphemia," my father swipes his hand out as I step up to the circle of people. "She will be your point person and has already arranged your living arrangements."

"You can call me Effie." My father grinds his jaw, hating my nickname, but quickly turns his sleazy grin back on—always putting on a show.

The women introduce themselves. The one that looks like a mercenary is named Linnie and has only a slight French accent. A short-statured and lean woman with tanned skin introduces herself as Hadis, her dark brown eyes with flecks of gold flit over the surroundings, constantly surveying, reminding me of a hawk. The last woman, with short buzzed, dark hair and fair skin is Marguerite.

The drive to our home is passed with my father jabbering and the women politely laughing at his sexist jokes. Though I watch Linnie's knuckles whiten around her champagne glass, and I half expect it to explode. *I think I'm going to like her.*

My mother greets us and presents the dining table full of home cooked Italian food as if she made it herself. I doubt she even got out of bed thirty minutes before we arrived.

"You all must be starving after that flight, how long was it now?" my mother asks as she flits around the table to her seat at the opposing head from my father.

"Just shy of nine hours," Linnie responds, tucking in her chair and flapping her napkin onto her lap.

Once we are seated and begin eating, I notice my mother skeptically observing Marguerite's shaved head and can practically hear her in my head. "What would possess a beautiful woman to do that to herself? Must not be looking for a husband, that's for damn sure." And a healthy dose of cursing in Greek.

My mother and father's marriage was political, of course. The merging of the Luciano and Papadimitriou families. Though, I do think they've learned to love each other in their own way. Like how a spoiled child loves his favorite toy simply because it's his and no one else gets to have it. I grew up knowing my worth was my hand in marriage.

Marriage for love is for princesses in the fairytales, not princesses in the Mafia.

Finn

I check my watch again. They should be arriving any minute. I straighten my respirator and cross my ankle over my knee. The room is empty and dark, I am sitting in the only chair in the room. The only light is coming from the three monitors mounted above the door streaming three of the many cameras covering every inch of this old hotel.

It was decommissioned years ago because the whole thing is riddled with asbestos and when renovations were needed there was nothing to do but abandon it.

Now, it's my playground.[2]

A black, windowless van drives through an opening in the construction fence that surrounds the dilapidated property. One of my men in a ski mask

2. *Fed Up*—Ghostmane | SummerOtoole.com/playlists

drags the fence closed behind the van.

A subtle sort of adrenaline leaks into my bloodstream. It's not deafening, but heightening. The blue light emanating from the screens is crisper, the air behind the respirator fresher, and the need to hunt growing stronger.

I used to be consumed with my thirst for violence. After my father's suicide, I wanted nothing more than to feel the slick, warmth of fresh blood spilled on my hands. The desire—*need*—is still there, but it's quieter, more patient and calculating.

It seethes through my veins as I watch a man being pushed out of the back of the van, a black pillowcase over his head and his hands zip tied in front of him. He stumbles, crouched and shoulders curled, as he tries to brace himself in his new surroundings.

Calvin, my second, jumps out of the back of the van and rips the case off Martin's head. His usually neatly styled Ivy League cut is mussed, and I'm annoyed but amused when his first instinct is to raise his bound hands to fix his hair. *The pretentious fuck.*

Pretentious *and* stupid. We hired him as a fence for a parcel of diamonds and he swapped half of the stones with fakes, pocketing the real ones.

And sure, we could have roughed him—broken a few bones, retrieved the stones— and threatened him if he ever pulled another stunt like that while representing the Fox name. But I needed *more.*

I use my phone to remotely unlock a door that used to be a back service entrance. Calvin opens it and ushers Martin in, my eyes track the movements on the screens. All the doors and elevators in the hotel were set up with electronic locks for key cards. I've reprogrammed them so that I can control which doors open from the palm of my hand.

I see Calvin's lips move as he explains the game to him and the corner of my mouth curls watching fear sink into his eyes. Now, the fun can really begin.

The rules to the game are simple: *Run.*

He jumps back when Calvin pulls a switchblade, but he only cuts the zip ties. I see but can't hear Calvin say one more thing and then Martin is off, sprinting down the hall. The monitors above me change as the motion sensors on the cameras follow his path.

His white dress shirt is stuck to him, sweat making a dark spot down the middle of his back. He paces and pounds the elevator buttons, running a hand over his face waiting for an elevator that is never going to come. After another few seconds of waiting, he ditches the elevator and decides on the stairs.

I watch him scamper up the steps, trying each door at every landing, but I keep them locked. On the seventh floor, he kicks the door and wails, pounding his fists.

This is always my favorite part. When they start to crack, to break. They regress to a child throwing a tantrum when it finally sinks in that they aren't leaving these halls alive. Any composure goes out the window with the last of their hope.

The next time he slams his shoulder into the door, I unlock it and he tumbles to the floor, the door finally opening. He regains his footing and looks around frantically, trying to decide which way to run down the hallway of rooms. He doesn't know that he's merely a mouse in my maze. It doesn't matter which way he chooses because every route is a dead end until I decide it's not.

It's the control as much as—if not more—than the violence that I crave. Total and complete control over his destiny, helps settle the anxiety that is always trying to eat away at me.

He arrives on my floor, red-faced and out of breath, and my blood hums with his approach. He starts down the hall straight toward me. The door to the old suite I am in has been switched with a stairwell door.

When I can hear his footsteps outside, I switch off the monitors and stand. *Time's up.* My pulse races under my skin. I love watching them scurry, but I love the anticipation of waiting blind. My breath quickening with every footstep that draws closer.

I roll my head, cracking my neck, and slide gloves over my fingers. The letters tattooed across my knuckles disappear under the black leather. They spell out two short words: CAN'T HIDE.

*You can run but...*The door cracks open...*you can't hide.*

"Hello, Martin." His backlit frame freezes in the doorway. "I'm so glad you could make it."

My phone vibrates in my hand, and I look down at the picture I've waited all night to receive. There's a torrent of feelings, making my head hurt. *Fuck,* I wanted to draw this out, but now seeing my confirmation proved correct—her face staring back at me from my screen—my already-thin patience snaps.

The dark room lights up for one blinding second. The next second, Martin hits the ground, a bullet hole between his eyes.

Chapter 2:

Chance

Hadis spreads out the latest surveillance photos on the table in our shared apartment, and I have to steel myself to look him eye to eye. Again.

We've rented an apartment under a fake name in the building across from the *Fox's Den*. We know Cash lives in the penthouse apartment above their restaurant. In fact, they own the whole building. I was honestly surprised they didn't own this one we're now staying in too.

It may be Cash's apartment but in the three days we've been staked out, documenting everyone coming and going and establishing lines of sight through the windows, we haven't seen the eldest brother once.

Instead it's him. Finn.

I'm beginning to wonder if my father gave me this job just to torture me. If he did, it's working.

I've spent the last ten years trying my damnedest to avoid all things Finneas Fox. When the Fox family shows up in the newspaper, I turn the page. When I'm obligated to attend an event he might be at, I suddenly come down with the flu. And on the rare occasion I go out with friends, I ensure we never choose one of the many clubs and bars owned by them.

"We need to get inside. What we're looking for is inside. I'm sure of it." Linnie stands and palms the table, shuffling the photos around.

"They only ever have two guards at the front door…," Hadis muses.

Marguerite leans back in her chair, rocking onto the back legs, "What are you thinking?"

"But the entrance from the roof terrace has no security." Linnie nods approvingly at her implication.

"But how would you even get up there? The only way to get there is through the apartment which we've already determined is always guarded," I say, and they all look at each other with hints of a smile.

Linnie sits down and laughs, "Finding a way into places we shouldn't be able to, is quite literally our job description." *Right.*

My phone buzzes in my pocket and I pull it out.

Please be at Il Giardino *in 30. Your father wants an update. -Bruno*

It's an unknown number, but it's not uncommon for him to get a clean burner every few weeks.

I don't typically jump to orders from my father's lap dog, but I'm grateful for an excuse to get out of this conversation. Despite the amount of time that's passed and all the bloody events that have transpired between our families, this plot still feels like betrayal, and it doesn't sit well with me.

It's a direct, premeditated, and unprovoked attack. If we get caught, it will be a blatant breach of our truce and I shudder to think about what will happen in retribution.

The Foxes aren't known for second chances.

Opened before the urbanization of June Harbor, *Il Giardino* is one of the oldest restaurants in the city; it actually has a quarter acre garden in the back. To this day, they still use produce harvested from it and their outside seating is dispersed throughout the garden. So you can eat your Linguine alla

Puttanesca next to the plant that grew the very same tomatoes on your plate. In my rush to get out of the apartment, by the time I step out of the taxi, I am ten minutes early. From the sidewalk, I can almost imagine the place in its glory eighty years ago. Candles dot every red tablecloth-covered table, making the place glow without being too bright. The low, wooden rafters are exposed with a rustic charm and black and white vintage photos of Italy hang on the walls.

Maria waves to me from the hostess stand as I walk in. "Table for one tonight, Ef?" Despite the several other couples waiting for a table, Maria reaches for a menu to seat me right away. I can't deny there are some perks of being a Luciano—I don't think I've waited for a table once in my entire life.

"Two, my father is coming."

"Inside or outside?" she asks while weaving between tables, me following behind her.

"Outside, please." It's a gorgeous evening, the temperature is cool enough to be pleasant, but not so cold I need more than a light, long sleeve.

As she leads me under an arching trellis of green beans to an empty table, my feet stutter to a halt, my heart leaping into my throat. I have to fight the urge to flatten myself on the brick pavers and hide behind the raised garden bed. Because through the climbing poles wrapped in green vines, I see *him*.

Finn is sitting at a table by himself, eyes on a book in one hand while he takes a drag from a cigarette in the other. Despite being bombarded with pictures of him daily, I am not prepared for the pure feeling of suffocation I get seeing him in person.

Do I leave? Do I tell him to leave? My father is going to be here soon after all.

"Everything okay?" Maria's voice shakes me from my trance.

"Hmm? Oh yeah, this is great." I don't bother to give her a fake smile to be polite, plopping myself down at the table trying to catch my breath. Finn doesn't have any plates on his table, only an espresso cup and saucer, so maybe he is done eating and will leave before my father gets here. *Here's hoping.*

Maria leaves me and it's a good thing I know the menu by heart because I stare at it but can't read a damn word. I pick at the corner of the menu just to have something to occupy my shaking hands.

The garden is surrounded by a brick wall and our tables are placed just in front of it, at the end of the rows of raised beds. There are no other tables in our row and goosebumps run down my arms, being as alone with Finn as I've been in a decade.

I can feel his dark presence, like a cloud floating in front of the sun creating an instant chill. *Can he feel me like I feel him?*

The smell of cigarette smoke wafts over to me and instantly transports me back to the night we climbed out on the roof and shared a cigarette while I taught him the constellations. I've smelled cigarettes a thousand times since, but for some reason that is the one memory the scent is intrinsically tied to. It makes something sharp in my chest pang.

I try to shrink myself in my chair, but I can't look away. I'm entranced by the way his long neck bobs as he takes a sip and how the setting sun makes his cheekbones look chiseled and cutting. He flips a page, and his eyes flick up briefly and my heart nearly stops. Luckily he doesn't notice me, and I check the time anxiously wondering when the hell my father is getting here. If it wasn't a busy Friday night, I'd ask to move inside, but I already skipped a line of waiting guests.

A server comes out with a bottle of wine I didn't order. "Compliments to your family," he says and pours me a glass while I wait. I quickly empty it before pouring myself another. I jump when my phone pings with another text message.

Change of plans. He won't be coming.

Thank god. I finish the wine that's left in my glass before throwing my napkin in my seat and standing up to leave, thanking Mary, Joseph, and Jesus that I can leave before—

"Effie?" His voice is deeper than I remember but instantly recognizable.

I bite my cheek and consider running, but that would be suspicious as hell and I can't pretend that a small part of me wants nothing more than to sit down at his table and pretend like the last ten years never happened.

I turn slowly and hope the mock surprise I have pasted on my face is believable. "Oh my god, hi. I didn't see you there." *God, what a terrible line.* "Are you leaving?" he asks, ducking his head to get a clear line of sight through the web of beans.

"I was waiting for someone, but they canceled," I say quickly and spin around hoping he'll leave it at that.

"And you're really gonna let that *brunello di montalcino* go to waste because some asshole stood you up?" He nods to the half-drunk bottle on my table.

"Oh, no, I was waiting for—it wasn't a date." My cheeks burn.

"Good." He leans back and crosses his legs at the ankles and takes a slow drag of this cigarette and my skin lights on fire as he blatantly trails his eyes down, then back up my body.

"Good?"

"Join me." The corner of his mouth tilts up, and he nods to the empty chair at his table.

"I don't think that's a good idea. I should be going." I try to leave again. Keyword being try. I can't tell you why I don't ignore him and leave like I ought to.

"It's been a decade, Effie. Our families have been at peace for years, right?" I stare at him, not knowing what to say. Technically we are at peace for all he knows. Denying the truce would be suspicious, but joining him would be a risk too. Finn can read between the lines better than anyone I've ever met. He notices the tiniest details, and I am terrified I'll give something away.

"Please..." he looks down and swallows deeply. When he looks back up again, his eyes have a raw vulnerability to them that tugs on my heart and makes me wonder if maybe he missed me as much as I missed him. "Just one drink."

"Okay," I manage to squeak out. I wipe my sweaty palms on my jeans and grab the bottle of wine from my table.

The first thing he says when I sit down is, "God, I've missed you."

And I wonder how the hell I'm going to get through this night.

"I think we are the last people here." I look around the garden, now empty of all other diners and servers. It's been three hours since I sat down, and my cheeks hurt from smiling so much.

"I don't want to say goodbye." Finn's dark green eyes look at me earnestly, like he's begging this night to never end.

But it has to.

It's a cruel irony that we reconnect at the same time I'm planning a heist to rob him of his family's finest possessions.

My mouth hangs open, still trying to formulate my response when the string lights lining the brick walls turn off. I look at him guiltily. "I think that's our cue."

"Fair enough," he sighs, standing and coming around to my side of the table, holding out his hand.

I shouldn't take it. I should walk away right now. Tuck this night away as a memory to hold onto but nothing more. But it's so dark in the garden right now and maybe they forgot we are here, and maybe if I just reach out and take his hand right now in the night, it will be like it never happened in the morning.

I must take too long to decide because he tucks his hand into his pocket and gives me a weak smile. I stand and we start walking back through the rows of vegetables, passing orange squash blossoms and a bush of fragrant rosemary.

It feels so natural to slip my hand in the crook of his elbow and lightly grasp his bicep. I feel him tense slightly, but then he leans into me and I want to stop time. This night has been a gift I never expected, and I know as soon as we walk out of this restaurant, the illusion will shatter.

I don't even realize I've stopped walking until he pauses and faces me. He gently peels my hand off his arm and holds it in front of him, picking up my other. My breathing slows as he looks down at me. "I meant what I said. I don't want to say goodbye to you. Not again."

His thumb slowly rubs circles on the back of my hand. The motion is so small but jarring. It's too comforting, too soothing, and I can't let that happen. We may have a truce right now but for how much longer?

"It's really late, I have to go." I bite my tongue to hold back all the words I want to say and tug my hands away.

I brush past him, but his fingers wrap around my wrist, and he spins me back. He catches me with a hand on my hip. The breath is snatched from my lungs when his fingers that were around my wrist raise to trace the edge of my chin with a featherlight touch.

His fingers trail up my jaw and into my hair, "Come home with me."

"I can't—"

"I'm parked out back, no one will see us leave together."

"But—"

"I've waited ten years. I'm not waiting another minute." His grip in my hair tightens and he pulls me to him, crashing his lips down on me. I'm only frozen for a moment, and then I'm melting into him, fisting the collar of his shirt and breathing him in like he's the only pure oxygen in the air.

My mind empties of all thoughts but the feel of his mouth on mine. He tastes like the sweetest forbidden fruit, and I feel more drunk on him than the wine. I involuntarily whimper when he pulls away, immediately missing his touch like a drug. His voice is thick and raspy. "Yeah. You're coming home with me."

He bends down and then makes me scream as he wraps his arms around my thighs and throws me over his shoulder. "*Finneas!*"

He laughs. "I like that, already screaming my name."

I gasp, my cheeks burn, and I clamp my mouth shut.

We leave through a back gate instead of going through the restaurant, and Finn opens the door of his coupe with one hand, the other still wrapped around my thighs. He gently deposits me in the passenger seat, and I blush when he leans across me to buckle me in, the smell of his rich cologne wafting past me.

Finn drives like a bat out of hell, his hand never leaving my thigh. I'm grateful that he uses the private underground garage. The last thing I need in all this is for one of *Les Arnaqueuses* to see me and have word get back to my father.

Before I even have time to unbuckle, he's already opening the passenger door, sweeping out his palm. "After you, princess." *Princess.* That one word makes my stomach flutter more than anything else he's said tonight. I convinced him to drive me to get ice cream once by saying, "I'm the Luciano Princess," and he replied, "Well, who am I to deny a princess."

"I can't believe you remember that."

"I remember every second I've spent with you."

My stomach twists into knots at his words. The knot only grows into a bigger and tighter ball as we take the elevator to the top floor. It loosens a bit when he pushes me against the door to kiss me ravenously before letting us into Cash's apartment—the same one we've been surveilling for days. It drops into the pit of my stomach as we step into the apartment, and I listen to the click of the lock. Standing here now, I realize the gravity of the fucked-up-ness of this whole situation.

But then he's wrapping his arms around my waist from behind and kissing my neck, and I can't bring myself to resist. *Just one night*, I tell myself.

I roll my head to the side, giving him more access and as he sucks the sensitive skin between his lips, a moan slips out of mine. "*Fuck,*" his breath tickles my neck, "you don't know how long I've waited to hear that sweet sound." He groans and bites down on my earlobe and my knees nearly buckle.

His hands inch down my stomach and pinch the hem of my shirt, letting his knuckles graze the skin of my stomach. "Please let me see you, Ef." He tugs the hem higher, and my eyes latch onto the big window to our right. Through it I can see the window of our stakeout place and panic grips me.

I spin around. "Let's go to your room." Luckily the blinds are down now, but who knows the next time one of them is going to look out the window.

He smiles giddily, and it's such a beautiful, light expression on his usually darkened features. Sweeping up my hand he leads me down the hall and into a room. It's a small room with a four-post bed and minimal other furniture and decor—what you'd expect of a guest bedroom, but I don't let on that I know this isn't his place.

Like he can't wait a second longer, he rips my shirt over my head and his hands hungrily roam the bare expanse of my curves. He pauses almost as if he's awestruck, and I find myself wanting to cover myself, not deserving of his adoration. If only he knew what we were planning.

I move to cross my arms over my chest, but he pulls them away and pins them at my side. "Don't ever cover yourself in front of me. Not when you look like Aphrodite herself."

With my arms still pinned, he bends down to kiss my throat, my chest, and across the tops of my breasts. I suck in a breath with each brush of his lips. He straightens and dusts a kiss on my mouth, before kneeling. He continues to travel the length of my body with swipes of his lips and tongue.

His grip on my hands doesn't waiver, but the urge to hide lessens with each roll, curve, and freckle he kisses. His eyes lock on mine as he teases the delicate skin above my waistband with his tongue making me shiver. "Every part of you is going to belong to me by the end of the night," he whispers into my flesh and begins to undo my jeans with his teeth.

Fuck if I've ever seen anything hotter than this man on his knees for me.

Releasing my arms, he pulls my jeans over my hips and down my thighs until I'm left in nothing but a black, lace bralette and matching panties.

He stands, fisting my hair and tipping my head back. Forcing my gaze up, I notice two eye hooks screwed into the canopy rail above the base of the bed. Finn's lips graze my ear as he whispers, "Ever been tied up, princess?"

"No," I breathe, my skin lighting on fire and a pulse beating between my legs. I've had boyfriends in the past, but no matter how much I initiated, none of them were even a modicum as rough as I wanted. They were probably all too scared of my father to leave bruises. Funny, since my father had no problem leaving them.

It's not lost on me that this might be my one chance to experience something I've craved, to be at the mercy of a man not under my father's thumb, and who can give me what I truly want. And if this one night is all I will get with Finn…then how could I say no?

Finn traces his bottom lip with his tongue, a wicked gleam in his eyes. "Good. Now stay right here." I stand unflinchingly still—save the rise and fall of my chest as my heart hammers under it— as he goes to a dresser and pulls out two coils of silken cord and something else small and white that I can't get a good look at.

He walks back to me, stopping to rake his gaze down my exposed figure. "Hands out." His voice is colder, more commanding, but still burning with lust and something else I can't quite put my finger on. Whatever it is, it makes my insides feel like molten heat.

The rational part of me wants to question what the hell am I doing? Letting a man I haven't spoken to in ten years tie me up, practically naked? But despite those ten years and all the boyfriends in between, I never, not once, felt a closeness with any of them like I feel with Finn. I could be holding onto an idyllic memory, to a teenage love that ended before it could even begin. Or Finneas Fox could really be the one man I've ever felt safe with.

[3]He methodically ties each wrist with some fancy knot that is tight yet comfortable. I get a pang of something bitter realizing, the ease with which he's using the rope means he's done this before…many times before.

He gently spins me by the hips to face the bed and then ties the end of each rope to one of the hooks above us. My heart beats erratically sensing him behind me but lacking his touch, wondering what he will do next and being so eager my inner thighs feel slick.

"You're so beautiful like this," I shudder at the finger he trails down my spine as he speaks, "You're gonna look even more gorgeous with your ass turned bright red—" *Smack!*

I cry out in shock, but it's instantly followed by a soft whimper for more.

"You liked that, hmm?" His voice is so low I barely hear it, like a whisper from a ghost. I hear footsteps and turn my head as much as I can to see him pull something else out of the dresser.

He catches me looking and shakes his head. I fix my eyes straight ahead

---

3   Pull That Trigger—Tommee Profitt, Fleurie | SummerOtoole. com/playlists

again, a slight thrill shooting through me at the idea of doing something *bad*. I feel him behind me again and then the cool, flat touch of something on my thigh.

I look down and see him drag a black, leather paddle up my leg. My heart thuds in anticipation. Tantalizingly slow, he brings to my hip and then caresses the round of my ass.

"I have one question before we begin—"

"What's my safe word?" I guess.

"No." His voice is shockingly cold, detached and starkly different to the tone he's used all night and dread sinks into me. "What the fuck are you and those French bitches planning?"

Chapter 3:

All is Fair

Effie

⁴"Do you really think I don't keep track of every single person who moves within a mile radius of us? Let alone right across the street? Come on, Ef, I know you're smarter than that." His voice is like ice dripping down my spine and moments from the night trickle through my mind.

The fact that he was dining at an Italian restaurant known to be a favorite of our family.

He was parked discreetly out back and there were no guards when we arrived at the apartment.

The texts from an unknown number, conveniently placed me at a table alone next to him.

Please be at Il Giardino *in 30. Your father wants an update.*

I don't think Bruno has ever said please in his life. And he always refers to my father as *he*. We all know which *he* he is talking about.

"The texts. That was you?" *How could I be so fucking easy?*

"Now, you're catching on," he mocks, and I yank on the ropes, trying to twist around, they remain taut, and steam rises in my chest.

Anger boils in me. *Played. I've been fucking played.*

"You said it yourself, Finn, I am a goddamn Mafia princess. If my father finds out you have broken the peace and have me fucking chained up, he will rain hell down on you." I seethe over my shoulder, irritated I can't look at him face to face.

"What peace, *princess?*" He tilts my chin further back with the tip of the paddle. "Any false pretense of peace was broken the moment you brought *Les Arnaqueuses* into my fucking territory."

He drops the paddle and tugs my head back by my hair. My eyes sting from the pressure on my scalp. "Now tell me, what are you planning?" he demands, and my body jolts as he brings the paddle down hard on my ass.

"*Nothing,*" I growl back, grinding my teeth together anticipating another stinging blow.

When it indeed comes, I huff out through my nose but keep my lips pressed tight together. I'm far too used to taking punishment without giving bastards the pleasure of my screams.

Finn grunts dissatisfied at my silence and spanks me again harder, the burn making me madder…and *wetter.* And I think I hate him the most for that.

Another spank resounds in the room, and I squeeze my eyes shut, focusing on the rage turning red behind my eyelids. I feel his breath against my neck, and then he drawls roughly, "If you won't tell me what you're planning, then at least be a good girl and *count.*"

Another blow and I squeeze my thighs together, the impact making my clit throb. He bends down again, and I feel his tongue lick my beading sweat in a path up the back of my neck and says into my ear, "Four."

"No." I bite out.

Smack.

"Five." I recognize a devilish glee in his voice now, and I realize that the soft, vulnerable Finn from earlier was never real. He isn't soft or kind or sweet.

He's a fucking sadist.

"If you think you can beat the answer out of me, we're both going to be in for a long night." Physical pain can be tuned out. And I'm so good at exactly that.

He chuckles darkly and then I hear a buzzing sound. "Oh, princess, this isn't about pain…" He dips under my arm and stands in front of me. My breathing becomes choppy as he trails a vibrator between my breasts and down my stomach. "…It's about pleasure."

He runs the buzzing toy across the most sensitive part of my lower stomach, right above my waist band. My abs constrict and I try to curve away from him, praying he doesn't go any further. "You've made your fucking point, Finn."

"Think about how good I'll make it for you…" he trails off as if he didn't even hear me, even though there's no other sound than our breathing, a distant foghorn, and that goddamn incessant buzzing. Dragging the toy lower to my inner thigh, he teases it up and down the sensitive skin but never quite all the way up. "So good, you'll hate yourself for how much you enjoy it."

"The only one I hate right now is you." I take the opportunity while he's looking down to use my limited mobility and headbutt him in the face.

"*Fucking hell,*" he snarls, checking for blood with the back of his hand. Unfortunately, his nose isn't bleeding. "I was going to be nice—"

"I hope it's fucking broken, you piece of shit," I spit, ignoring the throbbing in my head from the blow.

"You wanna play dirty? Then let's *play.*" His eyes are dark and unreachable as they bore into me, shoving the buzzing toy into my panties.

"No, *no.* Finn, please, don't."

I attempt to knee him in the groin, but he catches my leg instantly and laughs unimpressed. I try to wriggle my calf out of his grip but it's useless, he just pulls my knee out to the side and looks down at my bare thigh like he wants to take a bite out of it. For a second, I think he might.

He crowds me, hooking my leg around his hip so I'm forced to embrace him. I huff, trying to lean farther away but he holds me tight. His lips nearly brush mine as he says, "You know how to make it stop."

And then he's cupping between my legs, pressing the vibrator tight against my sex and the pleasure is instant and blinding.

I want to cry out in tortured rapture, my body responding so fiercely to the toy, the ropes—fucking hell, to *him.* But I don't want to give him this.

Not like this. So I bite my tongue and squeeze my eyes shut, trying to block out the feelings and not make a sound.

I don't realize I'm crying until he wipes a tear from my cheek with his thumb and then he brushes it across my gasping lips.

I hate him. I hate him. I hate him. I want him. I need him.

He gives me a wicked smirk before returning to my backside and lashing my burning cheeks again with the paddle, the toy still vibrating against my clit in my panties.

"*Oh, Go—*" I bite back a moan, my cries getting harder and harder to contain. Another hit of the paddle and the mixture of pleasure and pain has me riding fast and hard to my climax. I hate the sounds I'm giving him so freely, yet against my will. I bite my lip in an attempt to not give him anymore.

He hits me once more, the fiery sting melting through my core, and then he encircles my waist and palms my stomach, inching his fingers lower and lower until he's applying pressure again on the toy. I shatter painfully. "That's it. Come hard for me, princess. Tell me how good it hurts."

"Fuck you, Finn," I pant, trying to catch my breath as my orgasm subsides but barely, the vibrator still pulsing against my swollen clit.

"You can make it stop anytime," he taunts.

He continues a rhythm of spanks then pressing the vibrator harder against me, over and over again until I'm struggling for air as another orgasm builds. I'm still so sensitive, never getting a reprieve from the last one, and I moan involuntarily.

"Look at you, such a desperate little plaything." He caresses the side of my hip, and I realize I've been rolling my pelvis forward, searching out the relief I hate to *need.* Then before I know what's happening, he's ripping the toy away and clutching my throat in his hand. I feel a whiplash of sorrow that the sensation is gone, wanting it back but also happy relief that it's over.

"What. Are. You. Planning?" He tightens his grip on my neck, pinching the sides of my throat with each word, the restricted blood flow almost instantly making my head swim.

"Go to hell," I croak out.

He huffs indignantly and releases my neck, the black dots swarming my vision dissipate. "I *will* break you. "

And then the torture—because that's what this is—begins again. He alternates impact and toy play until every muscle in my body is strung so tight it hurts, every inch of skin is blazing, and every thought in my mind is consumed with rage-fueled desire.

"Are you close, princess? I know you are." He slips the toy back in, and my whole body convulses on contact. He drags the paddle down the back of my thighs and my knees. "Your legs are shaking. In fact, your whole body is trembling." He's right of course, my knees wobble and I'd collapse if it wasn't for the ropes keeping me up.

I suck in a heavy breath when he tugs my hips back, pulling me onto my tiptoes and slinks a hand down the back of my panties. I hiss as his fingers slide down the curve of my ass and between my legs. I try to thrust myself out of his reach, but he only holds me tighter.

"Don't fucking touch me there, Finn. If you do this, I will hate you forever."

"Mmm…" he moans, and I can hear my own wetness as he rubs over my pussy. "You'd be much more convincing if you weren't so fucking soaked."

He lifts my hips even higher and presses two fingers at my entrance. "Finn…" My throat is dry and raspy, and even I can't deny it sounds like a plea, not warning.

"Quiet now, Ef." He thrusts the fingers deep inside my hot, wanting cunt. "And fucking take it." He drives them in and out of me, my body tenses as another godforsaken orgasm builds, the vibrator making my clit throb until I'm teetering on the edge.

"Oh god, oh god—*Fuck, Fi—.* " He curls against my g-spot, and I cut myself off, refusing to say his name with any ounce of pleasure. He uses his other hand to hold my throat. I can sense his fingers itching to squeeze until I black out. A cry gets tangled up in my throat, bliss begins to bloom in all the right places—but then he slows his movements, draws his fingers so painfully slow, in and out.

I whimper, delirious with this incandescent need. "Don't—Stop—

Don't—Stop."

He chuckles dryly behind me, "Are you telling me: Don't. Stop. Or is my needy, plaything begging me not to stop."

"Goddamn you, Finn," I sob. "*Please*. Please don't fucking stop." I feel myself break like a crack in an icy lake. Brittle. Cold. Irreversible.

He begins to pump his fingers faster and firmer again. "Then tell me what I want to know."

"No—"

"I am not bluffing, Effie. I will tease you until you are nothing but a dripping mess, then I will leave you. Bound. Alone. Wanting."

I can hardly focus on his words when my body shakes with the need for release and he plays my body like a well-rehearsed instrument.

"I know how desperately you need to come. I can feel your cunt strangling my fingers. And I can give it to you. I *will* give it to you, if you just tell me what you're up to." My toes that are barely touching the floor curl and sharp pangs start to spark in my core. "What will it be, Effie? Are you going to be left wet and needy, or are you going to drench my fingers as I make you come?"

My breath pounds in and out of my lungs, my grip on reality slipping, my mind clouding. I can't even find the words to respond.

"What—" *Smack.* "Will—" he strikes again with the paddle. "It—" *Fuck, it burns so good.* "Be?" The next hit sends a jolt of pleasure radiating to my clit; I cry out.

"*We're going after your cache!*" And then I'm toppling over the edge, spiraling in aching euphoria.

My entire body shakes, the ropes swaying as my climax rips through me, the summation of so many competing sensations.

"That wasn't so hard, was it?" Finn spits as he swiftly flicks a switchblade and cuts the ropes keeping me upright. I groan as my body gives out and I tumble to the floor.

He crouches down in front of me, and I'm suddenly struck by the contrast of him being fully clothed while I'm lying in a near-naked heap. "I promised you earlier that I would break you. That every part of you would belong to me by the end of the night. Well, the end is here, and I fucking *own* you. Continue on with whatever you're scheming, but you report back to me. *Everything*. Got it?" He snarls, his lip curled and his eyes too fucking cold, I wonder who the hell this beast in front of me is.

Before I even have a chance to agree or disagree, he's up and gone, slamming the door in his wake. And with it any potential for a future happiness the beginning of the night let me foolishly believe was possible.

Chapter 4:

In Love and War

Finn

"Hot coffee. Leave room for milk." I pass a ten-dollar bill over to the barista and walk to the other side of the counter, waving her off when she asks about my change. A teenager looking down on his phone bumps into me, and I have to weave to avoid him spilling his caramel-frapa-latte-shit on me. God, I fucking hate people. *Why didn't I just make coffee at Cash's apartment?* I'm only one week into my stay, and shit's already hitting the fan. He wanted me to be here to keep an eye on things while he and Harlow are away for a month long fuck-a-thon on some tropical island.

Thankfully, it doesn't take long to pour a cup of coffee, and I'm out of there quickly. I cross the street to the *Fox's Den*, using my key to let myself in since it doesn't open for another few hours. Perks of owning a pub is never having a shortage of access to alcohol, even if it is before eight a.m.

I didn't sleep last night after I had Calvin walk Effie home. From the window, I watched them cross the street from our building to hers, trying to make myself feel an ounce of glee for the walk of shame she deserved, but instead I only felt shame toward myself.

I'm telling myself I didn't sleep because I didn't finish. Fuck, just thinking about how her tight, *dripping* pussy felt on my fingers has my dick swelling. I walk straight to the bar and find the whiskey, adding a healthy pour to my coffee. Like that will somehow stop every inch of my body feeling like it got mauled by fire ants.

She loved the pain, got so fucking wet every time I—

Fuck it.

I storm to the back office and login to our secure server on the computer. A few clicks and I'm looking at Effie tied up, crying, and so damn needy. *What a perfect little plaything.*

I press play on the video recorded by a hidden camera in the room's crown molding, tugging the waistband of my joggers down and fisting my dick. I can't help but suck in a breath, licking my bottom lip when I fast forward to right before I add the vibrator into the mix.

I watch her try to knee me in the balls, remembering the zip of fire that lit up my spine at the fight in her. *And how badly I wanted to fuck it out of her.*

But I couldn't. Last night wasn't about getting off. It was about power and control.

And showing Effie that I possess both in spades.

No matter how much time has passed, no matter what silly, little crush we may have once shared, I will not hesitate to make it hurt.

I stroke my cock, having no trouble getting hard watching her try to rear away from me, but I never let her get more than an inch away from my face. I groan, remembering the feel of her hot breath across my face as she seethed.

Christ, she was a goddamn vixen, getting so angry with herself for enjoying it. Just like I knew she would.

I don't think many people know Effie. I don't think she lets many people know her, not the real her. She has a good, kind heart—something I may have once sympathized with, not anymore—but it's been crowded out by all the ugliness around her. She makes herself small to avoid the attention and thus ire from her father and men like him. Like *me.*

But that's a survival mechanism, not who she truly is. Who she truly is, is a fighter. She wants to fight back, be broken down, and then have someone care enough to pick up the pieces.

Maybe one day, I can be the kind of person who picks up another person's pieces.

But not until I find out exactly what *Les Arnaqueuses* are planning and make them regret they ever whispered the name Fox.

I shake my head and bring my attention back to the screen, focusing on the graceful muscles of her neck as I pull her hair back and *goddamn,* does her neck look good with my hand around it.

She tells me to go to hell, and I stroke faster, harder, conjuring the feel of her pulse thumping beneath my fingers. Beautiful, delicate, but *weak.*

I rub my thumb over the tip of my cock, my balls drawing tighter the longer I watch her take it until her legs are trembling. She was trying so hard not to come, trying so hard not to give in, trying so hard to make me think she hated what I was doing to her. But then...

I watch myself slide my hand down the back of her panties and suck in a breath, my dick throbbing. She fucking *loved* it.

I throw my head back in the desk chair and squeeze my eyes shut, turning up the volume on the video. I pump my hand up and down my cock as I listen to her beg me not to stop.

Don't stop. Don't stop. Don't stop.

I grind my teeth as tension builds in my groin, my balls heavy for release.

"Goddamn you, Finn. Please. Please don't fucking stop."

Her pleas are the strongest aphrodisiac. I grunt like an animal as I thrust into my fist and come hard to the sound of her breaking.

I grab a tissue off the desk to clean myself up, and like an addict, already craving my next fix before I've even come down from the last, I pull out my burner and text her.

I'm sitting at one of our bistro tables outside the Den, my finger tapping on the table while I stare up at Effie's apartment. The angle isn't great, I can only see if someone steps right up to the window. But I don't give two shits if I can see them. I want them to see *me.*

I light a cigarette and balance it between my lips while I send another text.

I'm waiting, princess.

And then immediately another one:

I bet you're sore. Did I leave any marks? Step up to the window and let me see.

I snicker to myself imagining how riled up she'll be reading my message. Just like I hoped, that last text gets her to respond.

Effie: Why the hell would I do that?

Me: Why the hell not? I thought we had fun last night.

Effie: I'm not your fucking puppet, Finn. And I sure as hell am not your "plaything."

Me: You sure about that? Because it certainly looks that way.

Then I send her freeze frames from last night. Us kissing against the door, her hands tangled in my hair, hungry for everything I'm giving her. Me kneeling in front of her, stripping her pants off. Then to really make it clear that I own her, I send an audio clip I snipped earlier: *Please. Please don't fucking stop.*

I don't expect a response. Instead I look up at the window. When I see a face peek through the blinds, I wave with a charming smile just to piss her off.

Five minutes later, she's crossing the street with a murderous look on her face. Her dark brown hair is hanging like curtains on either side of her face under a baseball cap. As she approaches, I pull out a chair for her, but she just brushes past me to the pub door. "Inside. Now."

She may be stupid enough to move in across the street from me, but she isn't stupid enough to sit outside in broad daylight with me. Nonetheless, I take my time putting out my cigarette and strolling over to the door, enjoying how she looks around flustered the longer I draw out the short walk.

"You're gonna get me killed, asshole," she whisper-yells when I finally let us in.

She badgers me with questions as I walk to the back bar. *What do you want? Do you know how much I hate you? You think you can blackmail a*

Luciano? I ignore them all, only speaking once she sits down at a bar stool next to me.

"You look tired. Something keep you up last night?"

"Fuck you." She spits and I get a swooping in my stomach when I catch a slight wobble in her voice. *She brought this on herself. She did this to herself.* I remind myself and shove any shred of sympathy deep down.

"Drink?" I stand up and circle the bar and pour myself a whiskey.

"What do you want, Finn?" *You. Tied up. In my bed. Bent over this goddamn bar. Any which way, as long as my cock is deep inside you.*

"What do you know about the cache?"

"Isn't it a little early to be drinking?"

I set the glass on the counter with a thump and rest my elbows on the bar. "Answer another one of my questions with a question and—"

"*And what, Finn?*" She stands up, kicking away the stool. "And *what?* You'll chain me up? Beat me? You already fucking tried that." Red blooms up her chest and into her cheeks.

My lip curls. "It worked, didn't it? You're here, aren't you?" She huffs and crosses her arms, looking defiant and oh so fuckable.

"You're here because you know just how *interesting* your father would find those photos. So, sit the fuck down before I make you." She scowls but obeys. I step back and lean against the back bar, letting her stew uncomfortably in the silence until she answers my question.

"Not much. We know the rumors that everyone knows: that your family has a stash somewhere of all the stolen art, jewelry, gold, artifacts, et cetera, that you've acquired over the years. Your 'hidden treasure.'" She rolls her eyes, but that is exactly what it is. It's a trove of hundreds of millions of dollars' worth of stolen and legally obtained goods.

It's our family's safety net, four generations in the making. Bank assets can be seized or frozen. Hustles come and go and require exactly that: constant hustle to be profitable. One day, whether it be in a year or a hundred years, if we ever want to leave the game, we can.

"So that's it? You're starting a war—*another* war—over some fucking rumors?"

"It wasn't my idea." She looks down and I can't help myself. I close the gap between us and tip her chin back up with two fingers.

There's a desperation in her deep, amber eyes, almost like an apology. My eyes shift down to her mouth and my jaw clenches with the urge to push my thumb inside her full, pink lips.

"What would you do if I kissed you right now?" The question is out of my mouth before I can think to stop it.

She swats my hand away from her. "I'd bite your fucking lip off."

I laugh, getting hard at the idea of her being rough back. "How do you plan on finding out more than just rumors?"

"Break into your brother's apartment." Her lips tip up into a smirk, "It's your security headquarters after all." I keep my expression exactly the same, seeing her statement for what it is: she's fishing. She just doesn't know how right she is. Inside Cash's apartment is a double reinforced steel room called the Vault. It has every piece of data, security footage, and intel we've gathered over the years.

"Well, if breaking into the most secure place in this city is your big plan, then I'm not too concerned." Her eyes flare as if she's offended that I am unimpressed with the big reveal.

"We know how we're going to do it." She straightens on the stool and juts her chin out.

"Oh, really? Care to share, princess?" She bites her lip when I call her that and the small movement is like a live wire straight to my dick.

"Hmm." She makes an exaggerated face like she's pondering the question. "No, actually I won't be sharing. Have a good day, Finneas." She pushes off the stool.

"If that's your decision, then tell your father I'll be in touch." I shout after her, my eyes glued to her ass and her soft, long hair swaying above it.

She flips me off over her shoulder in response, and I let out a dark laugh. *She's calling my bluff...*

Well, this is about to get much more fun.

Chapter 5:

Run Your Mouth

Effie

"Are you sure you want to wear your hair down?" My mother passive aggressively twirls a lock of my hair, and I grip the leather seat of the limousine.

"Yes, I'm sure." I try to hide the irritation in my voice, but apparently not well enough.

"Okay, no need for the attitude." She scoffs and tips back her champagne flute, finishing it off. "I was just saying, because I know how your hair tends to get limp after a few hours."

Maybe I'll shave my head like Marguerite. "Thanks, Mom. I'll keep that in mind for the next charity event for blind wombats. Or is it endangered giant snails?"

"Don't be smart, this gala is a fundraiser for the Harbor Island Resort and Golf club's new equestrian center." Incapable of ending a sentence without some backhanded compliment she adds, "You have such a lovely tan, but that shade of brown makes you look jaundiced."

I actually quite like my dress and look damn good too. The corset-style bodice hugs my waist and lifts my tits without restricting my breathing, while the soft, draping sleeves hang off my shoulders. The skirt hangs perfectly around my hips and ass and opens in a dramatic slit, revealing just enough of my thigh to tease but not enough that my mom starts calling me a slut in three different languages.

And the light-mocha satin does *not* make me look jaundiced.

"Hudson will be there tonight," my father chimes in. I know he's speaking to me even though he sips his scotch while looking out the window.

"Who is Hudson?" I ask, and his head swivels to level me with a look like he's trying to tell if I'm joking. I'm not, but apparently my mother thinks something's funny as she titters into her glass.

"Hudson Campbell. Governor Campbell's son and—"

"And your future fiancé," my mother spills, and my father cuts her a glare. I, on the other hand, feel like a bucket of ice water was just dumped on my head.

My father straightens his bow tie and turns to me. "For the family." That's all the explanation I get. I guess I always knew this day was coming sooner or later.

I feel my mask slipping into place, my dutiful daughter mask, my easy pawn mask, my "it's easier to comply" mask. Like Tetris, I compartmentalize away my identity, personality and only leave what's acceptable for this world.

"Is he proposing tonight?" I didn't plan on getting engaged today, but I can't help the petty voice in my mind that whispers how much my mother would hate photos of me in my jaundice-inducing dress and limp hair splashed all over the society pages.

"No, but this will be a good time to start teasing your relationship to the public."

"What relationship," I scoff under my breath. Turning back to my father, I ask, "Does he know about this, or will he be just as blindsided as me?"

"He's been involved in the negotiations." *Of course, because who I marry is a business deal.* Always has been, just never knew who would be the one to close it.

"Did you even consider having me join these *negotiations?* It's not like it's my life being bartered off. "

"Euphemia, calm down. It's not like you didn't know this was coming. You're almost *thirty* for heaven's sake."

The rest of the ride is quiet, the air in the limo is thin, like the life is being sucked out of it the closer we get to the museum hosting the event. Our driver pulls into the queue of cars and my hand starts sweating around my clutch watching the flash of cameras a few cars ahead.

We crawl to the front of the line and my mother pokes a finger at the window. "Oh look, there he is. Isn't he handsome?"

I recognize the governor immediately. Governor Campbell is a prototype for rich, white politicians. Average height, decently fit for someone in their sixties and graying sophisticatedly. Looks like the kind of person who spends three hundred dollars on lunch and then tips the server with a twenty-dollar bill.

It's easy to tell who his sons are. They look like younger, stronger, versions of him. My eyes bounce between the two of them and wonder with surprising detachment which one is going to be my future husband and the father of my kids.

The car door opens. My father steps out first, then helps me and my mother out. I smile sweetly, keeping my focus blurry so I'm not blinded by the flashing lights and end up squinting in every photo. I know the drill. *Smile, stand tall and—*

I look up, startled by a tug on my hand. One of the governor's sons takes my hand and places it on his arm and leads me forward up the museum steps. "I'm Hudson," he subtly dips to whisper.

I speak out of the corner of my mouth, keeping my smile soft for photographers, "Effie. But you must already know that."

Turns out that enduring a dinner of dry chicken and overcooked carrots, followed by speeches on the intersection of golf and dressage, is actually much easier in Hudson's company. He has a dry sense of humor but a lightness to him that is refreshing. He has that sweet all-American charm that isn't intimidating and has been nothing but respectful all night. Almost making me forget that all of this is a pre-arranged destiny.

I sour at the thought. Will I ever have something good and true? Or will everything always be constructed and form-fit into what best serves the family?

As if Hudson can sense my shift in mood, he sweeps his auburn hair back with a hand and rests his arm over the back of my chair. "Listen, I know our families are who they are, but that doesn't mean we have to rush into anything." He lowers his hand onto mine resting on the table.

"I want to take things slow, get to know each other." He laughs. "You know, actually date the person I'm going to marry."

My chest squeezes, realizing how real this is quickly becoming. I try to blow off the serious tone. "Oh, so we're not meeting at the chapel tomorrow morning?"

"If only I'd be so lucky. You're drop dead gorgeous, Effie." His warm blue eyes melt into mine, and I feel he's being truly genuine. Maybe he really is just a good guy in a bad world.

"How about we start with a dance? Then we can talk about whether you prefer a spring or autumn wedding." He nods to the speaker podium that has been replaced by a DJ booth, and the people starting to trickle on to the dance floor.

I take his proffered hand, catching our fathers give one another approving looks. He sweeps me close to his body, and I'm surprised how comfortable it feels. We're still an appropriate distance, but I can feel his body heat and smell is masculine aftershave.

He twirls me around and I giggle, feeling light and...*happy*. "How about we just elope on some tropical island?" I tease when he catches me again.

He laughs and dips me low. "You know our families would kill us both if they didn't get to choreograph our wedding for the most political gain."

The smart aleck reply on the tip of my tongue is shut down when I lock eyes with someone across the room. Dark, dangerous and green eyes I'd recognize anywhere.

Finn's leaning against a back wall, dressed handsomely in a classic tux, his dark hair is combed smartly out of his face, showing off the sharp angles of his cheeks and jaw. I can make out his knuckle tattoos while he takes a sip from a whiskey glass. *Can't hide.*

It certainly feels that way. Especially as his gaze locks with mine, tracking every movement I make. He smirks, eyes dark, and spite flares inside me. I drape an arm around Hudson's neck and pull him closer, watching Finn over his shoulder. Hudson reacts warmly of course, placing a hand on my waist and swaying to the music.

Finn's jaw clenches and his lips press into a firm line as I whisper in Hudson's ear, keeping my eyes fixed on his. I'm only saying I like the song, but with the sultry look I'm sporting, I hope Finn thinks it's something much more scandalous.

He tips back his drink and finishes it, slamming the cup down on a table beside him. It's a thrill, goading him. And I don't plan on stopping.

I feel Hudson's hand slink to the small of my back, and I rotate us so Finn can catch the movement. His hand dips lower over the top of my ass. Heat licks my spine, and I know it's Finn's gaze burning into my back. *Let him burn.*

"I'm going to get a drink. Would you like anything?" he pulls away and asks.

"No, I'm good, thank you." We step off the dance floor, and he heads toward the bar. I look around but don't see Finn. I try not to inspect too closely at the wave of disappointment I feel at his absence.

Hudson shoots me a small wave from the bar while he waits. He smiles, and I scan his face looking for a hint of…something, I'm not sure what. He has a strong jawline and a sweet dimple on one side. He's clean cut and good looking but not playboy handsome. Many women would be delighted to have a husband like him.

"Princess," I hear roughly behind me and spin, coming face to face with Finn. The second I do, I realize what I was looking for in Hudson: darkness, hunger, ruthlessness. And I see them all staring back at me now.

"The fuck do you want?" I hiss as I see Hudson leaving the bar, drinks in hand. He only looks at me smugly and tongues his cheek. *I hate him.*

He ignores me and holds out his hand to Hudson who's just walked up. "Hi, I'm Finn—"

"Finneas Fox. Yes, I know who you are."

"Oh? And you are?" My jaw drops at his flippant reply knowing he damn well knows the answer.

"Hudson Campbell." His previous friendly tone is gone. "So, how do you know my fiancée?" I swallow deeply, stunned. So much for taking things slow. If I didn't know him so well, I'd think Finn was totally unfazed by the bomb just dropped, but there's a split second when his eyes flared, nostrils widened and then like shutters on a window, he closes every single emotion down.

"Old family friends." His gaze flicks to me and the corner of his mouth tugs up subtly. "Though we recently *reconnected.*" My face burns hot, and I am suddenly regretting not getting another drink.

Despite the death glare I shoot him, he continues, "She did some portraits for me. She's a very talented photographer, have you seen her photos?" My stomach roils, and I try to read any suspicion on Hudson's face, but he seems not to notice anything off.

Though I get the message loud and clear.

"No, you'll have to show me some time," Hudson says to me and pulls me to his side with a protective hand around my waist. Finn's jaw ticks at the display.

"Well, I'll see you around, Ef, perhaps for another photo session? And it was nice meeting you, Henry." Finn waves and walks away, my skin still crawling from the interaction.

I consider leaving it be, but then I think about how pleased Finn must be, catching me off guard and calling me out so blatantly. I don't want the smug bastard thinking he can get away with shit like that.

"I need to use the restroom. I'll be right back." I stalk after Finn and see him dip into the men's room. Without hesitation, I follow after him.

Finn's leaning against the sink counter, chewing on a toothpick, as if he was waiting for me. Like I said, *smug bastard.* I turn the lock shut with a click.

"You lost, princess?"

Finn

[5]It takes an ungodly amount of control to remain relaxed against the counter when she storms into the bathroom, cheeks flushed and angry, breasts rising and falling dramatically pushed up in her corset dress. The sound of the door locking makes my cock jump.

"You lost, princess?"

"You can't do this."

"Do what?" The irritation in her gaze is like a shot of the strongest scotch.

"You can't—" I kick off the counter and clamp my hand around her jaw, effectively cutting her off.

"Let's get one thing straight," Her pupils blow wide, but she bites her lip defiantly. "I *can* and will do whatever I damn well please. And no one, especially not the Luciano *whore* is going to tell me what I can and can't do."

I push her back against the door, sliding my hand lower on her neck so I can feel her pulse thumping. I snatch up her left wrist and look at her bare hand. "No ring, hmm?"

"It's getting resized." I can tell she's lying through her teeth. She yanks her hand away. "And don't call me a whore."

"Do you prefer plaything—"

My head snaps to the side, my cheek burning but my cock throbbing. She slapped me.

She fucking slapped me.

I trace my lip with my tongue, licking up the blood from a small split.

---

5 Run My Mouth—Ella Mai | SummerOtoole.com/playlists

I laugh darkly. "I know you like it rough, baby, but you only had to ask."

"I don't want *anything* from you, Finn." Her eyes are wild, like she can't decide if she's scared or turned on. I hope she's both.

"Really?" I tighten my grip on her throat and lower my other hand to her bare thigh through the slit in her dress. "So, I won't find your panties soaked from me watching you all night?" I slide my hand higher, feeling the heat from her cunt and her body tense the closer I get.

She sucks in a sharp breath as I brush the edge of her panties. Her hands ball into fists at her sides, and I wonder why she isn't pushing back more. I trail the tip of my tongue up her cheek to whisper in her ear. "I know it didn't work out too well for you last time, but you're not even gonna try to fight back this time?"

"Go ahead..." She shimmies out of her thong, stepping out of it and stuffing the soaked material into my jacket pocket. "...Feel how wet I get for my *fiancé*."

I resist the urge to turn her around and fuck that lie right out of her. I decide to play her game.

I'll let her run her mouth.

Right up until I make her scream my name.

"That so, huh?" I graze my fingertips up and down her slit and—*Christ, is she wet.* "So what did Harvard do to get you dripping like this?" She bites her lip as I part her folds and swirl her wetness over her clit.

"Finger fucked me under the table," she breathes as I apply more pressure to her swollen bud.

"At dinner with all those people? You dirty girl." I swipe my fingers lower and press against her entrance. She bites her lip and nods, but that isn't good enough for me. "What did he do, princess? Tell me."

"He slid his hand up my thigh, pulled my panties to the side and sunk two thick fingers into my pussy—" She gasps as I thrust two of my own fingers into her.

"And then?" I demand, my voice low and gravelly, my need to sink more than just my fingers into her so fucking strong. "Did he fuck you sweet and slow like the princess you think you are or hard and rough like the whore I *know* you are?"

"Soft," she mutters, and I huff, displeased with this answer. "And then hard." That makes me grin and shove my fingers, now coated so nicely in her arousal, deeper and then draw them out to do it all over again.

Her breath skates in and out on sweet little moans and then she pants, "He used his thumb to rub my clit." I do the same and look at her as if to say, *like this?* She nods vigorously, her heartbeat quickening, like a drum against my hand still around her neck.

Her eyelids droop and her pussy flutters around my fingers. My dick is fucking throbbing in my slacks, and I rock my hips forward to grind the painful bulge against her for a little goddamn relief. I curl my fingers inside her, and she bucks into my hand. "Fuuck."

"That's it, baby, ride my hand like my greedy little plaything." I can't tell if she truly hates being called that or actually loves it, but either way, her eyes slam open.

"If you think fingering me at dinner is dirty, you should hear what he did to me in the limo ride over." She sneers, and jealousy ignites in the pit of my stomach even though I fucking know she arrived with her parents.

"Tell me, princess." I pull my fingers out, loving how her breath hitches. "And we'll see who does it better." Her eyes heat as she watches me suck my fingers clean.

I gently part her lips with a thumb on her chin and spit into her open mouth. "Taste that, Ef? Taste how fucking sweet you are."

"Tastes like the best head of my life," she smirks.

"Is that what he did to you in the limo? Ate that perfect pussy?" She licks her lips and nods. "Well, then." I dip down to pick her up, her legs wrapping around my waist, and carry her to the sink. She looks like a goddess, even on a bathroom counter, and I'll fucking kneel at her altar.

There's a sharp knock at the door, and she slams her legs closed. "Un-uh, spread your legs, princess. Let's see who makes you come harder." She keeps her knees tight against my palm trying to push them apart.

There's another rap at the door and she looks at me then the door. "Someone's in here." I growl and force her knees open, clamping a hand on either thigh to hold her open for my worship.

There's a panic in her eyes, like she's scared someone is about to barge in, but I get her attention back by biting her inner thigh sharply.

Another pounding at the door and someone shouting on the other side. "It's fucking occupied!" I yell back. When I look up, her eyes are back on the door. "Eyes on me, princess. Watch me ruin you for all other men, especially that so-called fiancé."

"But—" she whispers nervously.

"Shh, I don't want you making a damn sound unless it's my name while you come on my tongue. Understood?" She clamps her mouth shut, blush growing even brighter on her cheeks, but she nods. "That's my girl. Now lie back."

I tug her ass to the edge of the counter with one hand and use my other to push her top half flat. Her legs clamp down on either side of my head at the first heavy drag of my tongue over her clit. Her body's instant reaction to me gives me a high like nothing else ever has.

I thrust two fingers back inside her dripping cunt. "So fucking sweet, baby," I groan as I lap the length of her pussy. She whimpers, and I notice only one of her hands is gripping the edge of the counter. I can only guess that the other is covering her mouth.

I can tell the moment she finally blocks out the people I am sure are lined up outside because she rolls her hips up and rides my face like it's the answer to all her questions. I focus on fucking hard but slow with my fingers and keep my tongue flat on her clit, letting her movements grind it just the way she wants it.

My dick leaks in my pants, and I couldn't care less about my own needs while she's getting lost in the pleasure I'm giving her. I feel her pussy quiver around my fingers and her moans, muffled by her hand, escalate.

I groan into her, not changing a single thing, while she rides hard toward her release. Her hands fly to my head and her fingers tangle in my hair as she shatters. *"Oh god, fu—fuck!"*

"My name, princess. Scream my fucking name."

"F—F—Finn," she cries in pure rapture, and it's a sound I will remember for the rest of my life. One I never thought I'd hear again.

Her saying my name without an ounce of hate.

And it chips away at the cold, black thing beating in my chest in a way I'm not sure I'm ready for. I swiftly push the uncomfortable feeling away and rip my hand away and stand abruptly, while she's still crashing down from her high.

I straighten my jacket and take in her heaving form laid out before me. Her dress hiked up to her hips, strands of her chestnut hair sticking to her forehead with beads of sweat.

"Finn?" She props herself up on her elbows and looks at me with a hurt in her eyes that I can't stand to look at.

"People are waiting. Get up," I say gruffly and refuse to look her way as she stands on shaky legs and pulls her dress down.

"You're an asshole." She brushes back her hair with her hands as she pushes past me.

"And yet, you still followed me in here." She pauses like she wants to turn around and say something in response, but then continues on toward the door.

I stop her, spinning her around with a hand on her shoulder. "*What?* I thought people were waiting," She's mad. I don't blame her. I *am* a fucking asshole.

"C'mon, I'll help you out the window. Unless you want everyone seeing you walk out of the men's bathroom after me looking freshly fucked." She twists her face up in annoyance but knows I'm right and heads to the back of the bathroom.

I crank the window open, then use my hand as a step to lift her up to the sill. She leans over and tries to swipe her panties from my coat pocket. I laugh, clamping my hand over them. "Nah, I'm keeping these."

She hops down off the window ledge. "Night, asshole," she says, walking away.

"I'll be in touch about that *photography session,*" I holler after her.

Chapter 6:

Pet

Effie

In the past week I've become a glorified babysitter to a girl gang of criminals, been blackmailed and married off. Not to mention getting finger fucked to high heavens by my enemy—and not entirely unwillingly.

To say it's been an eventful week is an understatement.

It feels like there's only one thing that's actually in my control. So, I look for Hudson's email on the investment firm's website he's partner at, because why would I have my supposed fiancé's phone number? That would just be too reasonable. There's no email anywhere on the site, and I end up having to message him on LinkedIn. *Fucking ridiculous.*

Hudson responds almost immediately, accepting my invitation to join me for lunch today. We need to get on the same page and ideally the not-engaged page. At least not yet and certainly not while Finn is still holding those photos over my head.

I know most people would be devastated to be told who to marry and when, but I grew up knowing that was what my future held. It was never a big deal to me because I never dreamed of anything else. And if I'm being honest, Hudson is much better looking than most of the men I knew were in the running. He was polite, decently funny, and I didn't totally hate being around him. He's Governor Campbell's son, so I'm sure he's no saint, but he's not a made man either.

Once we're married and the alliance secured, we may even have a chance at a normal life. If I even know what normal is.

Picking out my clothes for our lunch date, I feel like I need to overcompensate for my bathroom rendezvous at the gala. I was able to sneak back into the party without raising too much suspicion, but I want to wipe away any inkling he may have that I am anything but wife material.

So, I slip on a white shirt, no frills and minimal cleavage, paired with a red A-line skirt with small white flowers, I am the picture of innocence. *Okay, maybe not innocence.* But it's a start.

I'm waiting for an Uber outside of the apartment building when I get a text.

Cute skirt. Imagine how easily I could slip my hand under there.

Fucking Finn. I look around, trying to spot him, but he's not sitting outside, and the sun is creating too much of a glare to see into his window. I know he's watching though, so I don't look too desperately. I'm sure he'd love to see me flustered. Instead, I type back.

Effie: That's exactly why I wore it…

Finn: Trying to play, dirty girl?

Effie: Can't wait for the dirty things my fiancé will do to me at lunch when he discovers I'm not wearing any panties.

Finn: Be sure to count how many times he makes you come. So I can double it.

Effie: Goodbye, Finn. I have a date to get to.

Finn: Hudson.

Effie: Oh, so you do know his name.

Finn: Just wanted to remind you of it.

My driver arrives, and I slide into the backseat wondering what the hell

Finn is on about. But then I get another text and nearly throw my phone out the damn window.

Finn: Since you're so used to screaming mine.

I type out a string of expletives and a colorful description of where he can shove it. But then delete it and decide no reply is the best reply.

Leave the bastard on read.

Bella's Bistro is as sweet and charming as it sounds. A French American restaurant known for their long menu of crepes and decadent Sunday brunch. The decor is a mix of florals and antique finds.

The hostess points me toward the patio where Hudson is already waiting. I walk toward his table. The sun brings out the copper hues in his hair, his suit jacket folded over the back of the chair next to him. He has his back to me, and as I approach, I try to picture this being my life, my everyday reality. Meeting my husband for lunch at our favorite restaurant between meetings, because no matter how busy his day gets, he always makes time for us. The jasmine wound around the patio fence makes the air smell romantic and the aromas of the kitchen give it a homey feel.

But when I get close, he notices me and something about the fantasy of domestic bliss dulls. He smiles and stands, pulling out the chair across from him. I sit with a topsy-turvy feeling in my stomach, like maybe his teeth are a touch too white or his hair is coiffed a little too neatly. Like it all is just a mirage or a gilded front. Almost as if he isn't gritty enough to be tangible, to be real.

"I was so happy to get your email." He sits after tucking in my chair, his dimple popping as he smiles adoringly at me. It should make me feel beautiful the way he is looking at me, but instead it just makes me feel…*played*. I'm just a pawn in this game.

Which reminds me why I'm here. "I wanted to talk about the gala and what was said."

He scoots back in his chair, sitting a little bit taller, "And what exactly was said?" *And there it is.* There is that slight gleam of chicanery in his eyes, a touch of guile in his voice. It's something so subtle, barely imperceptible, if I hadn't grown up surrounded by men just like him that developed my sixth sense for these things.

"You know exactly what you said. And I just want to make it clear that I will not be caught in the crosshairs of some dick swinging match." His eyebrows raise, and I continue, "I'll play the dutiful daughter and we will get married, then I'll play the dutiful wife. But until then, you won't be throwing around words like *fiancée* before it is mutually decided upon. Do I make myself clear?"

I unfurl my napkin and lay it over my lap to give my shaking hands something to do while I steady my breath. I don't talk to people that way, especially not men who will soon hold my life in their hands. But there's been something about going toe-to-toe with Finn lately that is making me want to push back against everyone and everything.

Or maybe I'm taking the stress of being blackmailed out on Hudson…

"Yes ma'am." He chuckles and leans forward, pushing up the sleeves of his dress shirt. "As long as I make it clear that I will not be made a fool of. If there's anything between you and that little Fox shit, shut it down. I don't want scandal or…" he looks me up and down with an evil sneer, "a loose cunt."

Sit. Smile. Nod. Sit. Smile. Nod—No, fuck that.

I push out of my chair, throwing my napkin down and pitching forward, slapping my hands on the table. "You need me more than I need you. Don't forget that next time you think about speaking to me that way."

I storm out the way I came, my heart pounding in my chest and cheeks aching to smile in victory. Riding the high, I pull out my phone and text the one number I should be avoiding:

Meet me at Peaches.

Then I walk down the block to a jewelry store and buy myself the most expensive engagement ring in the place.

The strip club smells like Clorox and overly-fruity body spray. I scan the floor. There's only one dancer on stage and the crowd is minimal. Single men in trucker hats and groups of two of three in business attire. It is barely past noon on a weekday after all.

I suck in a breath as my eyes bounce around the edges of the ceiling, looking for cameras. It was a stupid fucking idea coming here of all places. But I was so high off telling Hudson to show some respect that I didn't think. I wanted to confront Finn and knew Peaches was close by and it wouldn't take much convincing to get him here if he wasn't already.

And if I'm successful, I'll have him delete any footage from the club today too.

I text him that I'm here, then remain standing and twiddle my new ring. The movement is subtle enough to make him think it's subconscious but obvious enough he'll catch it from wherever he's lurking. The corners and edges of the club are dark, intended for patron privacy I'm sure. Most of the purple-hued light is trained on the stage. My skin crawls knowing he is watching me. I'm certain he is.

I can feel his presence as precisely as I can feel the hairs on my arms standing and I hate that it's not all in dread. There's excitement there too. It pulses when my phone buzzes with a new notification. He replied to my text.

Finn: I know.

Effie: Why do you have to be so fucking creepy all the time?

Effie: Come out.

I pop my hip and stop scanning the floor. Instead I stare straight ahead with a look that I hope mimics teachers right before they say *I'm waiting.* If he wants to act like a child, I'll treat him like one.

Finn: How was lunch? Ended awfully quick. I knew he wouldn't be able to get you off, though I was looking forward to making you count for me.[6]

That's it. I spin on my heels and storm toward the door. This is all a fucking game for him, a way for him to get his dick wet. But this is my fucking life he's messing with. And I don't say that hyperbolically. If those pictures get out, I wouldn't be surprised to find myself dead in a ditch.

Which makes coming here even stupider. But I'm here now, so I'm going to fucking get what I came here for. I turn back around and make a beeline to a table of middle-aged businessmen. I pick up a high-ball glass and slam back whatever is in it, praying for something strong. I set the empty glass down and ignore whatever they're saying as I saunter closer to the stage.

My foot hesitates on the first step as I look down and see my cherry-red skirt brushing across my knee. I wore this damn skirt to refine my innocent, obedient daughter image, and somehow I doubt that climbing on stage at a Fox-owned strip club will help.

Then again, I guess some things are worth it to get under a Fox's skin.

I suppose my father and I have that in common.

I climb the steps and stare down the pole like it's an opponent, my heart beat surprisingly steady. My foot inches forward and my fingers fall to the buttons of my blouse.

One step. One button. Another step. Another button.

The stage shakes with thudding footsteps as Finn barges out of his creeper corner and leaps onto it.

"Oh, there you are. Come to enjoy the show?" I tease and hurriedly close the distance to the pole. I only get in one swing around before he's throwing me over his shoulder.

"There will be no fucking show." My stomach swoops, and I'm certain it's due to the possessiveness in his growl and not the change in elevation.

I pound on his back with my fists and try to flail my legs, but he has his arm like a steel bar across my thighs. "Finn, you goddamn caveman, put me down!"

He carries me off the stage and across the floor, busting through an office

---

6 ALPHA—Layto | SummerOtoole.com/playlists

door and unceremoniously tossing me down in a desk chair. I sweep my hair out of my face, seething. "You can't—"

"What did I say about you telling me what I can and can't do?" He slides in between the chair and the desk, leaning back against it. I try to stand but he tugs my seat closer so that if I stand, I'd be chest to chest with the asshole.

"I'm pretty sure that conversation ended with me slapping you."

"No, princess. It ended with my lips on that pussy and my name on yours." He chuckles smugly, and I freeze when he gently thumbs circles on my outer knee. "So what is it? You asked to meet so a real man can get you off?"

The upper hand I thought I had is slipping the more I let him toy with me. And he's so good at it too. "That's not—"

My sentence is cut off when he swiftly shoots his palm up my thigh and snaps the elastic of my panties. "Thought you weren't wearing any?" *Fuck.*

"I want you to delete the photos." He only raises a brow at my demands, as if I said something inconceivable, so I add, "I'll keep you apprised of our operation, but I want assurances that those photos are destroyed *first."*

He swipes his tongue across his teeth, a rueful grin teasing his lips. "That's not how blackmail works, princess. I hold the leverage, I make the demands. And if you *behave*—" I flinch at the insinuation in his words while his hand still rests under my skirt. "—Then those photos will never see the light of day."

I swallow hard. "You'd really do that? To me?"

"That and so much worse." There isn't an ounce of remorse in his tone. Only cold, calculating honesty. And it fucking hurts.

But like any good soldier, I know to raise my shield when going into battle. "Well then, where do you want to start?" I ask, and something tender, almost sorrowful flashes in his eyes but it's gone so quickly I wonder if it was all in my head.

"Let's start with what the fuck that thing is on your hand."

I look down at the diamond sparkling on my hand and wiggle my fingers before cutting my gaze back up to his. "My engagement ring. I got it back from the jeweler."

"You're not fucking engaged."

"Then how do you explain this, huh? You think I bought this for my-self just to convince *you* I'm engaged? Please, you're not worth nearly that much."

He barks a laugh, and it takes me off guard. "Yes, I think that's *exactly* what happened." His dark eyes gleam as I'm sure he sees the blush bloom-ing on my cheeks. *Damnit.*

He lightly wraps his fingers around my hand and lifts it to kiss the ring. I freeze as he locks eyes with me and says low and greedy, "Either way, it's a beautiful ring. You—I mean *he* has great taste. You know where it would look great?"

I humor him, "Where?"

He leads my hand to palm the bulge in his slacks. "Wrapped around my cock."

I attempt to rip my hand away. "Be fucking for real, Finn." I scoff but he keeps it clutched tight to his groin, even going so far as to grind his pelvis into my palm. And yet, at the same time I paint a look of disgust on my face, I can't help but squeeze my thighs together.

"Go ahead, princess: take what you want." He flicks his chin and coolly scans my heated cheeks, chest.

My lips tug in snarl. "You're fucking delusional."

"You want those photos deleted right?"

My eyes narrow and I stop trying to pull my hand away. "Every single one you sent me."

"Okay—"

"And the audio clip," I rush to add.

"Done." He laughs coldly and leans back on his hands as I swallow my pride and tilt forward.

Even as I reach for his zipper and tease it down, I know this deal is too good to be true. But it's also *true* that I am out of options. And hell, I gave a hand job to Mikey Carlorino in the eighth grade so that he wouldn't tell my parents that he saw me sneak out to go to high school parties from his next door window. If thirteen-year-old Effie could do it, certainly twenty-eight-year-old Effie can—and the stakes are much higher now.

I keep my eyes trained on the task, knowing that if I was to look up, whatever I saw looking back in Finn's eyes would make this much harder... or hotter. And the latter is much worse. My fingers creep under the waistband of his briefs, his abs tensing as my skin skims against his.

My breath hitches when I free his cock and realize...I suck my bottom lip between my teeth and feel my throat bob as my eyes take in the silver barbell piercing below the head. I shoot him a cutting glare when I feel, rather than see his smirk. He tongues his cheek like he knows exactly how my pussy flutters wondering what the jewelry would feel dragging over my clit.

"Whatever you're imagining right now, I guarantee it feels ten times better."

"Gross." I roll my eyes, but internally, I clench.

I tentatively circle his cock, the tip already glistening with pre-cum, and give a few testing strokes. I zero in on the flex of his thighs like he's holding back the urge to thrust forward.

"Come on, Ef, I know you can do better than that. I can take as good as I give." His chuckle is deep and gravelly.

I scowl and meet his eyes. I'm sure mine are full of malice as I gather saliva in my mouth and let it spill out of my lips. My spit drips down slowly onto his red tip. It's grotesque and resentful, and the moment he groans when it hits his dick it becomes hot as hell.

I remind myself this isn't hot. This is fucking bribery, coercion. And I should hate him. I *do* hate him.

I channel my confusing mix of lust and anger and smear my spit down his shaft, rotating my fist up and down. I rub my thumb over his leaking head and piercing on every upstroke making a deep rumble resound from his chest. "Fuck, that's it."

The husky sound makes my insides melt, and I tighten my grip, stripping his cock more vigorously, needing this to end. He pushes air out of his flared nostrils and rolls his head back, his dark hair sweeping off his forehead. I force myself to look away, to not trace the corded muscles of his neck as he bites back a moan.

"Christ, Effie. That's so fucking good." The way he's enjoying this makes me sick. His praise only makes me wilt because it's not *good*. It's fucking hate-filled. But he's too much of a self-absorbed fuckwad to notice.

I notice his hips jolt the more attention I pay to his piercing, so I focus on that, adding more spit to glide my movements. I want this over as soon as possible. He responds by clenching his jaw, and I yank my head to the side when he tries to reach out and stroke my hair. "Don't fucking touch me."

His laugh is interrupted by a knock at the door, and I freeze. The surprise is all he needs to thread his big hand through my hair and grip the back of my head, forcing me to look up at him. "You're not done."

"Finn—"

"Let them see that hand where it belongs. No matter whose ring is on it." He calls over his shoulder to tell whoever it is to come in. As the knob turns, he stares back at me, stony-faced. "I won't ask nicely again."

I recognize the white woman that steps in as the dancer from the stage earlier. Her neon green, sequined bikini is obnoxiously bright under the fluorescent lights. She spots me and stutters to a halt in her high stage heels. "Oh sorry, I thought you said come in."

"I did. What is it, Mira?"

"Uh—I can come back." She takes a step backward, but there's a hint of interest in her voice.

"Fucking hell, what is it? You came in for a reason. Now tell me," Finn snaps.

"I just finished my set, here's my cash for the safe." She crosses the room and sets a money bag on the desk. I catch her eyes going to his crotch and she licks her lip. *Fucking hell.*

"Mirabelle, this is Effie."

"Hi, Effie," she says sweetly, and I scowl back. This is the exact last thing I need. This is so fucking bad. Somebody witnessing me jacking Finn in his office. I grit my teeth and try to calm my beating heart. Deal with one devil at a time.

Speaking of, one devil opens his fucking mouth again. "She's going to marry the governor's son. See that ring? It's from him—supposedly. But doesn't it look nice wrapped around my cock?"

She teeters closer and peers down, nibbling her bottom lip. "It certainly does," she says breathlessly.

Finn's jaw grinds, his abs flexing, and he twitches with each stroke. "So. Fucking. Good." He growls as he comes all over my hand. Mira gasps, clearly turned on. He leans back against the desk as the hot liquid drips down my fist.

I rip my hand off, disgusted with him, with her, and especially with myself. I go to wipe my hand, but Finn's hand snatched my wrist, holding it in front of my face.

"Lick it up. Clean that pretty ring, princess. Make it *sparkle,*" he drawls, and my spine goes rigid as my lips draw into a tight line.

"Fuck. No." I growl back.

"If you don't do what I ask, I won't do what you ask." He pushes my hand closer to my mouth, and I pull my head back. My eyes bounce between Finn's and Mira's who looks like she's nearly salivating. It's obvious she feels something for him, the way her pupils blow wide, and she looks hungrily at his pearly cum coating my hand.

She can have him for all I care…which doesn't explain why it gives me a wicked ping of gratification to lick him off my fingers while looking her dead in the eyes. Her lips part when I suck my ring finger into my mouth.

Our weird, jealous showdown ends when Finn reaches out for my chin and tips it up with two fingers. "She makes such a pretty pet." I purse my lips, and he holds out his hand for me to spit the cleaned ring into his palm. He holds it up approvingly, letting the light catch on the finely cut edges. "That's my good girl."

Mira leans across the desk and whispers in his ear, "She'd look even prettier on her knees."

I hope he doesn't see the inexplicable jealousy in my eyes. I hope he doesn't see the thrill simmering low in my stomach at being watched, even when—or especially when—the stakes are so high. I tear my gaze away from his before it gives me away and instead turn to Mira, "Funny. I think *he'd* look much better on his."

I lick my bottom lip and part my thighs, my heart thudding heavy in my ribcage. I hold my breath in shock and anticipation when Finn grins and drops to his knees. Pleasure flies up my spine at the sight of him on the floor, between my legs.

I let my skirt hike up to my hips as I drape a leg over each armrest. "Go ahead, *pet.*"

Finn's eyes darken, like sinking to the bottom of a deep, frigid lake. Without words, I know exactly what he's telling me as he slides his rough palms up my inner thighs. *Watch it, princess.*

I know I'm playing with fire talking to him like this, especially in front of his inferior. But I can't help myself. I can't help the devil on my shoulder that always grows louder when I'm around him. And he knows it.

I wouldn't be surprised if he pushes me, not for his own gain, but just to spite me, to make me even madder with myself in the morning. He's playing along now for the same reason he used pleasure to force information out of me. It's psychological warfare. He doesn't need to break me down himself, because he knows I'll do it all on my own.

This realization infuriates me. Even if this ends now, he's won again. He's compromised me. *Again.*

Well, if he's already won, I might as well get an orgasm out of losing.

Mira teeters backward on her staggering heels, trying to excuse herself. I don't know what compels me, but I find myself ordering her to stay.

My skin lights on fire, both under her gaze and under his touch. He slowly drags his hands up my thighs and then makes me yelp when he rips my panties in half with a sharp tug.

"I'm keeping these too." He tucks them into his pocket with a wicked grin. "Look at that wet fucking cunt." His low timber has shivers running up my arms which turn into a full body shudder when he drags his wide tongue firmly up my slit.

"So fucking sweet, princess," he moans and wraps his hands around my ass to yank me to the edge of the seat. I get a small pinch of glee when I notice Mira's lip twitch at his pet name.

I intertwine my fingers into his hair as he works me with his sinful tongue. He sucks on my clit and makes heavy, steady strokes. A mewl spills from my lips, and he doubles down on his movements. His fingers dig into my skin while he traces perfect circles around my clit. The next time he applies direct pressure to my clit, he slips two thick fingers into me, and I buck against his palm.

He's too fucking good at this.

Pleasure makes my toes curl and heat coils up my legs and around my spine. I dig my stilettos into his back and the way his lathing increases in fervor I'm not the only one who enjoys a little bit of pain.

"Fuhh—" I bite my tongue as my pussy throbs, my orgasm building into a delicious tension. I throw my gaze to Mira's as my breathing quickens and he brings me closer and closer to the edge. I claw at Finn's scalp, tugging on his hair as I am pushed violently over into spiraling bliss.

"*Fuh-Fuckk,*" I cry, fighting the urge to squeeze my eyes closed as the pleasure rolls over me so that I can keep them locked on Mira's.

She swallows hard, wringing her hands in front of her and her cheeks burn a brilliant red. But not in a turned-on way, in an embarrassed way, and I can't deny that I enjoy that fact more than a little. Maybe I'm more ruthless than I've given myself credit for.

Finn sits back on his heels and licks his lip with a devilish smile up at me. I keep my returning gaze cold, not wanting him to know how hot he made me. How he lit me on fucking flame. I turn that same cold gaze back to Mira and say, "You can go now."

As she leaves, Finn uses my skirt to wipe his mouth before rising. He brushes his knuckles against my cheek. "Such a feisty little plaything."

He turns around and opens a laptop on the desk. I push out the chair to watch over his shoulder, ignoring the way my legs wobble slightly. After getting through several security measures, he pulls up a folder of dozens of media files.

I gasp when I realize the extent of it.

Every second. Every angle.

He sorts by downloaded files and highlights the ones he sent me, enlarging each image preview so I can see they are the same. Then he deletes them.

He turns to face me, "Done. A *pleasure* doing business with you."

"What about the rest of them?" I can't keep the panic from leaking into my voice.

He laughs, "You really thought I was going to delete everything for a fucking handjob? Nah, princess. Our deal was to delete everything I *sent to you*."

"That's before I knew you had a whole fucking museum of shit!"

"A museum? Maybe I should frame some."

I shove him in the chest, my voice strained with poorly-concealed emotion. "You're a fucking monster, Finneas Fox."

I realize this moment was the one he was striving for all along. The ultimate way to spit in my face and rub in my humiliation. I know there is no convincing him to delete more so I storm to the door.

I rip it open but pause in the frame. I look back at him and say with utmost sincerity, "If you leak those photos, I will never forgive you. *Never.*"

The door slams shut behind me.

My blood is pumping, my sanity hanging on by a thread.

Why do I let him play me like this? Like a fucking mouse to a candied trap. I'm a goddamn Luciano, and I'm being made a fool.

I weave through the club's tables, scrunching my nose at the sickly-sweet smell from before. I spy Mira's shimmery, green bikini disappearing down a hallway labeled employee only. She's a reminder of exactly how *fucked* I am.

So when I pass a table with an empty beer bottle, I pick it up and follow her.

The hallway is dark but lined with red toe-kick lights. My veins pulse with determination and the need to gain back an inkling of control. I grip the bottle by the neck and smash the body against the wall. The heavy bass of the music covers any sound.

I open the only door at the end of the hallway and quickly realize it must be the dancers' locker and changing rooms. A long vanity table trails along a mirror-covered wall lit up with big, round bulbs. A makeup bag is opened, and half its contents strewn out on the table next to Mira, seated in front of the mirror.

She's distracted by something on her phone, so she doesn't see me come up behind her until I have her high ponytail fisted and head yanked back. Her eyes widen as they meet my crazed ones through the reflection.

Her mouth opens for what I'm sure was supposed to be a scream, but she quickly smacks it closed when I push the jagged beer bottle edge to her outstretched neck.

"Do you know who I am?"

"Ef-Effie Luci-Luciano." Her trembling voice almost gives me pause—*almost*.

"That's right. And I'm sure I don't have to tell you what will happen if you speak a single word to a single soul about what you saw today." She nods her head as much as she can without grating the glass against her skin. "*Right?*"

"Yes, yes. Of course." Her voice shakes, and I press the bottle a touch harder until she spews, "I won't tell anyone. Not a soul, I promise."

"Terrific." I release her head with a shove and turn to leave, confident I've scared her silent.

I pause before exiting the changing room and turn back to see her dabbing a slight drip of blood with a cotton pad. "Oh, and I'd go with the purple eyeshadow. Complementary colors and all."

Chapter 7:

Girls' Night

Effie

It's a weird feeling, looking at your hands and wondering what they would look like covered in blood.

I was so close to pushing that bottle a little harder, a little further. In that moment, Mira was me, and I hated her. I saw the way Mira looked at Finn, and I saw myself. I saw the way she cowed and bent to his air of dominance, and I fucking saw myself.

My brothers killed their first man at age sixteen. Some kids get a car at sixteen for getting their driver's license. In our family, you got a car when you killed someone. And were born a son.

Instead I was taught how to sit straight, shut my mouth, and look pretty. Look where that's gotten me. Under the thumb of another fucking man.

I laugh alone in my temporary bedroom at the thought because I could be talking about Finn or Hudson. My father never taught me to fight back because he needed me to be compliant and dependent. It's dangerous when a woman starts believing in her own strength.

But despite not having any of the training my brothers received, I am still trying to fight back. I've lost some battles, but I haven't lost the war.

After all, I've gotten Finneas Fox on his knees…twice.

I wonder if he's realized the same thing because I haven't heard from him in two days.

If I've been able to flip the script one way, maybe I can flip the script again and use his own strategy against him.

I've been terrified the crew will find out he's blackmailing me and knows his family is their target, but these women are the best of the best. I'm sure they will be able to work with this predicament I've put us in.

I slide out of bed and open my door with a direct line of sight to the apartment's living room. Hadis, Linnie, and Marguerite are already in there, lounging on the basic navy couch and cream-colored armchairs. The apartment came furnished, and while it's nothing special, it makes temporarily living here comfortable enough. It reminds me of hotel furniture, meant to look pleasing but still durable.

I head to the kitchen and grab a bottle of wine, weaving four glass stems between my fingers before returning to the living room. I kneel by the coffee table and uncork the wine, "There's something I need to tell you guys—"

"I win," Hadis says, and the other women laugh. I look up confused.

"We had a bet going on when you were gonna tell us what was going on with you and Finneas Fox," Linnie explains, and I set the bottle down so I don't spill it.

"I see…" There's no point in denying it, even if they didn't already know, I was planning on telling them. I sit back on my heels and scan their faces. They don't look mad…or smug…more amused than anything. "What do you know?"

"He has something on you, but we don't know what. And we've assumed since we are still alive, he hasn't told his older brother about us yet." Linnie speaks casually, but her eyes bore into mine with intensity. "But we could play the guessing game all night or you could just tell us."

"Right then," I begin to pour the wine while I try to formulate my words.

"Only three glasses. Hadis doesn't drink," Marguerite adds, and I nod.

Once I finish and everyone who wants one has a glass in their hand, I begin. "Finn and I were once good friends. Families in business and all. But after—what do you know about his father?"

"All of it."

"Okay, well you can imagine we weren't friends after that. We recently *reconnected*—" I internally wince using the same word he used talking to Hudson. "What I thought was a chance encounter obviously wasn't. He has videos and photos of it all and wants me to pass him information on our operation 'or else,'" I say with air quotes.

Hadis leans forward, resting her elbows on her knees, an excited gleam in her eyes. "This is brilliant."

"Brilliant?" I take a big chug of wine.

"He doesn't know anything, because you don't know anything—"

"He knows the target," I confess.

She waves her hand. "That doesn't matter. Banks always know their money is the target. Museums always know their art is the target. But because he doesn't know anything, we can feed him exactly what we want him to know. So..." She sits back and pulls her dyed blonde hair into a ponytail. "What do we want him to know?"

"So how did you all get together?" I finally ask, two hours later. We've planned exactly what we—well, I'm—going to tell Finn, and what they are going to do instead, and at this point, are just talking about their favorite places they've eaten since they've been in town.

They all look at Linnie who chuckles lightly. "I guess you could say we all have family businesses. My father was a bank robber, as was his father and his father's father...you get the idea, no?" I lean forward, intrigued.

Marguerite laughs. "Some families have sweet Christmas or Easter traditions. Our family's tradition is robbing banks."

"Our?" I ask, trying to spot any familial resemblance between the two.

It's hard but not impossible to see, what with Linnie's bold curly blonde hair and Marguerite's tight buzz.

"Cousins," Linnie continues, "But we met Hadis when the diamond shop I was working at—to rob, of course—hired architects for remodels."

"I was an intern, still in university at the time," Hadis adds.

"And I noticed she would come in separate from her coworkers to request blueprints and information for things that had nothing to do with the job they were hired for. Layout for the air duct system, the blueprints of the vault room, name of the roofing company…" Linnie swirls her wine and looks amused at Hadis. "Like recognizes like."

"You were casing the store?" I look at Hadis who raises a brow with a sly smile.

"It's in my blood. I come from a family of smugglers. Growing up in Iran, it felt like nearly everything not Iranian produced was illegal. Western music and clothing, non-Islamic art or art with any kind of nudity, alcohol. But if you knew the right people and had enough money, you could get just about anything from people like my parents."

"You smuggled alcohol even though you don't drink it?"

"Just because that's how I choose to practice Islam doesn't mean everyone should be forced to do the same. Plus, our biggest clients were always in government. Hypocrites, the lot of them."

"Really? What types of things would you get for them?"

"Lots of things. *Juicy* tracksuits, playboy magazines, *Star Wars* DVDs. Once the *American Idiot* album for the Speaker of Parliament's daughter." She shrugs and I laugh, but it's hard to imagine Green Day as illegal contraband.

I pour the rest of our second bottle of wine into my glass. "And how did you end up at an architecture firm in Paris?"

"My parents immigrated to France when I was a teen. I went to university intending to become an honest architect, but my brain was constantly thinking about how to break into the buildings, not create them."

"I remember the day Linnie called me." Marguerite sits up. "She was so excited. She said, 'Who better to know a building's weaknesses than the people who built it.'"

"Our fathers hadn't been able to keep up with new banking technology, so we kept going for smaller and smaller targets. Jewelry shops, armored trucks. But I knew with Hadis's expertise, we could take it to the next level, go after targets we'd only ever dreamed of." There's an energetic flare to the way Linnie speaks. Pride in what they've created.

"So, she confronted me the next time I came to pick up materials." Hadis grins. "And *Les Arnaqueuses* was born."

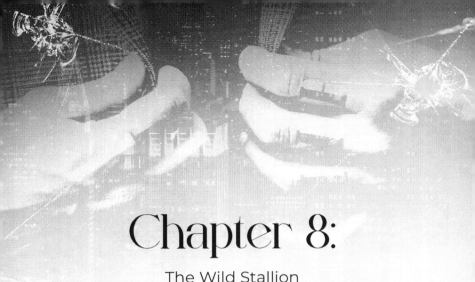

Chapter 8:

The Wild Stallion

Finn

I've grown impatient waiting for them to make a move. And it would be just my fucking luck that the one time Cash takes a vacation in ten years is the same time the most elite heist crew in the world decides to make us their mark. But I can't make a move without Cash, so I just need to buy myself time.

I don't trust Effie.

Not until she gives me a reason to. And so far, she's only giving me reason to think she isn't taking this seriously. Thinking she could strut into my place of business and make demands of *me*. What was that stunt she pulled with Mira anyway?

My throat goes dry remembering the silky feel of her thighs under my palm as I pushed her knees apart. I recall looking up from her lap, seeing the determined set of her jaw and heat in her gaze as she stared down Mira. She looked like a fucking warrior.

But she's spiraling. Lashing out and making rash decisions.

She's been thrown in the deep end and is desperately trying to stay afloat.

Even the strongest soldiers can still sink.

I can't figure her out. Which makes me want to grab her by the throat and fuck the truth out of her. But also makes me want to stay far away, keep my distance to just observe her, take all of her in like an animal in the wild.

She's unpredictable, that much is for sure.

And she still hasn't given me anything about this plan of theirs. And I'm done waiting.

Finn: Peaches. 20 min.

Effie: No.

I can't deny the way my dick jumps at her ready defiance, the way my mouth waters with the need to break her down to nothing but yes, please. *Yes, sir.*

Finn: I know you get off on being a brat, but we need to meet.

My foot taps against the leg of my chair as I wait for her response. I open my desk drawer in the Den's back office and pull out my growing stash of Effie's panties. I twirl the torn fabric of the ones from Peaches around my finger and smile to myself.

I pick them up and take a picture of it dangling from my finger, the other one in the drawer also in the frame.

Finn: I'm looking forward to adding to my collection.

That gets me an immediate response.

Effie: You're fucking sick.

Finn: Is that a yes?

Effie: Neutral territory of my choice. I'll text you an address.

The Wild Stallion Saloon.

I take in the weathered wood building. Its red paint has peeled and faded away to a rusty color, the door and windows are trimmed in a woody green.

Matching green columns hold up a corrugated tin porch covering.[7]

Over an hour outside of city limits, this is certainly neutral territory.

I wait in my car, assuming Effie hasn't arrived yet based on the fact that muddy, lifted trucks are the only ones in the dirt lot. We're in the agricultural part of this county, near Bartlett Farms and wonder if Effie realizes or it's simply a coincidence.

I can't be sure as she picked the location, but I'm thinking the obscurity of this place is just an overcompensation for her foolish decision to meet me at Peaches last time. I was worried she wasn't as smart as I remembered when she asked to meet there, but after Mira told me what happened in the dressing room, my concerns were abated.

She's spent her whole life on the bench and is only now stepping onto the field. Mistakes are inevitable, but she's learning quickly. Even if it is a pain in my ass to drive to the middle of nowhere.

A few minutes later a Mercedes SUV, just as out of place as my BMW, pulls into the lot. I watch in the rearview mirror as the car door opens and— *fuck me.*

The yellow sundress flowing over her curves is way too sweet for the things it makes me wanna do to her. But I'm sure that was her intention. She thinks she's just a pawn, but she knows how to play the game as well as anyone. She does it with grace and subtlety rather than rage and carnage. One may be more effective, but the other is just as deadly.

My phone buzzes and I pretend the battering of delight in my chest that she texted me doesn't exist. Fucking childish is what it would be if I did.

Childish and a liability.

Effie: I'm here, are you inside?

I don't respond right away, give myself just a few more seconds to soak her in. Her dark, chestnut hair is straight down her back. Her matching brown eyes sift through the parked cars. I know when she's noticed my car because she stands taller and drops her wringing hands.

I track her through the mirror as she walks over, small blooms of dust

---

7 Bottom of the River—Delta Rae | SummerOtoole.com/playlists

rising from her steps. I act like I don't see her, even when she steps up to my driver side window and taps the glass. Without lifting my head from my phone, I hold out a finger and can hear her huff through the window. Her frustration delights me.

When I finally give her my attention, she's glaring down at me. She crosses her arms impatiently, but the only thing I can think of is the way the movement pushes up her tits.

I roll down my window. "I'd be able to get out if you weren't standing in front of my door."

Her lips twitch. "I'll be inside at the bar," she bites out sharply. As she heads toward the building, I hear her mumble. "Christ, I already need a drink." My hands ball into tight fists watching her ass walk away.

The inside of the saloon is just what I'd expect from the outside. There's a yellowing American flag pinned on the wall next to beer posters and mounted deer heads. The crowd is blue collar, and a neon sign buzzes above the pool table where most of the people are gathered. It smells like old cigarette smoke and fried food, and the wood floor feels sticky under my shoes.

A woman in a tube top is behind the big oak bar fixing a drink for Effie. The hairs on the back of my neck rise as I watch every man in the place turn his lecherous gaze to her. Her dress sleeves are billowy and off the shoulder, showing her off her bronzed collarbones, and I bet every shithead in the place is imagining what that expanse of skin would look like with his fucking mark.

Like they have a mind of their own, my fingers inch toward the gun tucked into my jeans.

Not that she's mine.

But she sure as shit isn't theirs.

I pull out a stool next to her at the same time the song changes and the scraping against the floor is loud in the relative quiet. She gives me one sideway glance before finishing her conversation with the bartender like I'm not even there.

I don't like being ignored, it's disrespectful. And it would stoke the always simmering fire below my skin if I thought she was truly ignoring me.

But she's not.

She may not be looking at me, but all of her attention is on me. It's in the way she fiddles with her straw like it will soothe the itch my proximity causes. It's in the way she swallows deeply without ever taking a sip and answers the bartender's "enjoy your drink" with "thanks, you too."

She's flustered. *I* make her flustered. This realization isn't new, but it's delicious all the same.

When the bartender walks away, I spin her swivel seat toward me. Her hands fly out for stability, one landing on the bar, the other on my thigh. The thundering in my chest is instant with even the smallest willing—albeit accidental—touch from her.

"If I didn't know better, I'd think you missed me," I say, looking up and down between her hand on me and her eyes. She yanks it away, smooths her skirt and looks at me expectantly. "Do you have something to tell me, princess?"

A pair of men saddle up to the bar next to me, and she eyes them uneasily. She stands. "Let's dance."

My fist tightens into a ball at the same time my jaw clenches. "I don't dance."

"They're too close," she nods toward the men.

"Then we'll move." I stand and grab her hand, stomping to a high-top table.

She shakes her hand out of mine, and I have to fight the urge to hold on tighter. "And then what if someone gets close again? We can't keep playing leapfrog in the bar. It's suspicious as hell."

"I thought the point of picking a place in bumfuck nowhere was because nobody would know who we are."

"It's not a risk I'm willing to take. Now, fucking dance with me." She grips my bicep and I let her drag me onto the dance floor despite the protesting in my head. I stiffen when she places both hands on my shoulders and squares her hips with mine.

"Oh don't tell me you're scared of a little dancing?" Her lip curls in the corner and I bite my tongue. "You kill people for a living—and I'm pretty sure for fun too—but you can't dance?"

"You're stalling."

"And you're scared of *dancing*." She smirks and wraps her arms around my neck and tugs me closer so I'm forced to sway with her body. I can't even appreciate her soft tits pressed against my chest, or the way her hips grind across mine over the stupid fucking noise in my head.

The noise that demands a Fox never show weakness.

And as idiotic as it is, dancing is a weakness and years of survival training has me bursting at the seams to avoid it.

I tug her closer by the waist and lower my mouth to her ear. "Start talking, princess."

"What do you want to know?" Her own breath flutters against my neck. and a heavy, hot weight settles into my stomach.

How your voice sounds in the morning. What sounds you make in your sleep. How you'd look at me if you didn't despise me. "Everything."

"They're keeping me at arm's length, I don't know much."

"That's not good enough."

"It will have to be." She blinks up at me, a challenge glimmering in her eyes.

I tuck a strand of hair behind her ear and cradle her jaw. "You like playing games, don't you, pet?"

"Not as much as you. Though I have to admit, yours are getting a bit old." She steps back, taking my hand with her and spins beneath my arm, a taunting smile on her lips.

My eyes trail up the small bit of extra thigh exposed from her twirling skirt. I let her swirl back to me and lock her in place with a firm hand on her hip, the other caging her hand against my arm like they did in those old-timey dances.

To distract her from my awkward and stilted attempt at having rhythm, I throw out an offer she can't refuse. "Let's make it more interesting then. You give me a solid piece of intel, and if it proves to be helpful, I will delete everything."

Her feet halt and she sucks in a hopeful breath. "*Everything* everything?

This isn't some semantic trick or twisted wording?"

"Every single morsel of evidence that that night ever existed."

"Okay, it isn't much but..." She gives a quick scan of the bar floor once more before continuing—I'd do the same if I hadn't already been paying attention to every single person who's passed through the door since arriving.

"The rooftop. It's the only entrance you never have men on. I don't know exactly what they're gonna do, but they're going to create some sort of problem that requires you to build scaffolding to fix it—"

"They want me to give them a ladder right into the castle, huh?"

"Something like that." She shrugs, and I try to read her face for any minuscule hint that she's lying. Instead I find myself fixating on a small grouping of scratch-like scars by her eye that I've never seen before.

"When did this happen?" I don't even realize I've reached out to brush the scars with my thumb until I feel her hot skin, and then she jolts her head back.

"A lot has happened in ten years, Finn." She rips out of my arms and her boots clack across the floor to the exit. I feel each step like a lead ball landing in my stomach.

I chase after her and grab her wrist when I catch up to her in the parking lot. I spin her around and my throat ties into a knot when I see water misting her eyes.

"What the fuck was that about, Ef?"

She shoves me in the chest, and I drop her wrist, her voice strained with sudden emotion, "Don't start acting like you care. Not now, Finn."

I let her walk away. My armor is too tight for her words to cut.

I think.

Chapter 9:

Plates, Picture Frames, and Paintings.

Ten years ago

Sometimes when my father's angry, I can see it coming from miles away. There's a change in the air, a prickle at the nape of my neck. That eerie sense of knowing even without proof, like when you feel you're being watched.

When this happens, I know to lock my door before he shows up. Let him pound and pound on the wood and be grateful it's not my face.

But today, I didn't see it coming.

My mother's powder room is thick with the scent of her perfume and hairspray, but it has the best mirrors in the house. I want to try my hand at portrait painting rather than my usual landscapes. Figured self-portrait sketches would be a good place to start and this vanity table with three panels of mirrors would be excellent. The end two mirrors are on hinges to capture different angles. I unscrew half of the globe bulbs around the perimeter to dim the lighting—I'm not trying to draw every single pore.

I'm on my third sketch when the door slams open, ricocheting loudly off the wall. I catch my father's red, twisted face in the mirror.

"Like mother like daughter, who are you in here whoring yourself up for, Euphemia?" Spittle hits my cheek as he yanks my head by a rough fistful of hair.

There's no makeup on the table, only my pencils and paper. "I was draw—"

"And how in God's name did you manage to break every other fucking bulb? You're a spoiled brat, breaking everything you touch." Before I can explain they aren't broken, my head is flung forward and my nose smashes into the vanity.

My eyes instantly water, and I taste a trickle of copper down my throat. I try to shuffle my sketches out of the way so I don't drip blood onto them. They aren't great but I would like to keep them. Unfortunately, that only gets my father's attention.

"Yourself. That's all you fucking think about." He holds up a sheet of paper and examines my work with a sneer. "Heavenly Father, tell me what I did to deserve such a self-conceited bitch of a daughter?" I wince at the ripping sound as he shreds my work into pieces.

I should have predicted this. He has a tendency to destroy whatever he sees when he's like this. Plates. Picture frames. *Paintings.*

He snatches another off the table, and I use the few seconds it takes for him to tear it in half to stuff the only remaining one into my pocket.

"Clean this up." He pulls a silk handkerchief from his jacket sleeve and throws it at me. "And don't get fucking blood on my rug."

I don't watch him leave, just listen to his Italian loafers scuff against the carpet as he crosses the room and slams the door just as loudly leaving as he did entering. I dab at my nose, sniffing back and swallowing the rusty taste of my own blood that drips down the back of my throat.

My phone vibrates on the vanity, and I jump at the sudden sound in the now-quiet room.

I don't look at the caller ID, quickly answering to end the shrill sound. "Hello?"

"Hey, Eff, I'm at the corner." A soothing warmth sinks into my bones at the smile in Finn's voice, and I picture the way his left eye crinkles in the corner when he smiles.[8]

"I lost track of time drawing, but I'll be right there."

"Okay, see you soon."

I swipe my watery eyes with the back of my hand and inspect my nose bleed, which has mostly stopped, wiping the tip of my nose before cleaning up the shredded remains of my sketches and tightening the light bulbs.

As I crack the powder room door open, I listen for my father, trying to place his whereabouts in the big house. Luckily, I can hear him down the hall in the kitchen shouting at someone on the phone. Even though I can hear exactly how far away he is, I still race to the front door with a beating heart as if he's going to jump out at any second.

My brothers are in the driveway, smoking by their cars. "Hey, where you going?" Gianni shouts and flicks his cigarette butt to the ground.

"Out." I raise my brow and give him an impatient look.

"Yeah, okay, don't tell me." He laughs. "Dad know?"

"He'll be happy I'm out of his sight, trust me."

"Whatever," he waves his hand and returns to his conversation with Renzo. Not that I'd expect them to care given the sum total of zero times they've stood up for me.

Once I'm out of their sight, I climb the iron fence surrounding our property so I don't have to deal with the guards at the gate, and run the rest of the way down the sidewalk. I don't need to run, no one's coming after me, but there's always a nervous giddiness I get when I'm seeing Finn.

Like I'm buzzing with energy and just *need* to sprint to get it out.

I can hear his old truck rumbling before I see it. He's the only guy I know who doesn't have a luxury car worth at least a quarter-million. He says it's because new cars don't have enough problems. He likes tinkering under the hood and fixing the parts that are always breaking on an old car. I don't get the appeal, but I can't say I hate the way he looks in grease-stained overalls and no shirt underneath.

---

8 Something to Someone by Dermot Kennedy | SummerOtoole.com/playlists

I bite my cheek, trying to get the image out of my head as I climb into the cab so I'm not blushing. He leans across the wide bench seat to offer me his hand and pull me in.

"Hi." I say, slightly breathless and quickly add, "I ran," with a shrug to explain why I'm out of breath. Because it's most definitely *not* because of the way his dark hair brushes across his lashes and the way my lungs squeeze when I meet his forest-green eyes.

"Hey—" His smile morphs into a frown, "You're bleeding." His brows pinch in concern, and I quickly turn toward the window and wipe at my nose with my sleeve. *Crap.*

"Your father?" There's a black shadow to Finn's growl that's cold and vengeful and it equal parts scares me and thrills me. "This is the last fucking time." He veers away from the curb and slams on the gas.

"Finn, he's not worth it," I plead as he approaches my gate. Because the reality is, no matter how satisfying I find the image of Finn making my father's nose bleed instead of mine, this wasn't the first time and it's far from the last.

"But *you're* worth it." He cuts me with a deep stare, and it strikes a part of me that has been told my whole life I am *not* worth it. Not worth respect and standing because I wasn't born a son. Not worth a voice or say because I'm just a pawn.

He pauses in the road when I put my hand on his arm and urge him to look at me. I can see my father's men at the gate start to walk toward us, curious. "What's there to do? He's the Don. You storm in there and try to tell him how to run his family and he'll take a finger or bust a kneecap just because he can. If you even make it that far."

His knuckles whiten around the steering wheel, and he presses his lips into a firm line as he stares straight ahead at the men closing the distance and pointedly reaching into their jackets where we both know they are carrying.

"Let's go, okay?"

He works his jaw like he's chewing on words unsaid. His foot stalls on the brake for a long, heavy pause. Finally, he puts the truck in reverse and looks at me. "Promise me one thing."

"Okay." I nod and he removes one hand from the wheel to cover mine on his arm.

"Next time, you call me, and I'll be there."

Chapter 10:

Only Yourself to Blame

Present

Finn

After receiving an anonymous complaint, we sent a city inspector who determined that the brick facade of your building has lost a substantial depth of mortar. To avoid a building code violation a licensed contractor must be used to repoint all brick with a mortar depth at or above 1/4" of depth within 30 days to avoid resulting fines of no less than $5,000.

I read the letter from the city's code enforcement office again and can't deny the smirk that plays on my lips.

My naughty plaything decided to abide by the rules this time and gave me the truth.

I suppose that means it's time for her reward.

I make a mental note to find out who to bribe at the city office to postpone this violation—if there is even a violation. I'm betting *Les Arnaqueuses* greased some palms to get this letter, and I'll just need to find whoever they paid and offer them more.

I type out half a text but decide better of it and call Effie instead. While it rings, I tap my finger against my thigh.

She answers, but I only hear an aggravated sigh. I wait, my skin buzzing knowing how antsy she must be getting from my silence. I'm proven right when she huffs, "*You* called me, Finneas. What do you want?"

I chuckle and absentmindedly spin in the desk chair in the Den's office. "I want to see you."

"Oh boy, let me just hop to it then," she says in a sarcastic tone that has me grinning.

"Deflecting nerves with sarcasm is a common defense mechanism."

"You don't make me nervous, Finn."

"I make you feel *something*." I sense her being seconds away from hanging up on me, so I quickly add, "I, on the other hand, always keep my promises. Do you want to see for yourself?"

"You're gonna delete everything?" I can hear a reserved hopefulness in her voice.

"Yes. The Den doesn't open for a few more hours. Come over." I can't explain the beat that rises in my throat while I wait fucking...*nervously* for her reply.

"Okay," she says, and the call ends.

I didn't realize how desperately I wanted to see her until those few passing seconds clutched my lungs.

This is getting fucking ridiculous.

Against my will, she possesses my every waking moment—and if I'm being honest, most of my sleeping ones too. I can no longer pretend it's out of concern for my family and the war that is brewing.

In the office at Peaches, she told me to get on my knees, and I fell like a sinner begging for salvation.

Then something switched inside me when I saw her eyes well up in that dusty parking lot. I've always been possessive when it comes to her, but when I saw those scars I became protective too. Summoning back up old feelings that will do nothing but get people hurt.

I drum my fingers on the desk to the tempo I know by heart and pinch the bridge of my nose with a determined exhale. I'll use the next time I see her as an opportunity to remind myself that a cooperating blackmail target does not make an ally.

She's still a Luciano, she's still the enemy.

Ten minutes later, she's walking through the Den's heavy wood doors. Her dark hair is piled up on top of her head, like it was thrown up haphazardly, but the messiness suits her. Her eyes harden when they meet mine behind the bar; she lifts her chin in greeting.

She weaves through the tables to me and raises a brow. "Well, let's do this."

My hand finds the small of her back while I guide her to the Den's office. It's an automatic gesture. But the moment I touch her, I realize just how fucked I am. Because I don't want to just lightly lay my palm on her, I want to dig my fingers into her until my hold is bruised and branded into her skin. I want to brush the tendrils of hair falling down the nape of her neck and sink my teeth in until she carries my marks.

There's so much I want to do with her, *to* her.

And that pisses me off because I am realizing with disturbing clarity that I lack control when it comes to Effie Luciano.

I follow her into the office and leave the door open, dropping into the desk chair. I already have the folder opened and I look at her beside me, scanning her face as she looks at the dozens of photos and videos.

To Effie's credit, her face doesn't give much away. But then she bites her lip and I notice her thighs twitch tighter where she stands next to me.

I stand and she turns to face me. I dust my thumb across her lip, ghosting across the teeth riveting into it. "Should I press play for posterity's sake?" It's a husky whisper that makes her pupils blow wide, her eyelashes fluttering.

Her lips part, and her breath hitches when I drag her soft bottom lip down. *Fuck*, I want to ruin her.

"Delete the files, Finn," she says almost breathlessly. But I can't pull myself away, my control is hanging on by a ratty thread, I can almost hear the fibers tearing bit by bit while I coast the back of my hand down her neck.

I lightly collar the base of her throat, my thumb rubbing softly in the hollow between her collarbones. I feel her swallow, and my stomach flips. Her eyes are like ice, cold but fragile. And able to melt if the heat is strong enough. "Do you want me, princess?"

"I want you…" My pulse jumps. "—To delete the files." She juts her chin and pushes into my hand. "Now."

"As you wish," I say dryly and sit back down. A few clicks of the mouse and I read aloud the dialogue box for her even though she's watching everything over my shoulder. "Deleting these 237 files from the cloud will delete them permanently from all devices. Do you wish to continue?"

"Good. Do it."

Another click and all evidence of that night is gone. Except for the memories. Those will never leave me, like a brand from a hot iron.

"Well, pleasure doing business as always, princess," I spin in the chair to face her and my stomach swoops when I realize how soft her eyes are now. *Thawed.*

Her mouth moves subtly, then falls partly open as if she was about to bite her lip but stopped. "Ask me again."

I tilt my head in question and she raises her brows in implication. I sigh through my nose when I realize what she means, my body tensing like it's preparing for a fight. Despite the rapid fluttering in my chest, I thread my thumbs into the belt loops of her jeans and tug her between my legs. "Do you want me?"

Her thick thighs wedge between mine, and I drop my thumbs to glide my palms over her round ass. She nods and pushes her pelvis forward, a timid but excited glimmer in her eyes.

"Is that a yes?" It feels like my spine is made of kerosene and I can feel the anticipation of a match about to strike. She nods again, the smallest of smiles tugging on her lips.

I stand, tightening my grip on her hips, I crowd her until our foreheads are nearly touching. "Say. It."

We share a held breath.

"I want you." And the match is struck, lighting up my body.

Grabbing her thighs, I hike her off the ground, and she responds hungrily, wrapping them around my waist. The soft, needy moan she makes when our mouths crash together is all it takes for me to say *fuck it.*

I spin us around and set her on the desk in front of the computer. A gnawing hunger paws at me as she skates her hands under my tee shirt and urges it over my head. If losing control is what it takes to sate this hunger, then consider me off the rails.

I clutch her face in my hands to deepen our kiss. It's frantic and hasty, like horny teenagers, but it's also perfect. The way she battles back as I try to coax my tongue further into her mouth. Neither of us willing to concede. She's lighting little fires everywhere she touches. My chest. My abs. My back.

She gasps for air when I break our kiss. There's a flash of something in her eyes—wariness, regret, acceptance—I can't tell. But it doesn't matter because all I can think about is claiming her. Taking her. *Owning her.*

"I told you once that I own you, you remember that, Ef? That means *everything.*" I cup her pussy.

She mewls in response. And I work on the button on her jeans while I continue, "I own you, not because of some fucking photos, not to taunt some fake-ass fiancé, but because—" *We were always meant to be* is what I want to say but it's not what comes out of my mouth. "Because you're just as desperate for me as your cunt is for my cock."

I kiss and bite a path down her neck, and she leans back, encouraging the way I ache to devour her. One hand is knitted tightly into her hair while the other fights with her zipper—*these fucking jeans.* I'm so close to breaking out a knife and just cutting them off her.

I thrust my hips between her legs, and even with our clothes, she moans hungrily when my hard cock rubs against her pussy. I lean forward to whisper in her ear. "So fucking desperate for my cock, just begging to be fucking claimed and fucked full of—"[9]

I catch movement in the corner of my eye and my body floods with ice.

I grab her wrist and wrench it forward. She yelps at the painful grip. "What the fuck is that?"

Her fist tightens, but I pry it open. A USB stick. That she was attempting to slot into my computer.

"You think you're above all us pitiful little humans, but you're just like any other fucking man: led around by his cock." She snarls, and ice turns to white-hot rage.

She fucking played me.

I'm too stunned by how far I've fallen that I don't see it coming when she knees me in the groin and pushes off the desk. She sprints from the room, and I pound my fist into the desk with a roar.

Just once. Just once, and then I collect my wits and think fast. A few taps on my phone and seconds later I have the entire Den locked down remotely. She's trapped.

I hear her rattling the interior doors before the wooden doors, tugging on the handle and cursing. As beautiful as her sweet whimpers were, the frustrated, harried sounds she makes now may be even better.

"*Oh, princess,*" I sing-song as I step out of the office unhurried, hands in my pockets. There's no need to rush. She's not going anywhere. This is always my favorite part, knowing my prey is trapped and just waiting for me to find them.

It's easy for my mind to switch gears completely. From lustful fool to top predator. I settle into my skin, feeling at home. *This* I know. *This* is when I'm truly in full control.

"I gave you a head start, but you can't hide. I will find you. Better start praying I'll show mercy when I do."

I stalk into the dining room and see her scamper through the tables toward the kitchen. *Perfect.* I can't wait to spread her over the large counter

---

9 Houndin—Layto | SummerOtoole.com/playlists

and make her beg.

When I enter the kitchen, my heart's pounding steadily. She's yanking on the back door's handle, and my mouth waters for retribution, to balance the scales. She's broken the truce, and now betrayed me again with this double-cross.

"Knock, knock," I chuckle, and she whips around, eyes wide and frayed. Her chest heaves and falls. Her eyes ping-pong around the room until they stop and narrow on a distant wall. I know exactly what she's spotted, I know every inch of this place. The knives that are lined up on a magnetic strip.

"Think you'll make it?" I taunt and see her calculation process on her face.

She makes a run for it, but I'm faster, closing the distance between us right when she reaches across the counter for a knife. I flatten her over the counter and pin her down by the neck. And for a split moment, there's a flash of disappointment, maybe even loss, that it had to be this way.

But it's gone as quickly as it came.

I pull a gun from my waistband and swallow down the growing lump in my throat, pressing the muzzle firmly to the back of her head.

Right above the wispy bits of hair that just minutes ago I wanted to brush aside so I could breathe in the scent of her skin.

A goddamn fool.

"Give me one good reason not to kill you right now."

She stopped fighting my hold as soon as I put the gun to her head, but she now turns her cheek as much as she can to look back at me, a cutting glare so full of venom I can almost feel the sting. "You thought I could genuinely want you after everything you've done? You repulse me, Finn."

I ignore the blow to my gut her words cause, telling myself they're a lie, even though I'm not sure they are. "Is that supposed to make me want to kill you *less?* Saying that I repulse you?" I force a laugh, it's dripping with dark bitterness.

Her eye contact never wavers. "You're not going to kill me because you could never live with yourself if you did."

I scoff. "I've killed people for much less, princess. And I sleep just fine."

"You can tell yourself you hate me, but you don't. You despise yourself because you can't hate me, no matter how hard you try." The truth in her words is a bomb in my stomach. "It's why I was able to get so close today. Because even though I could never bring myself to fuck you, you couldn't wait to jump at the chance."

Another blade digs into my back, and this time, it's one I put there myself. Because she's right. My desire for her is holding a knife to my own throat.

But I can't let her know that. No, she can't know how dangerously true her words are. I reach for my belt buckle and make extra effort to ensure she can hear the clanking of metal. She flinches under me. "I should take you right here. Show you how wrong you are. How little I care."

She laughs but there's a barely-there wobble in her voice when she says, "You're right, *it* is little.*"

I growl, ripping her off the counter and shoving her shoulder down. "Get on your fucking knees, Effie. And watch your mouth before I fill it." I flick the gun between her and the ground, and she drops to her knees, a cocksure smirk flitting on her lips.

"Go ahead, Finn. Force me to give you a blowjob at gunpoint. I couldn't possibly hate you more than I already do. So go ahead, because apparently the only way you can get a girl to touch you is with blackmail or a gun." She licks her lips, then holds open her mouth, tongue out, welcoming, but the menace in her eyes is pure and unadulterated.

I look at her wet tongue and mouth, open and ready for me. I could so easily slide my cock between her ruby-red lips and make her choke as I ruthlessly fuck her. Her eyes would water when I force myself all the way to the back of her throat until she gags. Then I'd make her swallow me down, every fucking drop.

I could.

But I don't.

Instead, I tuck the gun back into my pants and step over to the back door. Entering the code on a keypad, it unlocks, and I open it. "Get the fuck out."

She looks over her shoulders at me warily but slowly rises to her feet.

She takes tentative steps toward me and freedom as if it's a trap.

"Go." I say bitterly

She hurries out after that, but when she's a few paces away, I call, "So long as we're clear…" She pauses and looks back at me. "Whatever happens next: you only have yourself to blame."

Chapter 11:

What Happens Next

It's been three days since my failed attempt to get into Finn's computer.

I talked a big game—and I'm proud as hell for keeping it together—but I thought I was going to puke all over his Italian leather boots when he made me get on my knees. My stomach drops uneasily just thinking about it. Sitting on the couch, I draw my legs closer to my chest.

I get a chill down my arms remembering the cold metal of the gun.[10] I've heard my father's men and my brothers talk about being shot. You don't always feel it like you might think. Your body reacts so quickly, pumping you with adrenaline and setting you in shock, that you notice everything but the pain.

The smell of gunpowder.

The sound of your body hitting the ground.

10 Lost It All—Jill Andrews | SummerOtoole.com/playlists

The warmth of your spilling blood as your body grows cold.

But sometimes, they say, you can feel nothing but pain. Hot, searing, mind-numbing pain.

When the muzzle dug into my spine, I wondered which experience I'd have when he finally shot me. I considered the location he'd chosen and thought perhaps I'd avoid both. He was sparing me this one kindness, a one-shot kill.

The crew is out right now, probably somewhere deciding whether this job is even worth it now that I've fucked it up even worse. So, I'm left alone to ruminate on how close I came to dying, how I've destroyed the one job my father ever entrusted me with, and how—

A sharp knock at the door pulls me out of my spiraling pity party.

I hop off the couch and go to the door, standing on my toes to look through the peephole. All the air in my lung escapes as panic settles over me.

Hudson.

His hair isn't in it's usually perfectly coiffed fashion and dark circles ring his eyes. The collar of his coat is popped only on one side and his dress shirt is untucked.

There is no reason for him to be here. None. He shouldn't even know about this apartment.

"Effie, open the door." He drawls drunkenly and leans his forearm onto the door to peer into the peephole like a parrot bobbing its head. "I need to apologize," he slurs so it sounds more like *I needa apawl-a-size.*

Christ, he's wasted.

He stumbles back from the door and clutches his mouth. "I think I'ma be sick…" He starts to curl over, and I whip the door open.

"Okay, just get inside, I'll get you to a toilet—" My words are suffocating in my throat as he wraps his meaty hands around my neck and pushes me back into the apartment.

There's not a whiff of alcohol on him when he pushes his nose against mine and snarls in my face, "You fucking slut." Words crisp and clear.

"*Huud—*" I can't get any air, let alone words, out as he squeezes harder, kicking the door shut. Panic crawls up my body like a thousand pin pricks, demanding my body to react, fight, do *something*. But every thought is over-ridden by the aching wrench of my lungs for air and the feel of his grip crushing down on my esophagus.

He throws me to the floor and my knees skid on the wood, skin splitting. But I can finally breathe again, even if it's in sputtering, painful gasps. My elbow throbs where it broke my fall.

"Recognize these?" A ball of fabric lands by my head and I prop myself up to look at it.

The underwear Finn tore off me at Peaches.

"If you're having trouble remembering, I can show you quite the video to jog your memory. Received it in an unmarked package but I'm sure we all know who it's from." *Fuck. This is bad. Really fucking bad.* My mind floods with filthy images from what Finn made me do and what he did to me. If Hudson has seen even a few seconds of what transpired...

My pulse is so loud, blood pumping in my ears. He drags me from the floor by my hair. I'm sure I scream at the tearing against my scalp, but all I hear is *thump, thump, thump.*

My body doubles over when he delivers a wrenching blow to my stom-ach. But I'm yanked right back up again, his grip in my hair strong as ever.

Spittle lands on my face when he presses on. "You throw that fucking fit at the lunch about being called my fiancée, and then turn around and jack off that piece of shit wearing a ring that's supposed to be from me?"

Before I have a chance to respond he punches me in the jaw, my neck whipping and pain radiating like I was struck by a baseball bat. The impact makes me bite my tongue hard and blood wells in my mouth.

"I'd ask if you have any idea how terrible that makes me look, but I'm sure that was your intention, huh?" His face is scrunched in rage as he bel-lows and I'm just catching my breath when I spit bloody saliva at his feet.

"Or maybe I just wanted a real man to get me off before I'm forced to marry you."

His jaw bears down and his nostrils flare, red spreading into his cheeks. Enraged, he reaches for me again, but this time I duck and dodge around him. He spews filthy cuss words and accusations while he comes after me.

I don't make it far, my airways feeling bruised and winded. He catches me before I reach the door, fisting the back of my shirt and flinging me back into him. I collide into his chest, and he hooks his arm around my neck.

"*You fucking bitch*," he hisses, and his elbow squeezes, pinching my circulation.

I claw at his forearm, but it's as immovable as a tombstone. Very quickly my vision blurs and black dots begin to speckle the room. I have an out-of-body awareness that this is a much better way to die than being shot. I'll black out before he completely deprives me of oxygen.

Perhaps it will be an almost peaceful death.

Something I never considered I'd get in this life.

A calm settles over me as my eyelids droop. My surroundings become fuzzy. Still, even in this state, my thoughts float to Finn. *Would he come to my funeral?*

Before my eyes give into the darkness, I spare a passing glance out the window to his building. There's a light on in the living room. A soft, cozy, warm tone. I picture him reading a book in a big leather chair. Perhaps his hair is ruffled and unstyled after doing whatever he does all day. Maybe he's in sweats and relaxed, or maybe he's still in his business suit but has the top buttons undone. What tattoos might be showing?

For some reason that final thought—the fact that I will never know what tattoos sprawl across his chest—spurs me into action. A sudden and inexplicable burst of energy makes me swing my legs, fighting back.

Hudson grunts against my renewed strength and bends backward so my toes dangle off the floor. The black dots are turning into fully-formed, encroaching shadows, but something gold breaks through my haze.

A gold letter opener on the foyer table.

I swing madly. Using every last, fading morsel of strength I have to distract him by flailing all my limbs so hopefully he doesn't notice me reaching for it.

The black has nearly seeped completely through my consciousness. I can't see anything but faint bursts of light. Yet somehow I manage to bring the letter opener behind me and not stop when the blunt tip meets the resistance of his flesh.

A strangled cry is ripped from my lungs as his grip begins to slacken while I put everything I have into plunging the opener deeper into his neck.

I feel the wet heat of his blood spill onto my hand, still gripping the handle so hard my fingers ache. I only let go when he crumbles to his knees with a garbled, choking gasp and releases me.

My head spins, feeling dizzy as the room comes back into focus with the pressure on my neck gone. I scurry back on the floor until I hit a wall.

Thump. Thump. Thump.

My pulse beats heavily in my ears, ringing hollow and deep. It keeps me from hearing whatever sputtering sounds Hudson makes as he chokes to death on his own blood. I watch him writhe until he stops but I don't hear anything other than the thumping.

I don't know if it's minutes or hours later but eventually my senses return. Hudson is no longer making any noise. His body lies lifeless, even the blood has stopped spewing with the halt of his heart.

My mind draws a blank on what my next steps should be. I feel like I'm in a dream, still in a daze and waiting to wake up. Maybe I will sit here forever next to Hudson's body until it turns gray, then blue, then purple and decays.

Somehow, I find myself holding my phone to my ear, the ringing feels distant and rumbly like the sounds of waves on a beach.

"Effie?" Finn's voice cuts through my cloudy mind, and I suddenly remember how and why I ended up with my phone in my hand.

"Do you—Do you remember when you made me promise to—to call you and you'd—"

"And I'd be there." He finishes my sentence and a weighty sense of relief I don't quite understand settles in my chest. I hear rather than feel myself heave a gulp of air. *I think I'm crying?* "Effie, where are you? Are you at the apartment?"

I nod as if he can see me and somehow he infers my silence as a yes.

"I'm on my way."

Chapter 12:

The Decision

Finn

I hate when anyone talks over the TV. Either turn the damn thing off or shut your fucking mouth. It grates on my nerves like a rusty, serrated blade. I fucking hate it. So right now, as Cash yells an endless stream, I have no idea what the fuck he's saying. The governor's press conference is blaring on the TV and his voice is like nails on a chalkboard.

I run my hand over my eyes to keep from ripping my goddamn hair out but can't stand it anymore and slam the power button on the remote. Cash stops mid-sentence and whirls his eyes between where I am on his couch and the now-black TV screen.

"You better be listening to that, because 'the evil people responsible who will be held accountable for their crimes' is you." He uses air quotes around what I'm assuming the governor said. "Your recklessness is gonna turn this city on its fucking head. The one fucking time I leave you in charge, and you start a goddamn war."

Cash clenches and unclenches his fists as he paces with a permanent scowl on this face.

"Christ, would you calm the fuck down. They haven't even found the body." I drum my finger on the rim of my whiskey glass before taking a sip. The whiskey slides down my throat warm and full of spice. "And even if they did—*which they won't*—but if they did, nothing will trace back to us. I even dug out the bullets myself before dumping the body."

"What bullets? I thought you said Effie stabbed him."

"I did." *God, this is getting boring.* I've repeated what Effie told me— once she stopped hyperventilating—to Cash at least a dozen times. I suck in a bitter breath remembering how she looked. Bruised. Bloodied. *Broken.*

"So what fucking bullets, Finneas?" Cash tugs on his hair like he's the one losing his mind.

"Mine."

She called me, whispering between sobs as if she was scared someone was gonna hear her. I didn't even consider it might be another trap. I could feel her fear through the phone, like ice down my spine. I recognized her scratchy voice, raw and raspy, instantly as the sound of someone's voice after they've been strangled.

Hearing that twisted my insides like a fucking wrench.

"Had to make sure he was really dead," I scoff with an ambivalent shrug despite the fact that rigor mortis was setting in when I arrived. He was plenty dead.

The truth is, as soon as I saw the angry red handprints marring her neck, I couldn't help myself.

One bullet for the brutal bruising on her neck. One bullet for the swollen red mark on her jaw. One bullet for her raw, skinned knees.

And one last bullet that should've gone in me, for ever putting her in that situation.

The sky is overcast and a hazy gray, my favorite kind of weather. My brothers and I exit the car. We look like a motley crew of grim reapers in our matching black outfits. I'm wearing a leather jacket, Lochlan only wears a tight black tee, while Cash and Roan are in full suits, but we still look like a reckoning all lined up.

Nonna Rosa's is a family-style Italian restaurant that doubles as the headquarters for the Luciano family. Apparently cozy and crime go hand in hand.

Roman, our head of security and Cash's second, has already scouted the perimeter and gives us the go-ahead from his post at the corner of the street. My brother called this meet, but stepping on Luciano's turf means you can never be too careful. On his all clear, Cash pulls open the door and we follow him in.

I don't know what to expect from this meeting so entering the empty restaurant leaves me weary and full of trepidation. The wooden chairs are flipped and stacked on top of the tables, the place closed to the public tonight. A man shuffles behind the bar, and while he's dressed like wait staff, I'm sure he's a foot soldier and has at least two guns tucked out of sight.

Luciano's men greet us with metal detectors, and we each step up to be wanded and patted down. There's a ticking like a clock in my gut, a foreboding that something is about to go down.

"Geez, buy me dinner first," Lochlan jokes behind me when, I'm assuming, he gets patted a little too thoroughly.

"This way," one of the men says gruffly, and we follow him through the restaurant to the walk-in freezer.

A shelf in the back is already moved aside, and a hatch, that I'm sure is usually hidden, is open on the floor. Silently, we are led down the steps, and I shoot Cash a questioning glance. *What the fuck have you gotten us into?*

I have a lot of confidence in my brothers and me, but being led down a trap door with no weapons feels like we're just begging to be ambushed.

Our steps echo, and I tap my middle finger and thumb together in my usual beat, steadying my breath and keeping my face blank. If we are being led to our deaths, I don't want to give them even a whiff of unease. *Show no weakness.*

We descend into a room that reminds me of a 1920s speakeasy. The windowless room is lit with several small chandeliers, casting shadows off the ornate gold and jade wallpaper. Well-polished tables dot the floor, and a curved wooden bar lines the right wall. At a large round table sits Luciano, his Capo and—my lungs feel halved in size—*Effie*.

It's been nearly a week since she killed Hudson, but the bruises on her neck are still garish and prominent. Her jaw is less swollen, but still purpled, and she averts her eyes as soon as they meet mine, making me want to raise the fucker from the dead to kill him again.

Luciano rises as we approach, Bruno and Effie follow his lead, and my blood boils when I notice a slight wince to her movements.

"Gentlemen," Luciano welcomes as we sit down. Cash is the only one of us who relaxes back in his seat. The others and I cross our arms or steeple our fingers, elbows resting on the table. "We have a clear and unavoidable problem that threatens both our families." His snobby voice pisses me off, and I can't stop thinking that his slicked back black hair looks greasy.

"You think? Breaking a decade old truce tends to make things a little rocky—"

"Finneas, shut the fuck up," Cash barks, and I shift in my seat, rolling my shoulders and neck. "It's now irrelevant how we got in this situation, what matters is getting out of it."

"I won't deny the role my family played." I balk at his audacity, and Roan curses under his breath. "But this outcome is not one we ever intended—"

"Yeah, no shit," I slam my palms on the table and rise, "You *intended* on robbing us blind and starting another fucking war." I can't look at Effie when she flinches at my raised voice.

"Sit down, son," Luciano orders, and I truly regret not sneaking in at least a knife.

"I am *not* your son." My jaw clenches, and my fingers whiten on the table.

"The governor's not going to let this disappearance slide under the rug. He won't stop looking, and he won't hesitate to bring the full force of the

FBI, police, and his under-the-table goons down on us. Because unlike you two," he pointedly flits his gaze at me then his daughter, "He's not stupid. He's seen what you sent Hudson, and he's putting the pieces together."

"It's all circumstantial and speculation. He won't find a shred of admissible evidence." I slump back in my chair and crack my knuckles.

"Maybe not, but he can subpoena people he suspects to be witnesses. He has plenty of legal measures and political power to bring this house tumbling down." Cash picks up where Luciano left off. "We have knowledge that can bring Effie down, and she has knowledge equally as damning. So we've come to a decision that will protect both our families and stop history from repeating itself."

I glance across the table and Effie looks just as surprised by this "decision" as I am. In fact, the only ones who don't look totally confused by what is going on are Cash and Luciano. I drum my fingers impatiently on the table, not caring about the side eye my brother shoots me.

My chest feels like a heavy weight is slowly settling onto it as we sit in prolonged silence, waiting for someone to catch us the fuck up. I can't stop my gaze from traveling to her. Her long hair is brushed over her shoulders and down her back, a headband pulling it out of her face, leaving every inch of her flawless features visible. Even battered and bruised, she's still fucking stunning, and I fight the roiling heat in my gut when our eyes lock.

Hers are heavy and sad, and it makes me want to punch something, namely myself, for sending that bastard to her doorstep. The thought that I could have gotten her killed makes my lungs feel like they're collapsing.

"Spousal privilege," Luciano states, "precludes spouses from being compelled to testify against the other."

"I know what spousal privilege is, what does it have to do with me?" As soon as the question leaves my mouth, I realize the direction of this conversation, and it seems Effie does too.

"No, absolutely not!" Effie pushes her chair back and crosses her arms defiantly. "He's the fucking reason we're in this mess in the first place!" Her voice cracks, and red deepens the olive tone of her cheeks.

"Consequences of your own actions," I volley back. "*This,*" I point at

Luciano, "is the result of you breaking the truce." I can't bring myself to blame her, not when I sent that package. But her megalomaniac father? Yeah, I can blame him.

"You started this, *you* fix this, Luciano." Cash tries to stop me from standing, but I bat his hand away. "You think you can plot against us, and then smooth things over with wedding bells? You're fucking insane."

"*Finneas,*" Cash hisses my name under his breath, and I reluctantly sit back down. He addresses the group again, taking an envelope from his pocket and unfurling the sheet inside. "It's already done."

"That's not my signature, no way that will pass as authentic."

"It will when you have friends in the right places." Luciano fixes me with a smug, sleazy smile. "All that's left is to consummate it. Better get to it, lovebirds."

The drive to Bartlett Farms is silent. Not a word is spoken between us. It's a painful contrast to the last time we drove out here together. She spends the entire drive staring at the passing landscape through the window, but unlike last time, she never turns to look at me with softness in her eyes and a faint smile on her lips.

After realizing that this marriage was happening with or without our consent—the right palms greased to pass the forged marriage certificate—Cash sent us off to Bartlett Farms to lay low for a while. The last residents passed a few years back, and the property doesn't have any financial trail back to us.

Objectively, it's a good plan. We can hide out without being too far from June Harbor in case shit hits the fan. And being legally married…well, it's a smart move. Protects both our asses if we both stay silent, but it's mutually assured destruction if one of us talks. I don't like the idea of being so precariously tied to Luciano now, but I don't completely hate the idea of Effie as my wife.

Though she certainly seems to.

All I can hope is that even though I failed to keep her safe, I can protect her now.

We pull into the farm's drive and my low-riding sports car sounds like it's being torn up driving over the gravel. I park in front of the old barn. It looks better than the last time Effie was here. The roof isn't sinking inward, and the gaps in the wood siding have been patched up. It's been a sort of project of mine, I guess.

"Do you remember this place?" I ask, while I remove our luggage from the small trunk.

"Of course," she says, almost bitterly, and it stings.

"I've been converting the upstairs loft into an apartment. We can stay there." A motion sensor light on the barn turns on as I guide us around the corner.

Effie looks back at the farmhouse. "Why aren't we staying in the big house?" *Because I can't stand the idea of you having that many rooms to avoid me in.*

"It hasn't been touched since Mrs. Bartlett passed. Trust me, this is smaller but much better."

The barn's ground floor has been split in two. The front portion is my garage where I used to tinker on my truck and other odds and ends I'd find at rummage yards. The back half is the small living room and kitchen of the converted apartment. I let us inside, and Effie cranes her neck to look at the high vaulted ceilings. The walls are the original wooden planks, but fixed up where it was needed. It gives the whole place an earthy scent, like you'd expect to be walking across straw on the ground. Except instead of straw and dirt, the ground is polished concrete with mismatched rugs I found at flea markets.

"Bedroom's upstairs." I nod to the handmade steps leading somewhat precariously up to the loft. Effie circles in place, looking around, arms wrapped around her midsection like she's cold. "There's uh...no central air, but um...there should be wood somewhere on the property. I can get the stove going if you're cold."

"I'm fine."

"Okay."

[11]Our words are so stilted, nothing like the sharp sparring words we've wielded over the past few weeks. Maybe it's being back here. Maybe it's just being around her. But I suddenly feel like the shy twenty-one-year-old who first took her here. My skin itches, like I can't get comfortable in her presence, waiting for the next shoe to drop. *Waiting for the phone to ring...*

At least not when she's like this. Shut down. Dejected. Like being married to me is the worst fucking thing in the world.

I know how to handle her when she's pulling my hair and screaming my name as she comes apart on my tongue. I know how to handle her when she's full of venom and spite. But this? This isn't a version of Effie I ever want to see.

And I'm the cause of it.

I notice she keeps looking to the corners of the room, and suddenly I realize why. "There's no cameras here."

"Yeah, alright," she scoffs, and that small bite back makes heat crawl under my skin.

I drop our luggage at the bottom of the steps. "I've been honest this whole time, Ef. *You're* the one whose lies landed us here."

"*Honest?*" she balks. "Sure, you've been honest, if that means being a deceitful, manipulating bastard." Her eyes harden and her shoulders set. She crosses the room to me. "You are not innocent in this, Finneas."

"Maybe not, but you're not some hapless victim either." I step closer. She takes a step back so she doesn't have to tip her head back to look at me. I can't resist the urge to tower over her. Make her choose between standing her ground or cowering back. "Bed's upstairs, *wife.*"

"Don't fucking call me that," she says sharply while brushing past me to climb the stairs.

I follow behind her, bags in tow, dropping them at the top with a heavy thunk. She's standing next to the bed with a death glare, her arms crossed.

---

11 you broke me first—Tate McRae | SummerOtoole.com/playlists

She says something under her breath I don't quite catch, then with a sigh, she bends over the edge of the bed and hikes her dress up.

I suck my lip between my teeth as my eyes rake over her full, dimpled ass. Faded stripes of stretched skin cover her hips and get lost under her purple panties. I've never had a stronger urge to sink my teeth into anything more than I want to take a bite out her perfect, fucking ass right now.

My feet decide to break their stupor and I cross the room with reverence, gazing upon my offering. My dick swells in my pants, and I groan when I undo my belt and relieve some of the pressure on it.

My breathing deepens the closer I get, the stronger my need to slide my fingers between her legs and see if my wife is already soaked for me.

My wife. Effie Luciano. Fuck.

I slide my pants down my hips and stroke my cock, my piercing already slick with pre-cum. I spread my palm wide on her lower back and skate it up her spine. I watch with delighted fascination as the fine hairs on her arms, draped on the mattress by her head, stand on end. *I make her fucking shudder.*

I smooth both hands down her sides and grip her hips. I hear her draw in a deep breath, as if in preparation. I toy with the waistband of her panties. But then I pick her up and flip her over, pushing between her knees.

Her eyes are sharp, her tone just as cutting. "What are you doing?"

I stroke her thighs, inching her legs wider. "I'm going to look my wife in the eyes the first time I take her." I reach for her panties again, but she pushes my hand away. My brows pinch in confusion, and her next words are worse than getting fucking shot.

"I don't want to see your face." She flips back over and plants her feet on the ground to bend over the bed. She shimmies her underwear down her legs almost spitefully.

My stomach churns, and my jaw clenches painfully tight seeing her pussy presented to me with such...such *hatred.*

I swallow down the sour taste in my mouth and reach around her waist with one hand. I use two fingers to slide over the seam of her pussy, my cock jumping at the warm slickness waiting for me.

"Finn…don't…" She looks over her shoulder at me as I part her lips and press gently over her clit. Her brows are pinched and her eyes…they make something cold and grating twist around my heart.

When I speak, it's a whispered plea. "Let me at least make it good for you." *Please.* She shakes her head and swallows deeply. I wonder if the same caustic taste is coating her tongue.

"Just get it over with." Her words slice my heart in two, like wire through a block of clay. My stomach twists painfully as I realize she probably said something to a similar effect before bending over the first time. And I came at her like a clueless fucking caveman.

"As you wish," I say through gritted teeth as I drop my hand and position my dick at her entrance. I suck in a painful breath as my head kisses her tight heat. It's everything I've ever wanted in the worst possible way.

"Please, Fi— Just do it." The resentment and sadness in her voice makes my throat squeeze around a rock with jagged edges. My teeth ache as I push in into her, my jaw so excruciatingly tight as I hold back hot tears.

A small gasp spills from her lips as I sink fully into her. I draw out slowly knowing my piercing is dragging against her inner walls and wanting to give her a chance to adjust to the new sensation. My hips punch forward again, and I bite back a moan. She feels so fucking good. Her cunt is hot and tight. My dick doesn't know the difference. Doesn't know that my chest is splintering with every inch I bury myself.

The loft is uncomfortably quiet. The only sounds are the soft punches of my breath with each thrust and the slight creak of the bed. Somewhere outside, an owl calls into the night.

Every cell in my body is screaming to thrust harder, deeper. To dig into her hips until my fingertips are imprinted on her skin. To bring my hand down hot and fiery on her ass for the spark of causing a little pain. I so badly want to reach around and lathe her clit with attention until I feel her clench around my cock in a rapture of her own.

But I can't do any of that. Not without her hating me more. So rather than give into my carnal drive to break her down and reshape her as my own, I tap a rhythm lightly on her hip to keep from squeezing until she bruises.

As my pleasure—if I can even call it that—builds, it's sickly-sweet. The sensations that usually make me feel like a god, now make me feel dirty and perverted. I try to concentrate on pumping in and out, keep it mechanical and impersonal, but then I see her fists twist into the quilt, and it breaks something in me. I squeeze my eyes shut as I focus on the rising tide, my balls drawing tight and tingling heat zips up and down my length.

"Fu—fuck," I curse as hot, blinding pleasure pulses through me and into her.

I keep my eyes closed a moment longer, scared to open them. Scared to see the one person I was supposed to protect and treasure, bent over, used and leaking my cum.

I gather my breath on shaky legs. When I tenderly pull out of her, she doesn't move, just lays there, cheek against the mattress, intimately exposed. She looks heartbreakingly vulnerable.

I know I should leave, just walk away, not prolong this experience any longer than necessary. But I feel physically ill leaving her like this.

So without a word, I gently smooth her dress back down and brush a kiss on her shoulder.

I go straight to the garage and hit the punching bag until my knuckles are raw and bleeding.

Then I hit it some more.

Chapter 13:

Lucky

Effie

[12]I'm going to kill him. *I'm going to fucking kill him.*

I throw on whatever clothes I find on the floor after I rummaged through the suitcase last night and left everything like a bomb went off. Before I stomp down the stairs, I spy a lavender cardboard box on the nightstand. I thought I couldn't get any angrier, but I guess I was wrong. I pick it up, seething, and barrel straight out the door.

When I get outside, Finn has the barn door to the converted garage wide open and just like he was *all fucking night,* he's pounding a hanging punching bag. The sun is barely cresting the tree line. Morning fog is still clinging to the berry fields.

He doesn't hear me as I approach him from behind. He moves fluidly and light, his lean back muscles dripping with sweat. Each punch radiates raw power, and I swallow a humbling breath. It's not until this moment, watching the strong, sinewy muscles of his arms flex, that I realize how much rage and violence he's been holding in, taking it out on the bag.

I shout his name. He doesn't respond, and I try again, raising my voice. Fed up, I slip one of my slides off and fling it at the back of his head.

"The fuck—" He spins, rubbing the back of his head and pulling out an ear bud. His scowl melts when he realizes it's me. Mine doesn't.

"It wasn't enough to keep me up half the goddamn night with the sound of you punching away, but you had to wake up at the ass crack of dawn to continue and ruin the little sleep I was able to get?"

He dips his chin and flicks his tongue out to suck his bottom lip under his teeth. He levels me with a heated stare that makes me squirm. He breathes heavily through his nose as his eyes rake over me hungrily. I can't deny that my own breathing grows shallow under the smoldering weight of his gaze.

"Did you hear—"

"Are you—Is that my shirt?" He cocks his head to the side, a lifted eyebrow and curious amusement spreading across his face. I look down in horror, heat rushing my cheeks. I must have swept it up by accident in my angry rush.

"Don't change the subject."

He steps forward like a hungry predator but stops himself, and my eyes roam the canvas of his body. His tattooed chest rises and falls, and sweat runs in rivulets down his chiseled abs. The black ink spelling out *VULPES* in an arch above his diaphragm is a handsome contrast to his fair skin. Celtic knots twist and turn into the shape of a fox's head on his sternum, and a patchwork of smaller, traditional-style tattoos decorate the rest of his skin.

My hand crunches around the small box in my hand, and I throw it at his feet. "And what the fuck is this shit? *Plan B*? You really think I'd let you stick your dick in me and risk having little Fox brats running around if I wasn't on birth control?"

He glances at it but doesn't pick it up and swallows hard. He fixes me with a stare that's both angry and apologetic, as if he's mad I didn't accept his gift, but sad he thought it was necessary. "I didn't know."

"Of course you didn't, because you didn't bother to fucking ask." My blood boils, temperature rising with my voice.

Last night was terrible, I tell myself while I'm trying to remember how to breathe.

I'm still sore, because despite what I said in the Den, it's *not* little. Far from it and before last night, it had been a while. A moment that I've thought about for years as an intangible fantasy was ruined by the fucking mess we've found ourselves in.

I meant what I said last night. I didn't want to see his face. But not for the reason he thinks.

I didn't want to see the apology in his eyes because I'm not ready to forgive him. I *don't* forgive him. He's hurt me in so many different ways, and I still come crawling back for more. Maybe he's right, and I like the pain. Whether it comes in the form of a paddle in his hand or the emotions behind his eyes. Maybe I need the sting and burn and hurt to feel something more than the cold detachment permeating my everyday life.

I knew if he fucked me face to face, he would try to kiss me. And I would let him. And whatever hope I tasted on his lips would make it all hurt so much worse.

"Looks good on you." He flicks his chin at my outfit with a wolfish grin. I get the feeling he's purposely trying to annoy me to avoid addressing the fact that he was too eager to get his dick wet than ask about protection.

"You're the fucking bane of my existence, you know that?" I tug the shirt over my head and throw it at him. His jaw slackens and nostrils flare as his eyes comb over my thin bralette. "I picked it up by mistake. Maybe I would have noticed if I'd gotten a lick of sleep last night."

He balls the shirt up, and I notice blood is seeping through the tape around his knuckles. "You're welcome to my shirts anytime. What's mine is yours, wife."

"Thanks for the offer, but it won't happen again. Now I'm going back to bed, and you're going to find something to do that doesn't sound like a fucking army of rhinoceros is going to bust through the floor."

He calls after me as I walk away, "Next time, lose the bra and I'm sure your body will entertain me for a long time."

And then the infuriating pounding of fist on leather resumes again.

Maybe I should have killed him.

[13]I'm puttering around the small apartment looking for something to entertain myself with while Finn is thankfully somewhere out of sight. I find a ring of keys by the door and decide to go exploring. *What's his is mine, right?*

Two keys go to the garage and apartment in the barn. Not super interesting. The other three keys are clearly meant for doors, so I figure the next best option is the big house.

Climbing up the steps, I have a strong rush of déja vu about the night I was here last with Finn ten years ago...

The truck's headlights swept across the dirt drive, and I looked out the window to the aged but clearly well-loved farmhouse. A few hours earlier, Finn got into a fight with a cashier who was rude to me. I can't remember what started it, but when Finn told him to watch his mouth, he told him to fuck off.

Then Finn broke his nose. The tired look in his eyes walking out of that gas station is burned into my memory. Even at twenty-one, he had a reputation to uphold, but he didn't get any joy out of it. Not like now.

Now, I can see the way his eyes light up at the promise of inflicting pain. And despite any rational logic, I want to feel that pain.

Christ, I'm fucked up.

The second key I test in the front door unlocks it. The door creaks as I slowly open it. I feel as if I'm breaking into someone's home though I know it's empty. I try to tuck away the memory of the last time I was here and everything that followed, and distract myself with what's in front of me.

Finn was telling the truth. The place looks completely untouched. Like

---

the previous owner just evaporated and nothing changed save the buildup of dust. There's a rocking chair in the front room with a hand-knit blanket draped over the back and a book face down on the seat, still spread open to hold their page.

The house looks suspended in time, glass lamps and doilies on most side tables and surfaces. Porcelain angels and other figurines are amongst the knick-knacks strewn about, the typical stacks of Stephen King and James Patterson books piled on end tables. Embroidered pillows and chunky blankets are piled on the corners of the couch.

There's a sign by the front door that makes me smile. *Have a berry good day*, it reads, and I can picture a wife kissing her husband goodbye as he rises with the sun to work in the fields. Maybe she wakes up before him to start a pot of coffee and make his morning eggs. Or maybe he slinks out of bed and dresses in the bathroom quietly so she can continue sleeping undisturbed, only brushing a passing kiss on her cheek on his way out.

I stroll through the rest of the house with a sort of deference for the life and people who lived here. It's so easy to walk past the collection of floral casserole dishes and China plates and picture a happy family around the dinner table saying grace. To look at the height markers on the door jamb, written in crayons and pencil over the years and imagine the house full of kids playing or coming in muddy from a day outside.

I find a hallway filled with black and white and sepia tone photos hanging on the walls. They clearly tell the story of Bartlett farm from the earliest generations. A pair of men stand in a freshly tilled field in work overalls, their arms draped around each other's shoulders. Accomplished smiles light up their faces even as they squint into the sun and one of them proudly has his foot on a shovel head staked in the ground.

I recognize one of the men in another photograph. He's older and has a woman at his side with a baby on her hip. They are posing in front of what I assume is the original hand-painted sign for Bartlett Farms.

I watch the baby turn into a young girl, gain a younger brother, learn to ride a tricycle, and jump off the pond's dock as a teenager.

I know these are idyllic snapshots of years of life. Life that is bound to be full of laughter and tears, joy and heartache. But still I can't help but feel a bittersweet pinch in my chest seeing happy, *normal*, childhoods. More bitter than sweet.

The resentment that suddenly overcomes me is suffocating. I mourn what I never got to have. It's a sad kind of anger that makes you want to scream into a pillow and cry in a dark room.

But at the same time, I don't want to stop looking. Like watching a movie you know has a tragic end, I am drawn to the fantasy of the charming, farm-family life even if it hurts.

There's a photo that shows the barn in its just-built glory, another of a Fourth of July parade, and then one in particular that catches my attention. It looks like the family inside some sort of bunker or low-ceiling concrete dome, simple bunk beds built into the walls and cans of food lining shelves. A bomb or fallout shelter?

I pull out my phone and snap a picture of the frame, curious if this structure is still on the property, and making a mental note to find out.

The pounding sound has returned, different from the bag but still just as annoying. I leave the farmhouse and walk around back to investigate—even though I already know who the culprit is.

Finn swings the axe above his head and brings it down hard on the log of wood. He's in jeans now, but just like this morning, he's still shirtless, still sweaty, and still so gorgeous it hurts.

Last night, he fucked me slow. He didn't grip my flesh nearly as hard as I expected him to. He was unsettlingly gentle, but I wonder, was his head thrown back as he rocked into me, or did he keep his eyes on the job in front of him like the wood? Was *I* just a job to him? Or a hole? Was I even a fucking person?

Was the entire act a dream turned nightmare like it was for me?

I kick a piece of gravel as I walk and Finn spins at the sound. "Where you've been?"

"Around." His lip quirks at my short response.

"So, is this what you do when you're not killing men and ruining lives? Play lumberjack in the country?"

"Thought a fire would be nice." He looks down and brushes wood chips off the stump before looking back up at me. "It was cold last night."

"Oh." I don't know what else to say to the uncharacteristically thoughtful gesture. In fact, it makes me uncomfortable, and I fidget with the keys in my hand.

"Anyway." He clears his throat, as if my awkwardness is contagious. "I, uh—Come with me. I want to show you something." He swings the axe to lodge in the stump and picks a white shirt off the ground, shrugging it over his head.

"What is it?"

"Just fucking—" I widen my eyes at his tone, and he pinches the bridge of his nose. "I mean, will you please come?"

"I'm shocked you didn't gag getting that out."

He shakes his head. "Follow me."[14]

He walks in the direction of the woods and cold grips me when we enter the forest. Like the memories of what happened here linger in the air. Last time I entered these woods, life was never the same.

The path has narrowed since last time I was here, but Finn continues as if he's sure of the way. The pond is visible through the trees, and I wonder if the dock is still there, it looked on the verge of collapsing ten years ago.

As if reading my mind, he says, "The dock is a quarter mile that way. I can take you on the way back."

"It's still standing?"

He chuckles. "Surprisingly."

We walk in silence until we arrive at a clearing and stop in front of a semi-circle concrete structure that disappears into the earth. I recognize it as a similar shape to the shelter I saw in the photograph.

"Effie…" Finn starts but looks up, a crease between his brows as if he's struggling to find the words. "We're on the same team now. Whether we want it or not, it's the truth. You're stuck with me now." He forces a dry laugh. I don't join in.

---

14 Stop playing *Fine*

"Right, well, my point is, we're a team—"

"And we better get our head in the game? Where are you going with this, Finn?"

He sucks in a breath before trying again. "My brothers and I? We're unbeatable because the two things we value most are loyalty and honesty. We all should have died on the streets years ago, but we didn't, and now we're the most powerful fucking family in this country.

"Look at what happened with us, I wasn't honest with Cash—I should have told him as soon as I learned about *Les Arnaqueuses*, but I didn't and here we are." I give him a *speed it along, buddy* look. "The point is, you're my wife and I'm your husband. Which means no more secrets, no more plotting, no more backstabbing, or double crossing. Honesty and loyalty."

Honesty and loyalty.

Two words that make my stomach roil, especially given the earnestness in Finn's eyes. His hand opens and closes into a fist as if he wants to reach for mine but decides against it.

Honesty and loyalty.

I don't know if I will ever be able to give those things to a Fox—especially now. But more importantly, can I ever expect those things *from* a Fox?

"So I wanted to start with this." He turns to the metal doors of the structure and slides a panel to the side. He places his palm on an electronic screen and steps forward, a blue laser scanning his eye. Then he enters a pin on a keypad.

I can hear the sound of locks as mechanisms disengage on the other side of the door and my stomach drops. Finn only confirms my suspicion. "This whole thing started because you wanted our cache. Well, here it is."

He pushes the unlocked doors open, the metal hinges groaning. "Biometric and password-based security. And before you get any ideas, the hand has to be attached to a person with a beating heart."

"Dammit," I quip. He gives me a wink over his shoulder, and it helps diffuse some of the tension knotting in my body.

We climb a ladder down into the bunker, and the air grows distinctly colder under the layers of earth and concrete. "It used to be a fallout shelter, built during the Cold War," Finn explains. "Added some security features, and it's now one of the biggest, most secure safes in the country."

I take in the large room filled with stacks of art, wooden crates full of priceless artifacts, piles of gold and jewelry made of precious gems like something out of an Indiana Jones movie.

"I can't believe some of this stuff even exists," I say in awe, my attention captured by a Renoir painting. I feel Finn come up behind me, every nerve in my body attuned to his presence.

"Do you still paint?" he asks in a low, tender voice and brushes hair off my neck, a cold burst of air on the exposed skin.

"No," I say, tilting my head at the painting, and Finn dusts a finger down the slope of my neck, making the hairs on my arms raise.

"Why not?"

I turn around, and he looks down on me, eyelids heavy and gaze locked on my lips. "Same reason you drive a million-dollar sports car and stopped tinkering on your old truck."

He scoffs. "Touché, princess. I guess we've both given up things we love." And wanders away slowly.

I carefully flip through a lost sketchbook that once belonged to Picasso when a loose sheet of paper slips out and flutters to the floor. I pick it up, turning it over before tucking it back in place.

My heart stutters looking at the drawing. I struggle to get in enough air, as if the oxygen has been sucked out of the bunker. Staring back at me is my own reflection, ten years younger.

My throat goes dry as I realize it's one of the last things I drew before I stopped. The self-portrait I'd drawn when my father flew into a rage and tore up my drawings. Before rushing out of the house to meet Finn, I shoved one in my pocket. It must have fallen out of my pocket at some point...

I'd forgotten all about it.

Remembering that he brought me to the Bartlett Farms that day—and by the tattered look of the drawing, I wonder if Finn found it on the ground here. There's brushes of dirt and the pencil lead is smudged in some areas.

I don't know how to feel. I don't know what to think. My jaw grows tight, and my eyes sting with tears. I have so many questions, most of all why is it here? Why is my silly, little sketch among gold artifacts and long-lost masterpieces?

I'm not sure I can handle the answer, so like a coward, I close the journal and tell Finn I'm ready to leave.

I'm silent on the walk back, my thoughts so preoccupied by what I found and what it means, that I don't realize he's led us right to the dock. The sun is touching down, and the last bits of rusty sunset are giving way to indigo and stars. The moon is tucked behind a cloud, but crickets still sing to welcome her rise.

Hit with a wave of emotion and what we could have been, I barely feel Finn sweep my hand in his and guide us to the edge of the dock. Just like that night, water lilies float on top of the inky water, catching the final bits of sun in their white petals.

Finn faces me and brushes a piece of hair behind my ear. "I should have kissed you that night."

His words take me by surprise. "It wouldn't have changed what happened."

"I know." He slowly rubs his thumb in circles in my palm. "But it may have changed me."

"How do you mean?"[15]

"Sometimes, I think…maybe I could have kept more of my humanity if I had shared it with you. Even if only for one night." Like a razor-sharp blade, his words carve into my chest, clawing apart something already too brittle.

"What humanity? Did you ever have any to begin with?" I don't realize the rage seeping through the broken pieces until I hear the anger in my own voice. I shove him hard in the chest, "Where was your humanity when you killed my people? When you tied me up and tortured me? When you nearly got me killed because of videos you leaked?"

Tears stream down my face, cathartic yet bitter. I push him again and again. "When you held a gun to my head? Where the fuck was it then?"

---

15 Tears of Gold—Faouzia | SummerOtoole.com/playlists

He takes each blow with a step backward, but no words. Doesn't even give me the dignity of a reply. Stone-faced and cold. *"Answer me, you fucking—"* my breath catches on a sob, *"bastard."*

He's only an inch from the edge of the dock, but it doesn't stop me from slamming into him with all my weight. His eyes fly open as his feet slip and he falls back. Grasping out, he grabs my wrists and we both go flying into the frigid water.

The sting of the cold water fuels my fight, and I come up for air, sputtering but intent. I find Finn's shoulders and try to push him back down. Our legs tangle in the water lily vines and water splashes in our struggle.

He tries to shove me off, but I swing around to his back and wrap my arms around his neck. "Why, Finn? Why are you so determined to destroy me?"

He still hasn't said a word, only grunts and gasps as I kick him in the stomach or plunge his head under the surface.

"Say something, you coward!"

He dips under the water again, but this time, he twists on his ascent and grabs my arms, propelling us until my back hits the small metal ladder off the dock. I fight in his vice grip, screaming and kicking.

"Effie, *Effie!"*

"You ruined me. You *ruined* me, Finn." I sob, thrashing in the water. He pins me with his hips, and I buck against him, pushing as much as I can with my arms captured.

The paddle. The ring. The sketch.

All these things flash through my mind and my heart, and it feels like my soul is being torn in two different directions—

Suddenly, hot lips are on mine, rough, cold hands are clutching my face. My head spins and I give in to the urging tongue, licking at the seam of my mouth, I melt into the palms on my cheeks.

Finn breaks the kiss but keeps my face held tightly to his. "Christ, I didn't know what else to do," he says breathlessly, and I'm sucking in hungry gulps of air.

"I hate you."

"I know," he sighs, pressing his wet forehead to mine.

"So let me go." I twist and turn, but he keeps me pinned against the hard edges of the ladder. "Finn, goddammit, let go of me!"

"I *can't*," he says like it physically pains him, and I get the impression he's not just talking about right now, right here. His hand skates down my waist and bunches in the soiled material of my dress caught up in the water.

The tighter he holds me, the harder I fight back, tearing and pulling at his shirt until it rips. My hands hit his bare chest, and a bolt of lightning courses through me. I can't help it.

All the energy put into pushing him off begins fighting to pull him closer. He desperately palms my bare thigh, pushing away my dress.

Our mouths crash into one another again, and I can hardly breathe but can't get enough of him either. I twist my finger into his hair until he groans against my lips, and I eagerly swallow it down.

His hands are everywhere at once. Roaming my thigh. Pulling away my panties. Groping my breast. Pinching my nipple. Collaring my throat. Tugging my hair. I am lost in the heat of him and the cold of the water.

His torn shirt flutters at his sides, and I rip it off his shoulders, baring him all to me. My fingers dip deeper to wrestle with his soaked jeans and once I undo the button he kicks them down.

"*Finn,*" I breathe.

"I'm here." He rocks into me, and I feel his erection slide up my stomach. I reach out for it, and he bites into my shoulder when I twist up and down his shaft. "Fuck, Effie. If I've ruined you, you've *obliterated* me."

I need him. More than I've ever needed anything. I can't explain it. I definitely don't understand it. But there's not a cell in my body that doesn't ache to feel him consume me the way he seems ravenous to.

"Reach behind. Grab the ladder," he growls into my ear. Then he rakes his teeth down my neck.

He cups my cheek in one hand, delicately plucking my lips in a kiss as he slots his dick along my entrance. "Do it, Finn. *Please.*"

Once his head is positioned just inside me, he wraps his arm around my waist and slams into me, sheathing himself in my pussy.

"*Oh—god.*" I feel so full, but unlike last night it's a sense of being completed. It's a moment of genuine intimacy, not duty.

"*Effie—*" He cuts himself off with another sharp thrust of his hips that slams me against the ladder and brings water spraying between us.

I remove my hands from the ladder to clutch his face and demand he see my eyes even in the quickly fading light. "Fuck me and tell me how lucky you are." He stills his thrusts and breathes heavily, taking in my words. "How lucky you are that after everything that's happened, everything you've done, I'm still here, still *wanting* you."

I see him swallow and close his eyes before gently plucking my hands off him and placing them back on the ladder. He fixes me with a darkened stare, imploring me to hold on.

My fingers dig into the rusty rungs, and then he's giving himself to me, pouring himself out with body and words. Each punch of his hips is another apology, another praise, another expression of gratitude.

I don't know when the tears start again, but he licks them up, leaving kisses in their place on my cold damp face. I squeeze my legs around his waist and moan as pleasure skitters like sparks over my body. He pulls me down while lifting my knees, hitting a new angle which makes my pussy throb and flutter around him.

His movements become hurried. "Effie," he pleads, "Come with me."

I mewl, leaning into the high building in my core. "*Yes.* Don't stop, please, don't stop."

"You feel so. Fucking. *Right.*" He pumps fiercely into me on each word, holding my body tight and my knees high. I tip over the edge, and my orgasm crashes through me until I can't feel the cold of the water. "Fuck, keep coming like that on my cock and I—" He slams into me once more and buries his face in the crook of my neck.

I hold his head, breathing heavy, and stroke his wet hair. His body envelops mine as I tether us with a hand on the ladder.

I don't know how long we stay like this, sharing one another's rawest forms in the water. Clinging to each other's broken souls. But I do know, when he finally carries me out, we are not the same people we were when we fell in.

Chapter 14:

Flowers and Gold

Finn

[16]Her teeth are chattering by the time we arrive at the barn, her wet dress clinging to her body. I climb the steps with her in my arms, bringing her to the bathroom. It's a tiny fucking thing with a slanted roof, tucked into the eaves. I set her on the toilet while I turn on the shower and grab a blanket from the bed.

"Let's get you out of this thing." Gathering up the hem, I lift the dress up and over her head. She shivers when her wet hair lands on her bare back, and I quickly wrap the blanket around her.

She's silent, hasn't said a word since the lake. I'm worried she might be going into shock until she delicately slips her icy fingers into the waistband of my jeans, tugging me forward. My chest swells as her numb fingers struggle with the button and soggy denim. When she finally gets it, she pulls them down, and I step out of them, waiting for her to look up at me.

Steam starts rising from the shower. She shrugs the blanket off her shoulder, and we're left naked in front of each other for the first time. Her eyes stay fixed to our feet, but I need to see her amber eyes. I lift her chin up with two fingers. I need her to see my eyes, see the truth in them when I say, "You're so fucking beautiful, Ef. Sometimes it feels like I can't fucking breathe."

The crease between her brows slackens, and she rises on her toes to kiss my nose. I don't think I've ever been kissed there before and the casual intimacy of it makes my heart lodge in my throat. Her eyes are soft and her lips curl ever so slightly as she takes my hand and pulls back the shower curtain.

The shower is cramped, and our bodies are forced to shuffle against each other. I use both hands to brush the hair out of her face as I take her in. *Truly fucking stunning.*

She looks up at me, and there's a reluctant comfort in her eyes, like she can't quite let herself feel secure in hoping for this new version of us. I don't blame her. I've given her no reason to trust me. I can only hope that she saw the cache as an olive branch. Not as an attempt to wrap everything up neatly with a pretty bow. But the first step on a long path toward redemption, of becoming a man deserving of her.

Because deep down, I've known, it's always been her. And it always will be.

"Turn for me, princess." I can't help but run my hands down her arms as she faces away from me, her ass just barely brushing up against my cock. I shampoo her hair, and she lets her head fall back as I massage her scalp. Her eyes are closed, and she sighs the sweetest little hum. It's such a contrast to the explosive, defensive, and rage-filled Effie, and I feel distinctly honored that she's showing me this side of her. She may just be too exhausted to push back, but maybe—hopefully—she's slowly letting down her walls.

She's been so quiet, that when she asks me a question as we towel off, it almost startles me. "Where did you sleep last night?"

I ruck the towel over my hair. "In the garage. In the bed of my truck." Though I didn't get much sleep, haunted by her words.

I don't want to see your face.

Just get it over with.

I follow her to our bed—*her* bed—taking particular pride in the new flush of her skin that has replaced the goosebumps that covered her body before. She pulls the quilt back, but instead of getting in, she turns to me. She worries her lip with her teeth and avoids my eyes. I know whatever she's about to say is gonna hurt like a bitch.

"You don't have to sleep in the garage, but maybe the couch?" *Fuck. Yeah, that stings.*

I take a deep breath, tying the towel around my waist. "'Course."

"Thank you," she says meekly.

I give her as much of a smile as I can manage and lean forward to kiss her. She turns to give me her cheek, and it feels like an arrow to the chest.

I step back and give her the space she clearly wants. I hope the hurt isn't evident in my eyes. I don't want her to feel bad for doing what she feels she must.

"Good night, Finn," she says as I walk away, and I look back over my shoulder and see her wringing her hands, a sad smile on her face.

"Night, princess."

"Well, you could go with something like this or like this." The most unhelpful art store associate says, holding up two canvases that are basically the same fucking thing.

"Will both fit on the easel?" I'm actively trying not to pull my gun on this dude to speed up this process.

"Uh, let's see…" He tries to place one of the rectangular canvases on the standup easel I've picked out and it doesn't fit between the spacers. "Damn, guess not."

I grab the canvas from his hand and flip it on its side and it lays perfectly. I fucking hate incompetence.

"Oh yeah, and you can adjust this," he says, pushing up the top rail. *Would you look at that.*

"Good. Fine. What paints are right for this type of canvas?"

"Man, you have a lot of good questions." He chuckles. I'd rather poke my eyes out with a hot fire poker than spend another second with this man.

You know what, google is fucking free. I walk away from him and pull out my phone. Ten seconds later, I'm in the acrylic paint aisle throwing one of every color and the brushes next to them into my basket.

At the register, the man begins to scan every tube of paint at the speed of a ninety-year-old woman and my foot taps anxiously. The only reason I was comfortable leaving Effie alone at the farm was because I thought this would be a quick visit. My skin itches thinking of her on the property by herself. No one would hear her—

The next thing I know my gun is drawn and the man is shaking, hands in the air. I throw my credit card on the counter. "Just charge it for three thousand, that should more than cover it."

He looks at the card like it's a ticking bomb and stutters, "I—uh—I can't—I have to ring each item."

"Jesus fucking Christ," I groan and pull out a wad of hundreds from my wallet, at least a couple thousand, and drop it on the counter. Then I toss everything back into the basket, card and all, hike the easel and canvases under my arm and leave before I fucking kill someone.

Though the store owner would probably thank me for taking out his incompetent ass.

When I get back to the barn, a mouthwatering smell fills the space. My heart squeezes, seeing Effie cooking on the wood stove, in tiny shorts that disappear almost completely beneath a long sweater. There's soft music playing in the background, and she sways ever so slightly, I doubt she realizes she's doing it.

I'm frozen in the doorway soaking her in, she looks good here. Like she was always meant for the slow life. She starts singing along into the spatula, and my heart goes from being squeezed to being crushed as I realize why she looks so good. It's because she looks happy.

I'm mesmerized by her hips, rocking back and forth, making her sweater rise and giving a little peak of her perfect ass in tiny black shorts. She twirls with her spatula-microphone and jumps with a scream when she sees me.

"Fucking hell, Finneas!" Her hand clutches her chest like she's trying to keep her heart from jumping out of her chest. "You scared the shit out of me." I lift a brow, and she glares back.

"What are you making?"

"Breakfast hash," she says, still pouting and crossing her arms.

"Smells delicious." I head straight for the stairs before she starts asking questions about what's in my arms.

I set the easel up by the far window, I feel like I've heard artists talking about natural light or some shit. There's not a lot of room in the eaves, but enough to stand in the middle. I drag one of the nightstands over and put all the paints and brushes I bought in the drawer. I step back and look at the set up and know something's missing.

It clicks, and I hurry down the stairs. Calling to Effie as I leave, "Don't go upstairs."

My first stop is the garage, but I come up empty. Luckily, I find what I'm looking for in the big house. Returning to the barn, Effie isn't downstairs. *Of course, she isn't.*

I told her not to do something, so she obviously did exactly that. I should have known.

I climb the steps and find her staring at the easel and canvas, paint drawer open. She's toying with the long sleeve of her sweater, and I can't read her face properly from this angle. She hears me and turns. My stomach drops seeing tears in her eyes.

"It wasn't done yet," I say defensively, placing the stool I found next to her.

"Is this—Is this for me?" Her voice cracks and her bottom lip trembles. Her eyes are so sad and heavy that I can't stop myself from wrapping her stiff body in my arms.

"I'm sorry, I didn't know it would make you sad. I will get rid—"

"No!" She rears back but keeps her balled fists against my chest. "No, please don't. I'm not sad."

I brush a tear at the corner of her eye with my thumb. "Princess, you're crying."

Her mouth cracks in a small smile. "I'm just surprised is all." She wipes at her eyes and fixes me with a warm stare. "I love it. I promise."

I bite my cheek, feeling so relieved I could pick her up and spin her around. I'm not a gift giver. Hell, I'm not a giver at all. And I definitely don't think I've ever made someone cry anything but terrified-for-their-life tears.

"Oh, there's one more thing," I say quickly, remembering my coat pocket. Her mouth pinches, holding back a smile as she looks up at me all doe-eyed, and I temporarily forget my own goddamn name. I pull the sunflower out of my pocket and— "*Fuck*, it's all wilted."

I go to shove the smooshed flower back in my coat feeling like an imbecile. *Who puts a delicate flower in a pocket?* Christ, I'm hopeless at this stuff.

But she stops me, taking the stem from my hand. "Thank you, Finn."

"I passed a bunch on the road, I can go back and get a new one."

"Finn, would you calm the fuck down?" My eyes snap to her. "You're the only person I know who gets more frazzled giving someone a flower than disposing of a body."

I laugh dryly. "Yeah, well…"

"Sunflowers are my second favorite flower." She looks at the yellow petals with a smile.

"Yeah? What's your favorite?" I brush a lock of hair off her neck and twirl it around my finger.

"Water lilies." *Fuck.* Warmth spills down my spine and pools in my stomach. My fucking chest hurts hearing her say those two words. I want nothing more than to pick her up and throw her onto the bed. To stay there all day, fucking until we lose track of time and space and all I know is every inch of her body, every note of her sweet scent.

But I remember last night and her not letting me in her bed and decide I better not push my luck. Especially not right now when she's looking at me like she not only doesn't hate me, but she might even like me.

"Enjoy, princess." I tug her in by the hip and press a kiss to her forehead, walking away before I lose the ability to control my darkest urges.

"My dad called," she says as I retreat, and my skin crawls thinking of that fucker. "He wants us to go to the Children's Hospital charity gala next week. The governor will be there, and he wants to put on a united front."

Memories of the last time we attended a gala together flash in my mind and I smile. "Are you asking me on a date, Ef?"

She rolls the sunflower stem between her fingers. "I guess."

"You want me to be your boyfriend, huh? A little arm candy to show off," I tease.

"Well, you *are* my husband." She pats my chest and smirks. "Remember?"

And fuck, those few words nearly bring me to my knees.

My hand is falling asleep tucked behind my head while I'm lying on the couch, staring up at the ceiling. I listen to the final ashes of the fire crackle in the stove, providing the faintest orange glow while the rest of the room is shrouded in darkness.

Effie went to bed a few hours ago after painting all day. I wish I could blame not being able to sleep on the lumpy couch under me, but I know that's not true. It's the woman curled up under the quilt upstairs. I imagine her wrapped in the white sheets, and I bet she would look like a water lily with silvery-white petals if the moonlight hit just right.

I don't know where we go from here. There's nothing keeping us apart anymore. No family rivalry, no heist, no fiancé or arranged marriage. Only the sins of our past.

She's mine by law but not mine by soul. Not fully. Not yet.

She was for a few precious moments in the lake. I could feel her breaking open, letting pieces of her soul drift out to me, trusting I would catch them. She wanted to be ravaged as much as I wanted to consume.

I perk up at the sound of footsteps upstairs. I listen carefully to see if she's just going to the bathroom. She isn't.

I lay still for another few minutes, my heartbeat growing heavier, louder, like it's drawing me to her. I throw back my blanket and head upstairs in nothing but sweatpants. I find her in her makeshift studio, bathed in moonlight and the same shirt of mine she wore yesterday. Her bare legs are on display and my fingers itch to brush the smooth skin, hoping goosebumps raise on her skin at my touch.

She turns her head as I slowly approach. I move unhurried as if she's a mirage that might dissipate if I go too quickly. "Can't sleep," she says and tugs on the shirt neckline.

"Me either." I close the distance between us and sweep her face up with a finger under her chin. "What's in that pretty head, princess?"[17]

She pulls her bottom lip between her teeth and swallows slowly. "I'm lost, Finn." My finger trailing up her jaw stops in its tracks, her voice so despondent it makes my whole body cold. Her eyes fall back to her canvas of abstract swatches of bold colors and gold paint.

"I feel like I can't trust myself when it comes to you." Like a physical blow, her words make me take a step back, dropping my hand. "I've never had anyone I could trust, until you. But then what my family did to yours... we went to war, and I didn't have you anymore, but I always had myself. Now, I'm not sure I do.

"Sometimes I feel like a body, bartered and bought, not a person. What happens when you realize you've been sold damaged goods? Will you still want me?"

My throat constricts and any reply dries up. Words fail me, nothing seems adequate. No apology big enough. No comfort strong enough.

I don't know what compels me, but I step up to the easel and squeeze some gold paint on a palette. Picking up the first brush I see, I swipe it through the paint and lift the hem of the shirt until she pulls it over her head.

My heart slams against my ribcage seeing her completely bare on the stool. She curls inwards and wraps her arms over her breasts. I don't tell her to uncover herself. I don't tell her I need to see. I kneel at her side, facing the curve of her hip and thigh as she sits with one leg crossed over the other.

17 Darkest Hour—Andrea Russett | SummerOtoole.com/playlists

I remember the stretchmarks I saw our first night here and thinking I'd never seen anything more beautiful. She tenses when the cold paint touches her skin but relaxes under the brush strokes. I trace each line until her hip is striped in gold.

I move to her other side and highlight each mark and scar with adoration. She sharply inhales when I kneel in front of her and nudge her knees apart. I gently lift her leg and set it on my shoulder, gathering more paint on the brush before tracing the stretch marks on her inner thigh. I place her other leg on my shoulder and her hands fly to fist my hair for balance. I can feel the heat of her cunt and smell her arousal, making me groan and run my nose up her thigh before painting her stripes.

Once I'm done, I press a kiss to her pussy, hoping she can feel the reverence in it. She shudders as I drag a long, wide stroke from entrance to clit. I look up at her, her teeth notched in her bottom lip and make sure her eyes are on me. "Tell me all the ways I've hurt you."

She stays silent, and I lap her pussy again with a slow and heavy drag of my tongue. Then I hover a breath's width from her sweet heat, waiting.

"You manipulated me," she breathes, and I take another purposeful lick, pausing again at the top until she speaks again. "You forced me." Another heavy stroke.

She sniffles, and I rub circles into her thighs. "That's good, princess. Keep going."

"You humiliated me..." My tongue drags from bottom to top.

Another grievance, another apology.

And we continue like this until her thighs are shaking on either side of my head and her raspy, close-to-tears voice has turned to breathy moans. Her fingers pull on my hair, and I groan into her.

"*Finn...*" her voice floats out, and I know what to do next.

I carefully set her feet down and stand, grabbing her hand and pulling her off the stool. She trails behind me, her hand feeling so small and trusting in mine. I position her in front of the full-length mirror by the small wardrobe.

"Look at you, a fucking masterpiece." I stand behind her and skate my hands over her shoulders and down her arms. She leans back, settling against my warm chest, and I melt at her trust. Laying my arms over her shoulders, I cup her breasts and fill my palms with them. I tease her nipples, rubbing a thumb over each one, and she rolls her head to the side and onto my shoulder.

I watch her eyelids fall closed, and her lips part on a contented sigh in the reflection. I gauge her reaction as one of my hands slips over her stomach and between her thighs. Her eyes open and they lock with mine through the mirror drunkenly, telling me it's okay. Maybe even better than okay.

So I spread her lips and drag a finger over her wet slit, feeling her swollen clit. Blood rushes to my cock, and I try to push my hips back, so she doesn't feel it, but she reaches behind her and wraps a hand around it over my sweatpants.

"*Fuck,*" spills from my lips with the slightest tug of her fist.

She looks at me, a silent plea in her eyes. I know what she wants, but she doesn't want to ask for it. So I swallow down the ball in my throat and whisper in her ear, "Hands on the mirror, princess."

She leans forward, arching her back. Her eyes never leave mine in the mirror even as I strip and slot my cock at her entrance and push in slowly. Her mouth falls open, and I fill it with my finger. She sucks on it, and I sink myself to the hilt, a deep groan pulled from my chest.

"Again. Tell me more." I pull my finger from her lips and rub it against her clit, still buried deep in her.

"You…" I slowly withdraw, dragging my piercing against her g-spot. "Made me feel safe and then took it all away." And I punch my hips forward, pushing all the way into her. She gasps.

I pull out carefully, and she continues breathlessly as I continue to circle her clit, "You made me feel like I wasn't worthy of gentle love." I pound back in, my heart cracking at her confession.

"*Oh god,*" tumbles from her lips as I drag against her inner walls and firmly rub her clit. I feel her body begin to tighten around my length.

"Don't stop, princess."

"And I hate—*oh fuck.*" I thrust again and her body trembles, her orgasm cresting.

"What do you hate?" I say through gritted teeth. Her clenching cunt feels like heavenly torture.

"I hate that I *can't* hate you," she cries and shatters.

"I know. I'm so sorry." I groan as her pussy contracts and demands. This moment of raw vulnerability is seared in my mind forever. It pulls my own release from me, and I hope she can feel she is so much more than just a body, that these bodily pleasures are just the bridge to something more, beyond family rivalries, forced marriages, lies, and betrayals.

I fold over her, breathing hard and sated. My arms tightly wrapped around her waist even as my legs threaten to give out. I gently pull out of her, and she whimpers like it's a loss. I pick my sweatpants off the ground and tenderly wipe away my cum spilling out of her, though I can't help but push a little back inside.

I pick her up and cradle her tight to my chest, soaking up these last moments of her warm skin against mine. I set her on the bed and pull the quilt over her. She's curled up on her side, and I kiss her temple, breathing in her addictive scent.

When I walk away, a hand reaches out and stops me.

And she says one word that has me carving out my heart and handing it to her, bloody and beating: *Stay.*

Chapter 15:

Married Man

For someone so cold in affect, Finneas Fox is a goddamn Bunsen burner. His front sticks to my back with a thin sheen of sweat as he breathes into my neck. I slowly try to extract myself from his koala grip without waking him. I pick up his wrist and carefully lift it off my waist, but it clamps back down and he growls behind me, "Where do you think you're going, princess?" His morning voice is raspy and warm and makes butterflies erupt in my stomach.

"You're a thousand degrees, Finneas. I'm going to shower." I roll onto my knees and kiss his cheek before making another attempt. He grabs my ankle and tugs me back.

"I like that you smell like me," he moans and pins my body under his. He lightly rocks his pelvis against my ass and heat strikes my core. *Oh, how easy it would be to flip over…*

But I'm sweaty and covered in paint—*Shit!*

"The sheets!" Anxiety throttles through me, and I thrash under Finn, trying to get a look at the damage. Gold paint is smudged all over the middle of the bed. "Oh my god, I ruined them."

Like a rising tide of guilt and shame, I feel the strongest need to fix it, hide it, anything to avoid the repercussions. "Finn, get off me!" He keeps me trapped and nerves turn to frustration. *Doesn't he see the problem?*

"Effie, what the fuck is going on?" There's annoyance in his voice, because of course there is, he must be pissed.

"Let me go and I'll fix it," I beg, and he flips me over, pinning my wrists by my head and looming over me. I flinch, tensing, waiting for a hit that never comes.

"What are you on about?" He peers down at me, and there's nothing but concern and confusion in his eyes. Which concerns and confuses me.

"Your sheets." Anxious tears choke me. "I ruined them, there's paint all over."

"Okay. I'll buy new ones." He shakes his head and brushes the hair out of my face that got all mussed from the struggle. "I bet there's paint all over my face too…" I look at the side of his face, and there is indeed paint smudged on his cheekbones and flecks in his hair. "From being in between these gorgeous thighs…" He slinks down my body, biting my stomach and kissing each inner thigh.

"I'm sorry." I can't handle the caring intensity in his eyes when he looks up at me, it makes me feel off balance.

"For *what*?" He sounds exasperated. "I don't give a shit about the sheets."

I close my eyes, trying to quiet the racket in my head.

You ruin everything, I can so clearly hear my father's rage-filled voice at my carelessness, his face turning beet red.

"Effie, look at me." Finn plants his hands by my sides and hovers above me.

I slowly peek open my eyes. "You're not mad?"

"Why would I be mad? I was the one who painted you for Christ's sake. And I'm certainly not mad that you spent the night in my bed." He leans forward and kisses under my jaw and down my neck.

I lean into the comforting weight of his body on mine, the way his hair brushes against my skin. *He's not mad. He's not my father. Just breathe.*

He licks a trail up my throat and dusts his lips over mine. "Now, can I convince you to stay in bed a little longer."

I run my fingers through his dark hair, pulling him closer to kiss him hard, letting him grind in the cradle of my hips, and I explore his mouth with my tongue. He moans softly, yet hungrily. I bite his lip sharply and he rears back, a mix of heat and mischief in his eyes.

"You cannot," I say with a small laugh as I weasel out from under him and leap from the bed. "*Ow.*" I whip around, my ass burning from a fiery slap. He's completely stone-faced, but then the corner of his lips tug up into a smirk.

When I get out of the shower, Finn's standing with his back to me, dressed in black jeans and black button-up. He turns around, rolling up his sleeves and wetting his bottom lip. He looks like he wants to eat me alive.

And I want to let him.

"I have business in the city to take care of today. Calvin is on his way here for security."

I cringe. "Does it have to be Calvin? Anyone else but him please." I understand people like me need protection, so I won't protest that. I've had security all my life. The only reason I didn't have a bodyguard while living with the crew was my father was worried his men would be too conspicuous.

"I wouldn't leave you with anyone I don't have full confidence in, he'll keep you safe." Finn reaches out to stroke my cheek with the back of his hand.

"It's not that," I say looking down.

He tilts my chin back up, "Then what is it?"

My lip trembles, humiliation tumbling in my chest, "He was there that night…He saw me…" As terrible as the interrogation was, being found half-naked, covered in sweat and tears in a ball on the floor was ten times worse.

"What?" Realization dawns on Finn's face and he sniffs, pulling his hand away as it clenches into a fist. "I see...I'll make some calls, get someone else out here."

"Thank you." I clutch the towel tighter around me. There's hurt in his eyes that for some reason makes *me* feel vulnerable.

"I should have never put you in that situation." He doesn't try to touch me, but I can tell he wants to, his shoulders rolled back, hands in fists. Like he's preparing for a fight, but he's his own worst enemy.

There's a lot of things I could say right now.

It's okay, look where we are now.

It doesn't matter anymore.

I'm fine, don't worry about it.

But why would I?

"Yeah, you shouldn't have. It was fucked up and cruel." I enunciate each word clearly to make sure he knows what I'm asking of him: Own up to your shit.

The emotion on his face shutters closed, tucking everything away neatly behind a mask of cold apathy. A defense mechanism, but I see through it. He nods and heads downstairs and out the door.

There's a brief moment when I feel bad. The deep programming all women have to protect men's emotions even at the expense of your own. I shove that feeling down, because *fuck that.*

Last night may have changed things, but it didn't fix things.

After he leaves, I check my phone to find a dozen missed calls from my father. My heart drops to my stomach. There's a single text. I read it, my blood going cold.

Euphemia. I won't tolerate another disappointment.

I delete the text and all the missed call notifications. I don't trust Finn not to go through my phone. My father must be getting desperate to be so reckless and text me so blatantly, without any precautions.

I slip on a pair of underwear and Finn's big t-shirt, some band I've never heard of on the front. It smells like him and rather than soothe me, it makes me want to cry on the heels of my father's message.

Honesty and loyalty.

That's all he's asked of me.

I wander over to my makeshift studio after making a pot of coffee. Clutching the warm mug in my hands, I sit on the stool and look out the window.

It's humbling looking out there, seeing the dense forest and knowing all the riches and masterpieces that are hidden away under it. So much history, so much talent. Knowing that the cache was the start of all this and it's so close to my fingertips.

I return my attention to the canvas in front of me, rolling all these thoughts in my mind.

I hop off the stool and go to my luggage. It takes a little digging, but finally I find it: a burner cell phone I packed for situations just like this.

I dial and listen to it ring.

"*Oui, allo?*"

"Linnie, it's Effie…I have a job for you."

Finn

It feels like my lungs are full of glass. My fingers tap on the stick shift like a fucking maniac. As if anything can rid me of the sick, self-hatred I felt seeing Effie's face when I mentioned Calvin. Fucking tore a hole in my chest.

I'm pushing ninety miles per hour, and it doesn't feel enough. Nothing will be fast enough to outrun this feeling.

Guilt fucking sucks.

I much preferred not caring, not feeling, not having my ability to fucking breathe tied to the emotions of another person.

I called Roman as soon as I left the barn, and he's sending soldiers to Bartlett Farms. Then Calvin and told him to turn back. Now I have one last call to make, and it makes my palms sweat.

I ring Stella. When she doesn't answer, I give the Den's office number a try. They open in half an hour, so she's probably there.

"What?" Cash's gruff voice answers, and my fingers tighten, annoyed, around the wheel.

"Stella there?"

"Yeah—*Oh fuck, baby, just like that—*"

"Fucking hell, Cash! Stop picking up when you're balls deep in pussy!" I'm about to hang up, but before I do, I shout, "Tell Stella to call me, you sick motherfucker."

When I'm twenty minutes out, I answer the phone to Stella's cheery, "Finneas."

"Meet me at Phantom in twenty."

"Dude, we're opening in five minutes—"

"I'm not asking," I growl, beginning to regret this entire idea.

She scoffs. "And I'm not going, goodbye Finn—"

"Wait." I'd rather get in a full-speed collision than tell her what I need her help for, but somehow I get it out without intentionally crashing.

"Why didn't you lead with that?" She sounds disgustingly excited. "See you soon."

I groan, wanting to turn the fuck around. But I remind myself who I'm doing this for, and *Christ,* is she worth it all and more.

Stella is waiting for me at the bar. The club is completely empty, not opening for another six hours. I see she's already poured herself a drink and I think I'll need one too—or three.

"First, if you tell anyone about this—"

"Yeah, yeah, you'll kill me." She sucks on the skinny cocktail draw and rolls her eyes. *This was a terrible idea.* "What's the second?"

"Pour me a scotch."

She hops over the bar and slides a glass with two fingers down the slick wood to me. I tip it back and down it in one go. Like a game of shuttle board, I send it back to her. "Another."

"I'm all for loosening up, but let's try to get a little work in sober first."

I sigh. "Fine."

She walks out from behind the bar and starts playing music from her phone on the club's stereo system. "I made a playlist that will be good for covering the basics."

I meet her in the middle of the dance floor and feel like I'm crawling out of my goddamn skin. "Let's start with the easiest: pop."

Some boy band crap plays on the speakers, and Stella starts bobbing and weaving her head. "Okay, so just relax and move with the energy of the music."

I try to mimic her movements, my back rigid and muscles tight.

I've skinned a man alive. I've been stabbed four times, and I've defused a bomb with three seconds on the clock. Yet none of that is even close to how I feel right now. Effie was right, I *do* kill people for fun, but a little dancing? Fucking terrifying.

"You look like a goddamn chicken, loosen up a bit." Stella laughs and my jaw clenches, wanting to put my fist through a wall. "Don't just move your head. Flow organically with the movement, you know? Roll your shoulders a bit, bend your knees, rock side to side."

I hold out my hand, "Whoa, slow down, that was like ten different things at once." I shove my fingers into my hair and yell, "*Fuck.* This is a fucking disaster."

"Okay, let's try something else," she says calmly, using her hands in settling motions as if I'm a wild horse and she's trying not to get trampled. She changes the music to something slower, almost sensual.

"Come here." I go over to her, my chest hammering like I'm walking into enemy territory. "Put your hands on my hips." I reach out hesitantly, and lightly do as she asks, keeping a foot between us. She quickly closes that gap, wrapping her arms over my shoulders and pulling me in until our pelvises are pressed together.

I jump back like I've been burned. "Christ, lady, I'm *married*."

"Boy, please." She purses her lips. "I love you Foxes, but y'all are bat-shit crazy, like if someone gave a bunch of toddlers guns instead of a nap. Now, do you want to learn how to dance like a fucking man, or like you're attending a catholic middle school dance, leaving room for Jesus?"

Stella is the only person outside the family who can put me in my place without getting shot. It annoys the hell out of me, but I respect her for it. And I really need her help, so I swallow my fucking pride and grumble, "Like a man."

She sets her arms back on my shoulders, and I clutch her by the hips. She smirks and speaks slowly, like when trying to get a child to say thank you. "*Sorry for being a dick, Stella.*"

I cut her a glare. "Don't push it."

Chapter 16:

Rocky Balboa

Effie

The villain is about to kidnap the princess…or maybe the knight is about to save her from a dragon or…I have no fucking idea what has happened these last three chapters because while I've been trying to peacefully read in bed like a half normal person, Finn has been up boxing.

I slide out of bed and aggressively shove my feet in some slippers. I stomp down the steps and out the door, wrapping my arms around myself at the unexpected chill. *It's a perfectly reasonable request,* I tell myself as I make my way to the garage.

There's a bright flood light aimed directly on the bag, throwing the corners of the garage into shadows. Finn works his way around it with lithe agility, weaving and bobbing around an imaginary opponent. He notices me and stops, grabbing hold of the swinging bag.

"Hey, princess." He's slightly out of breath and lifts his shirt to wipe at the sweat on his forehead.

"Finn, it's nearly ten at night, do you need to be doing this right now?" I look at him sideways.

"I didn't know you were sleeping already," he says, stretching and flexing his taped fingers.

"I wasn't but—"

"Ten more minutes?" He gives me what I think is supposed to be a puppy dog look and while it's not adorable in any traditional sense—more of a Belgian Malinois than a Golden Retriever—it still makes me crack.

"Fine, but you have to teach me. If we both have to be awake, I might as well get something out of it," I throw back, thinking he'll call it a night and head in rather than train with me.

He perks up. "You got yourself a deal." He looks me up and down and shrugs. "That'll work, but maybe lose the slippers."

"Are you serious?" I ask, getting tinges of excitement and nervousness.

"Of course. Do you have one of those things for your hair?" He waves his hand in a circle above his head.

It takes me a second, but then I laugh. "Do you mean a hair tie?" I flick the elastic around my wrist.

"Yeah, sure. Put your hair up and then we can get started."

As I wrap my hair into a ponytail he peppers me with questions about what training I have, what I already know, and I quickly get overwhelmed. Growing up with killers and fighters, I should at least understand half of the things he asks, but most of it is gibberish.

"Jesus, all I know is that punching you in the face right now sounds really good."

"Okay." He smirks with a confident chuckle. "I always say learn by doing. Go ahead, try to punch me."

"*What?* You can't be serious," I balk.

"As a heart attack." He clasps his hands behind his back and sticks his head forward. "Tick tock, princess," he jeers.

God, he's so annoying. I lunge, swinging my arm, and he dodges to the side, arms still behind him. I huff, peeved, and try again. And again. And again. Each time he dips or bobs, and my fist goes flying past his face, hitting nothing but air.

"Dammit, I thought you said I could hit you," I grumble, and his lip twitches in amusement.

"I said *try* to punch me."

I throw my hands in the air. "Well, I *tried.* Are you going to teach me anything or just point out how incredibly useless I am at defending myself?"

"You're giving yourself away, keep your movements small and varied so I don't see your punch coming from a mile away. Keep your hands like this." He brings his fists to his face in a guard and moves them dynamically, bouncing on the soles of his feet.

I try to mirror his movements, and he circles around me, nudging my feet into proper position, pushing my shoulder to get me to bend my knees, tucking in my elbows.

"There ya go." He comes back to my front and nods approvingly. "Now jab with your left, quick and fast, sharp and tight foot movements." He does it once and then I mimic him.

"Good, good. Again, and this time add your right, drive through your hip." His left fist snaps out and back and is immediately followed by a strong, powerful twist of his hips and right hand.

We go back and forth, working different combinations of these two punches. I know there are more punches, but he keeps me practicing just these two basics, tweaking my form or reminding me to bring my guard back up. After only ten minutes, my heart is pumping and I'm feeling encouraged.

He stands behind me. I can feel his breath on the side of my face as his left arm stretches out next to mine. "Your jab isn't a power punch, it's more like a pesky mosquito. You're not trying to knock anyone out, so get it out there and snap it right back, okay?" He demonstrates, moving so fast if you blink, you'd miss it.

I try, and he repeats *faster* after each jab. His hands drop to my hips and I try to keep my breathing even. On the next punch, he rotates my hips with his grip and calls, "*Right.*"

As he twists my hips, I shoot my right arm out with more power and force than all night. "There it is!" He claps and walks back in front of me. "Nice work, princess."

He gives me a tight-lipped smile, and I squirm under the intensity of his focus on me. I try to shake it off and say, "Same time tomorrow?"

"See you then." He flicks his chin with a grin. As I begin to walk away, he chuckles, "Maybe next time you'll land a punch—"

[18]I'm fast and powerful, just like he taught me, spinning on my heels and throwing my fist into his cheekbone. His head whips to the side from the impact. He straightens back up, a burning heat in his eyes that makes my stomach flutter.

"That felt good, didn't it?" His eyes darken and he takes a step toward me. "Do it again."

I try to brush him off with a roll of my eyes and shake of my head.

"Do. It." He repeats, a hunger in his eyes that calls to me.

"Why?" I eye him suspiciously as he continues to close in on me, corralling me up against a workbench.

"Because I deserve it. Now fucking hit me." His words sink in, and I search his eyes for a trick or a trap. But all I see back is the same hunger as before, but this time I understand it.

I push on his chest making him take a few steps back so I'm not caged in anymore. My fist closes, achy from the first punch, and I look at the red welt already forming by his eye. He pleads with me wordlessly, and like some fucked-up version of couples therapy, I give him what he wants: A fist to the jaw. To the temple. To the cheek.

Each hit, he straightens back up and looks ready for more, like I haven't even put a dent in the penance he thinks he deserves.

I roll my neck side to side and try to make a fist again, but I wince, my knuckles and tendons sore. He reaches for my hand and gently massages the pads of my palms. "I'll get you a pair of gloves for next time," he says with a weak laugh.

There's a strange energy hanging between us, like I've given him a gift and he has nothing to give me in return. I swallow the uneasy feeling and try to make a joke. "Are you gonna tell people you got beat up by a girl?"

"Nah." He shakes his head, looking down and bites his lip. His eyes roll back up to me. "I got my ass handed to me, but I had it coming." He winks and brushes a kiss over my red and swollen knuckles.

His lips feel like satin over my hot skin, and I'm about to lean in to kiss him when he pulls away. "I won't keep you up any longer." He drops my hand and steps aside.

"I don't feel so tired anymore," I joke, but go to leave nonetheless. As I'm walking out, something on the bench catches my eye. "Is that a projector?"

I walk over and pick it up, checking it out. "Does it work?"

"Yeah, I think so."

"Cool, well, good night." I leave, already excited and thinking of how to turn the barn into a rustic home theater.

Back inside, I decide to take a shower after working up a bit of a sweat boxing and go through my minimal night routine. I was never someone with a lengthy routine, but having brought only a small toiletry bag to the farm, it's even shorter.

By the time I'm done, Finn still isn't inside. I hope he's not planning on sleeping in his truck again. I know I just punched the shit out of him, but he told me to, and I think it was possibly more cathartic for him than me.

I find a bag of corn in the freezer and take it out to him, a peace offering of sorts. When I walk outside, the side of the big house is lit up in a glowing indigo. I turn the corner and feel my stomach drop at the same time my heart somersaults.

The bed of Finn's truck is layered in quilts, knit blankets and throw pillows. There's an old, metal camping lantern on the edge and half-lit up string of Christmas lights dangling off the side view mirror. On the top of the cab is the projector, pointed right at the broad, white side of the big house.

I look at the ramshackle set up and feel warmness spread through my body, like drinking hot cider on a winter night. "Finn?" I call out.

He pops out from deeper in the garage with an oil smudged cloth tarp in his hands. I look at him then look at the truck and everything. He half shrugs. "In case you couldn't sleep."

He throws the tarp over the flood light and walks toward me. "You said you weren't tired." He draws me to him with a hand on my hip.

I chew my cheek, not knowing what to say. "I'm speechless...And quite frankly a little concerned about that fire hazard." I brush past him and throw the oily cloth off the flood light. "What was the point of that?" I laugh.

"I don't know, ambience or some shit, right?"

"That explains the half-lit string of Christmas lights."

"Plugged them in and half the bulbs were blown."

"I see..." I nod, trying to fight my smile. "Well, what are we watching?"

His eyes light up at my question, and his mouth dances in a devilish smile before I'm thrown over his shoulder with a scream. *"Finneas!"*

He sets me down on the tailgate and hops up next to me. "Have you seen *Rocky?"*

"That seems fitting." I scoot back into the nest of blankets, a gentle kind of comfort settling over me as he sets up the movie and presses play.

Finn cuddles in next to me, scooping me under his arm, and I rest my head on his chest. The opening credits begin, and the sound is old and scratchy like vinyl. It's barely louder than the chorus of crickets and frogs.

There's a small gust of wind that blows into the garage and Finn tugs me closer, folding a blanket over our laps. He holds the bag of corn I brought to his cheek proudly, like it's a trophy. There's a small popping sound and when I look behind us, the rest of the Christmas lights have gone out. Finn gives me a look that says, *well, I tried,* and then he goes back to playing with my wet hair.

I guess I was more tired than I thought because I don't make it through half the movie before my eyelids start growing heavy and Finn's warm chest with the rhythmic beat of his heart seems like the world's best pillow.

As I drift off to sleep to the iconic theme song playing in the background, there's one thought I keep coming back to: I've never felt so safe.

Chapter 17:

Shuttle-Dicks

This is so weird.

This is *really* fucking weird.

Cash, Roan and Lochlan all sit on the couch, sunken into the cushions, relaxing back, they smile at me. "Great to see you all…" I say through a gritted smile. I turn my head to Finn next to me. "Finn didn't tell me you were coming."

"I didn't know," he hisses under his breath as if all three of his brothers aren't able to hear him five feet away.

Cash uncrosses his legs and stands, thrusting—dare I say, passive aggressively—a pastry box into my hands. "A little quality time, a chance to get to know the newest member of our family." His words are warm, and his tone is charming, but his eyes look like he could gut me alive without breaking a sweat.

"Sounds lovely." I don't worry about disguising the forced friendliness and sarcasm in my voice. Cash Fox knows exactly what he's doing. This isn't a good-hearted house call, so why would I act like it is.

Cash is checking up on his assets. Or his liabilities.

"Dude, put your fucking shoes on—your feet smell like ass." Roan shoves Lochlan, who has, in fact, removed his shoes, in the shoulder. *Make yourself right at home, boys.*

I look back to Cash. "Sorry, we don't have more to offer. Maybe we can run to the store for something." I lock eyes with Finn, hoping he gets the hint.

"No worry, *sister.*" He says the word like a threat. "The girls are bringing barbecue."

"Delightful. Can't wait." *Who the fuck are the girls?* I'm picturing the family picnic equivalent of cigarette girls.

Cash walks away, and Finn sweeps me aside, his big hand on my hip. "I swear I didn't know they were coming."

"It's fine, but what are they expecting us to do? We have one table with two chairs." My mother's aggressive and demanding attitude around hosting was beaten into me growing up and this situation is about to give me fucking hives.

"Lochlan is torturing Roan with his rotten ass feet, I doubt they're expecting a Michelin star experience, Ef."

"I mean—I just—Shit, I wish I had a little notice." I rub the heel of my palms into my eyes and try to think. I'm overwhelmed.

"You don't have to do anything, just relax." Finn tries to calm me down, and sure, maybe that's what he *thinks* but it's not really how he feels. He'll say that now but then will start dropping the passive aggressive comments in a few hours about how I embarrassed him in front of his family.

"Okay, I'm just gonna put some water out for everybody." It's the least I can do. It's not like we have lemonade or iced tea or anything remotely decent. *Are there even enough cups for everyone?*

I give a tight smile to everyone as I walk across the room to the kitchenette. Opening up the cabinet, I only count three glasses. *Shit.* Then I remember there's one in the bathroom.

"Excuse me," I say, crossing the room *again,* feeling like a fool pacing back and forth. I climb the steps and go straight to the bathroom. I pick up the cup by the sink like it's the holy grail and—*Jesus Christ!*

Finn appears in the doorway, startling the daylight out of me. I squawk and drop the glass, it shatters on the floor. The stress of everything compounds until it weighs on my chest.

I can't do anything right.

I break everything.

I'm never good enough.

"Oh my god." My throat burns and tears threaten to spill.

I can't do anything right.

I break everything.

I'm never good enough.

"Effie...*Effie.*" Finn tugs on my hand and I can't bear to look at him. "Do you want to tell me what is going on?"

I suck in a choppy breath. "We already didn't have enough cups, and now I've broken one, and—*Fucking hell.*"

"Okay...?" Finn tilts his head to look me in the eyes, his brows fretted together. "My brothers can drink out of the goddamn toilet for all I care."

I ignore his absurd and unhelpful comment and squat down to frantically sweep up the broken glass. "Ah shit," I hiss when a shard slices my fingertip. *Great, now there's going to be blood to clean up.* My head pounds as anxiety beats like a drum through my whole body. If I can just make it right, make it perfect, maybe my ribs will stay intact, and my heart won't leap through my fucking chest.

Finn bends down next to me and snatches up my hands in his, wrapping a hand towel around my bleeding finger.

"Ef, hey—" My eyes are glued to the shattered glass, my hands feeling itchy and uncomfortable being held still instead of picking it up like I should be doing, *need* to be doing. "Effie, look at me. *Effie.*" His voice is like the sharp crack of a whip, my head jolts up to look at him. "We'll get it cleaned up. I'll have someone go pick up some cups. It's not a big deal, okay?"

"I know that!" I snap but instantly regret it, knowing he was just trying to help. "I know that up here." I tap my temple. "But it *feels* like a big deal."

"Remember when you busted into Peaches like you owned the damn place—"

"What does that have to do with anything?" I gawk at him.

"All I mean is—You—" He clenches and unclenches his fists like he just wants to shake me. "You told me I had a small cock when I held a gun to your head. Do you know how many men have been in that same position and pissed themselves, crying for their mama? You're the fucking bravest person I know, so why are you freaking out over a goddamn cup?"

He sounds frustrated but genuine, and I just wish it made sense. How I feel, how I'm spiraling over something that is admittedly stupid. "That was survival, Finneas. Do or die. But this…this is just me, and just me is never enough."

He looks truly wounded by my words and shakes his head.

"It's just—I want everything to be perfect."

"Who says it has to be perfect?" His question stuns me.

"Uh…I don't know, everybody?"

"Who's everybody?" he asks, and I look at him like he has three heads.

"My parents—"

"Aren't here." He cups my face between his palms. "You're perfectly enough. And all this?" He swipes his arms wide. I open my mouth in retort, but he presses a finger to my lips. "They're only things." I try to absorb his words and quell the hammering in my chest, but I still feel the anxiety like a storm.

"You don't believe me." It's not a question, he's making a statement, an observation and I nod. I don't believe him. "Fine."

He drops his hands and storms out, my heart sinking like lead.

I tentatively poke my head out, and I see Finn taking a pocketknife to the bed sheets. "*Finn—*"

"They're just things, Effie." He cuts into the fabric, then rips a long tear down it. The second set of sheets ruined in as many days. Next, he picks up a lamp off the nightstand. "Just. Fucking. Things." He throws it at the wall, and I gasp as the shade is knocked off and the glass stand shatters.

"Shall I keep going?" he asks, and I'm momentarily paralyzed. It makes it hard to breathe picturing all that broken glass. He stalks toward the mirror with a testing look.

"No, Finn, I get it." I step in between him and the mirror, hands on his chest.

"Do you?"

"Yes, they're just things." I repeat his words back to him with not nearly as much conviction, then add, "And I like this mirror…I want to keep the memory of us." I like the way his eyes light up when I say *us*.

He sits at the foot of the bed and pulls me in between his legs, holding the back of my thighs. "I'm not him, Effie. I'm not your father. You won't be punished for being human." His words make a gnarly knot twist in my throat. "Honesty and loyalty are all I want from you. Not some Stepford-wives shit, okay?"

I swipe my knuckle at the corner of my eye. "Okay."

"Now, tell me, princess, and be honest." He looks at me earnestly, and I nod. "Are those scared tears or those other types of tears like when I gave you the easel?"

I can't help but bark out a laugh at his preciousness. The smile that spreads on my face feels warm and right. "They're the sunflower type of tears."

He sighs and folds forward, resting his forehead on my stomach like he's never been more relieved in his life. "*Thank fuck.*"

More and more people keep arriving. Okay, only four more, but it feels like ten when I only vaguely remember who they are from the surveillance we did with *Les Arnaqueuses*. Finn helps me set up a fold-out table that he dug out of the big house—along with more than enough cups.

Cash is helping Lochlan set up a badminton net in the lawn after he unearthed it in "all that old people stuff." I absolutely can't picture the most dangerous gangsters on the East Coast playing badminton. I'll believe it when I see it.

I throw an orange, purple, and green tablecloth straight out of the '80s over it. I scoot closer to Finn and whisper, "So, who are all these people?"

He loops his arms around my lower back, and I mirror him. He pulls me tight, and it looks like we are just having a cute, couple conversation. "The two men who just arrived are Roman and Alfie. Roman is the man who makes sure we don't get ourselves killed, and the twig with him, Alfie…" He narrows his eyes in thought. "Honestly, I have no idea how he made it this far, but he's loyal as hell."

"Okay, and I recognize Harlow. She was in the news a ton a few months back."

"Yeah, she's a real one. She certainly matches Cash's crazy, and she's proven she deserves her spot at his side." I nod along, trying to imagine someone equally as crazy as Cash and thinking only his brothers compare.

"And this is Stella." Finn gestures over my shoulder and I turn, greeted by a woman I've seen many times across the street at the Den.

"Hi, thank you for bringing the food." I shake her hand, and she gives me an approving smile.

"Giving her the run down on everyone?" She looks at Finn. When he only lifts a brow, I'm reminded of how shuttered he is in the public eye and feel a swell of honor that he's shown me so much more the last few days than most people ever get.

"He probably told you I'm the manager at the Den, but most of the time I'm just managing these four numb-nuts and making sure they don't kill each other."

I laugh at the picture she paints and quickly realize she must be very important to the Foxes if she can talk about them like that. "Didn't you say Roman was the person making sure y'all didn't get killed?"

"Yes," Finn says gruffly, then gives me a mischievous smirk. "He stops other people from killing us, Stella keeps us from killing *each other.*"

"Exactly, and they're damn lucky." Stella gives Finn a nudge in the shoulder and walks away.

"He'll never admit it in this lifetime or the next, but Stella is Cash's best friend. She's family."

"Best friend?" I bite back a laugh. Men like Cash don't have *friends*. They have associates, acquaintances, mutually beneficial relationships, but not friends.

"Like I said, he'll never admit it, and you didn't hear it from me." He brushes a piece of hair behind my ear, and his jovial expression shifts to something more serious. My stomach twists for whatever he's going to say next. "You're so fucking beautiful."

My cheeks warm and my heart skips. Words get twisted on my tongue, so I just rise on my toes to kiss his nose. "I'm going to help get the food plated." I turn away, a smile on my lips.

He grabs my hand as I walk away. "I like when you kiss me there."

I bite my lip to hide the ridiculous grin trying to break free. "Finneas Fox, the romantic," I tease while leaving.

"Tell anyone and I'll kill 'em," he shouts after me.

I laugh, and all I can think is *how the hell did we get here?*

Who knew lunch with your family's biggest enemies and rivals could be so pleasant?

Harlow and Stella are lovely and funny, and it feels good to not be the only girl in the room—or outside table.

Alfie has not shut up about the mac and cheese, and why didn't they get macaroni salad instead so that he doesn't "blow up the bathroom" later. While on the other hand, Roman hasn't said more than three words.

And the Foxes…well, they almost seem like normal brothers. If you ignore the fact that when someone makes a joke about stabbing the other, they actually pull out a blade.

But there's an air of camaraderie and equality that I never see between my brothers. Sure, my brothers are close, but there's always the edge of competition and the need to prove one is more deserving of the Luciano name.

I find it fascinating. Observing them all together, picking up small character quirks. Cash is the clear leader, but he doesn't act like he's better than the other three. Roan is easy to read, wears his emotions on his sleeve and is the quickest to get upset. Lochlan, the baby of the group, seems to annoy everyone the most, yet makes everyone laugh the most.

Finn is just as quiet and brooding as ever, but there's a lightness to the set of his shoulders, a loosening of his jaw. He brushes his hair out of his face, and his deep, green eyes lock with mine across the table. I feel a zap of energy crackle between us and settle in my core. His eyes darken subtly and the corner of his mouth ticks like he knows exactly what I'm feeling. His eyes drop to my lips while he licks his own and—

"*What the fuck did you just say?*" His head whips at Lochlan seated next to me, and anger twists his features.

Lochlan laughs it off. "I was commending Effie on a great home video."

"You fucking watched it?" Finn growls. He stands and leans across the table, his fingers whiten on the table and his muscles are wound tight, ready to pounce.

"An Oscar-worthy performance."

Humiliation lands like a fucking bomb in my stomach. I look down at my plate and wish I could evaporate into thin air.

"That's my *wife.*" Finn reacts as fast as a viper, grabbing him by the collar and yanking him out of his chair. His other hand holds a switchblade right under Lochlan's eye. "I should carve your fucking eyes out."

No one else at the table has moved, looking, quite frankly, unbothered while I'm frozen from embarrassment.

"Chill dude, if it was gonna get your panties in such a twist, you shouldn't have left it on the family cloud. Plus, I didn't think you'd care after you sent it to half the city." Another bomb detonates in my stomach. *Half the city?*

Finn's face flashes from rage to hurt then back so quickly that I almost miss it. "It wasn't half the city. It was one fucking person, and I'll have to live with the knowledge that I almost killed the one fucking good thing in my life because of it." He releases his brother with a shove. "Now sit the fuck down, and if you ever disrespect my wife again, it won't matter that you're my brother."

The table is quiet as Finn takes his seat. A heavy silence hangs in the air until Alfie clears his throat and all heads turn to him. "Um, weren't we gonna play badminton or something?"

The tension is cut as the table breaks into laughter, but I'm still stewing in the fact that the person sitting next to me has seen me in my most degrading moment. I look up at Finn and he's already staring at me, apology rich in his eyes.

I know he regrets what he did, but that doesn't mean it didn't happen. Doesn't mean I don't feel violated all over again. As people move to the lawn, Finn and I are the only ones left at the table.

"Which parts?" I finally speak. "Which parts of the video did he see?"

Finn takes a deep breath before responding, "If he watched what I sent Hudson, then just enough to get the idea."

"How much, Finn?"

"You unzip my pants and the first stroke, then I cut it to you cleaning up," he says it so clinically, devoid of emotion. It hurts him to relive what he's done. He's no longer pleased with my humiliation or satisfied by taunting me.

"You warned me something like this would happen," I say, remembering his last words as I left the kitchen the day I failed to hack his computer. He nods solemnly. "Do you still believe what happened is on me?"

We've been sitting across from each other like colleagues at a meeting, but now he gets up and comes to sit in the empty chair next to me. He spins me in my seat, hands on my thighs between his legs. "Listen to me, Effie, what happened is *not* your fault. We've both hurt each other, double crossed each other, but you almost getting killed? That's on me and me alone."

I sigh, a relief lifting in my chest because I know I'm not innocent in this, far from it, but hearing Finn acknowledge his role in the damage heals something inside me.

"And I will spend the rest of my life trying to make up for it." He cups my cheek and I lean into the warmth of his rough palm. "I'm not a good person, and I'll never be able to atone for all my sins. But if there's one sin I'll pay penance for every fucking day, it's ever putting you in danger."

I let his words sink in and feel the honesty and earnestness behind them. When it's clear I don't know what to say in return, he adds, "If you'll let me."

Finneas Fox is not a good man, but he is *my* man. "Okay."

He fights a small smile, and there's a hint of hope in his eyes that I haven't seen before. "Okay."

It's almost a relief when the intense moment is broken by Roan shouting, "Go get your fucking shuttle-dick!"

"It's a shuttlecock, you dumbass," Lochlan hollers back, and both Finn and I break into laughter. The smile on my face feels good and right, and the man in front of me feels good and right.

"Your brothers are ridiculous." I laugh.

He shakes his head. "Fucking clowns."

Chapter 18:

Actions and Consequences

What are you supposed to say to the man whose son you killed?

I guess I will find out soon. The car to take us to the charity gala should be arriving any minute. In a way, I'm relieved it's almost time. I've been so anxious about tonight, and running into the governor, that I've been on the verge of throwing up all day.

I'm ready on time, all that's left is for Finn to help me into my dress. It's a gorgeous strapless, form-fitting dress in heavy, emerald satin, with a daring slit in the back and a large playful bow that covers my entire back. We're at his condo in June Harbor, so I walk down the hallway to his suite from the guest bedroom I've been using to get ready in.

I find him in a walk-in closet easily three times as big as the bathroom at the barn. His back is to me, and his white dress shirt is at his elbows, his strong, capped shoulders bare. He's not even halfway dressed. "Finneas, I can't believe you're not dressed yet," I whine, anxiety coursing through me.

He turns slowly, tongue in cheek and gives me a lazy look up and down. His gaze rakes my skin and my stomach flutters. "That's rich coming from someone in nothing but lingerie."

"I need you to help me with my dress. The car will be here any minute."

He slowly shrugs his shirt over his shoulders. "You'll wait for me, the car can wait for us."

"Why are you being so fucking difficult?" He only replies with a smug coolness. "Jesus Christ, come to my room whenever your *highness* decides he's done making everyone else wait on him."

I storm back around. My palms sweat and my heart rate increases.[19]

A heavy hand grips the back of my neck and tugs me back. Finn spins me around and gets so close our noses nearly touch. "We've been playing a sweet game of house lately, but you're dancing with fire. Do I need to remind you the kind of man I am?"

His eyes darken intensely, and his dominant display is making me feel something other than stress for the first time all day. My heart thumps against my sternum, and I can't help but push him, riding the high of a small reprieve from the anxiety. "We don't have time for that either."

"The moment you became my wife is the moment you stopped letting anyone or anything else dictate your life. The car will wait. The gala will wait. And the governor? He can kiss your fucking feet."

"That's not how the world works, Finn." I bite back. "Point A, I'm married to *you.*" I shove him in the chest. His hands clamp down around mine on his bare chest. I feel his heart pound under my palms.

"You're right. And as your husband, it's my responsibility to get you out of your head."

He whips me around and bends me over the island of drawers in the middle of the closet. My cheek presses against the cool glass top. He hums in my ear and his breath sends chills down my spine. "Don't move an inch."

The island is taller than my hips, so I'm stretched on my toes to lay flat. He releases my neck and grabs a tie from the drawer. "Hands."

I bring my arms behind my back, and he ties them with the silky material.

---

19 Love Is a Bitch—Two Feet | SummerOtoole.com/playlists

I test the restraint, and the next thing I know a blinding pain is burning across my ass. I gasp, too shocked for words. The sting is so good I instantly crave more. He trails a finger up my spine. "I told you not to move. From now on, every time you fidget even the slightest bit, you'll earn another one. Do you understand?"

Fuck me, I know I should be pissed, but instead my body raises ten degrees, and my inner thighs slicken.

"I understand." Immediately I want to defy him, move just to spite him. And to get his hands back on me, because when he's touching me, I finally feel like I can breathe.

He steps into my line of sight, and I practically drool watching him slowly—*painfully so*—button his shirt. I've never seen anything hotter than Finneas Fox getting dressed with his eyes intently on me.

One by one, he does each button and covers a bit more of his tattooed muscles. I'd mourn the opportunity to see the work of art that is his body, but he's just as striking when so sharply dressed.

"One," he says, low and deadly. I didn't even realize I'd moved. Heat burns in my core.

He slowly walks behind me and my entire body lights up in anticipation. He caresses my cheek, still stinging from the last blow. "You look fucking divine bent over like this."

My pulse races waiting for the strike. His presence behind me is so strong and palpable he might as well have his hands all over me. His palm glides down my thigh and then in between my legs. His light touch as he approaches the edges of my panties makes me squirm. "*Two.*"

"Fuck," I whisper.

He laughs darkly. "No, princess, I won't be fucking you. That wouldn't be a punishment, now would it?" He drags his fingers over my pussy, and I inhale sharply, every muscle in my body struggling not to writhe. "But I promise you'll enjoy being punished just as much."

His hands leave me, and I feel cold without him. He grabs cufflinks out of a drawer in front of me and begins tediously fastening them. My arches ache and my calves burn from the position. "You can't go any faster?"

"Three."

"You never said I couldn't talk—"

"*Four.*" I bite my tongue and glare at him, he lifts one brow and smirks. *Arrogant bastard.*

Why do his cufflinks make me want to drop to my knees and undo all the work he's just done getting dressed? Why do my insides melt when he straightens his sleeves, giving each wrist a little tug?

There's also something about the way his gaze is constantly roaming my skin, soaking in every inch of my exposed body like a predator stalking his next meal, which heightens all my senses and demands all my attention. I could be late to meet the goddamn Queen, and I wouldn't care less, because all I can think about is the beautiful man in front of me and the delicious moments hanging in the air before he touches me next.

He picks up a bow tie and turns away from me to tie it in a mirror. I sigh in relief and take the brief moment of his back to me to stretch my back.

"Five." My breath catches in my throat, and I look up to see his eyes locked on mine through the reflection. I don't know how he does it, but he's able to finish his task without ever taking his eyes off mine.

The tension and silence gnaw at me. Eagerness and electricity hum through me. I can't handle it a second longer. "I thought you said I would enjoy this, and so far all you've done is bore me."

His lip curls menacingly as he slowly turns. "Then get up, princess," he taunts. "There's nothing stopping you."

He's right. The restraints on my wrists would do nothing to stop me from standing up and walking right out. But of course, I won't do that. I love the game too much. His eyes glow like embers when I refuse to move. He takes a tux jacket off a hanger and slips it on.

He rounds the island in slow, predatory movements. I sense him behind me, everywhere all at once. He kicks my legs apart and I have to stretch even further on my toes to remain flat. His fingers ghost over my clit and down my slit, so lightly it would tickle if it wasn't such an infuriating tease. "Are you always this wet when you're bored?"

And then his hand is gone, and my body vibrates in his absence. I hear him retreat and my heels sag, inching a touch down the island.

"*Six.*" His voice wraps around me like smoke.

I hear the clinking of glass and the sound of liquid pouring. "I'd offer you a drink but…" he drawls. Of course, he would have a bar in his fucking closet.

He comes to stand behind me, and I feel high with anticipation. He's so close I can hear his breath, steady and strong. I can see his hands in my peripheral vision, hovering over my hips. Every cell in my body stands to attention, craving what only he can give me.

Finally he touches me.

His hands feel cool against my searing skin. He begins to leisurely lower my panties and I hear him suck in an awed breath. This shaky inhale is the first time his control cracks, and I'm pleased to see I'm not the only one so affected. "How many, princess?"

"Six." The urge to thrust back into him is powerful, especially when I consider how he might punish me if I do.

"You know why I'm doing this don't you?" He asks, my panties mid-thigh and his hands lightly roving up the swell of my ass.

"Yes." I hardly consider his question because somehow I intuitively know the answer. He's doing it for me. It's not just about the tease, but about the care he has for me. He knows how the anxiety of tonight has been eating at me and these tantalizing moments are the only time it's melted away.

"Good. Because I won't be gentle. You may be a princess, but I'm gonna treat you like my whore." I brace for the spank I'm sure will follow, but instead I feel cold liquid spilling down my ass.

I turn my head the smallest amount to see Finn letting whiskey spill from his mouth onto me. "I'll let you get away with that one." He smirks and kneels behind me. My pussy clenches when I feel his breath flutter against my hot skin. He groans quietly, as if he didn't mean for me to hear, and spreads my cheeks, taking one long, indecent lick from hole to hole, lapping up the whiskey.

He stands and grabs my jaw, twisting my head so he can give me a long, lascivious kiss. He pulls away and my head spins, my breath completely snatched. "Doesn't your patience taste sweet?" I moan, savoring the taste of him, the whiskey and my own lust.

And then without any other warning, his fist closes around my bound wrist while his other hand comes down hard and sharp. It takes a moment for the burn to settle in, for the heat to spread, and *fuck*, nothing has ever hurt so good.

Except for the next slap, and the one after that and the one after that. Each one layers sensations on top of sensations, the pain and pleasure both building exponentially. By the time he finishes all six, I'm ready to beg for more even though my wrists ache under his bruising hold and my ass is nothing but white-hot fire.

I'm breathing so heavily the glass by my face has fogged up and I can hear my own heartbeat. I'm still coming down when I feel another spill of something wet on my ass. The cool liquid is like sweet honey against my raging skin. My mind is a haze, not even trying to deduce what is happening until a finger spreads the coolness between my cheeks.

He's thoughtful and confident in his movements. I never doubt I'll enjoy whatever he does next. He knows when to push me and when to hold me. His finger wanders to my back entrance and smooths the gel-like liquid around the hole, pressing softly. I whimper pleasurably as his finger breaches the tight ring. "Tell me to stop, and I will. But I don't think you want me to. Do you, princess?"

I suck in full breath and on the exhale, he pushes further, sinking in. "That's it, good girl," he praises as I relax and welcome him in. There's something uniquely vulnerable but comforting in relinquishing control like this. It makes me feel both scared and cared for.

He continues to lavish me with encouragement and begins to slowly pump in and out of my ass. Soon, I become lost in the rhythm, feeling fully in my body and in this moment.

"*Fuck,* if you keep making those sounds, I'm gonna forget about my plans and fuck your tight little ass right here." Finn groans and squeezes my hip harder. "You like this don't you? Such a filthy little plaything."

"Yes," I breathe on the next moan as he works his finger in a wide, sweeping circular motion inside me. It's mesmerizing and so fucking hot, I find myself pushing my hips back, eager for more.

"I'm gonna pull out, but stay just like this, okay, princess?" The hand on my hip slides up my back with a firm pressure and I nod. He withdraws slowly and the sensation is just as overwhelming as when he entered.

I hear him move several paces away but then he's back. He opens a sealed box at the side of my head so I can see as he pulls out its contents. "I want you to wear this tonight." He twirls the butt plug so I can see its size and shape and the jeweled base. "And every time you feel it, I want you to remember what happened here tonight. If you get anxious or overwhelmed, come back to this place where nothing matters but me and you." He strokes my hair and searches for understanding in my eyes.

"Okay." I swallow, oddly touched by the gift.

He circles back behind me and again gently pushes a lubricated finger into me. I relax much quicker this time, enjoying the fullness instantly. He pulls it out and next I feel the hard, metal tip of the plug prodding where his finger used to be. I focus on my breathing, relaxing my muscles and putting all my weight onto the island.

"Look at you," he says with awe, "my perfect, little wife."

He takes his time fitting the whole thing and once it's fully seated he kisses each dimple in my lower back. He gently pulls my panties back up and I hiss at the thin fabric against my smarting skin. He unties my wrists, and my hands fall to clutch the edge of the island.

He drags a soothing palm down my back. "Let's get you into that dress."

The car did, in fact, wait for us.

However, it feels like the driver is determined to hit every pothole and any other goddamn hump in the road. Each jostle and bump I feel ten-fold on my sore, full ass. Finn is casually sipping a drink with his arm along the window, his fingers drumming lightly on the rim. He looks at me from the corner of his eye every time we hit a bump, but I won't give him the satisfaction of a reaction. I'm sure he'd love to know I can still feel him even when he's not touching me, but taunting him feels just as gratifying as giving in.

He looks downright wicked in a full tux. His dark hair is swept back, but two small strands have fallen making him look polished but still rough around the edges, like he could kill you without getting a speck of blood on his crisp white shirt. My fingers itch to loosen his collar and dust a kiss as teasingly light as he did earlier. I'm getting lost in thoughts of us, and I'm taken by surprise as the limo turns sharply and I gasp, squirming.

At the sound, Finn's head slowly rounds on me, tongue in cheek. "Something bothering you, princess?"

"Nope," I say and sit taller.

He lifts a brow. "Is that so?"

"Mhmm." I grind my teeth as the car stutters to a stop at a redlight, my muscles aching.

He nods thoughtfully, but a devilish glint sparkles in his eye. He sets his glass down without ever taking his assessing gaze off me.

"Seems like I left my wife wanting." His hand lashes out and grabs my wrist, dragging me quickly and effortlessly across the limousine seat and over his lap. My stomach and hips rest on his legs, my ass facing up. He slides a heavy palm languidly from my ankle to my thigh.

"Finn, what are you—"

"I promised not to be gentle, and if you're still able to sit, I didn't deliver." His words are rich and goading. He smooths a palm over one of my cheeks, and even the light pressure wiggles the plug and rubs at the ache. "If six didn't do it, maybe we should try for ten."

He raises his hand and my heart pounds deliriously. "Wait—wait, Finn."

"What's that, little wife?"

I turn over in his lap and sit up, settling myself between his knees while my legs hang over one side of his. "Every bump in the road, every inch I move, I feel you." He looks down his nose at me and I trail a finger down his cheek, and I feel his jaw clench under my touch. "Thank you."

His lip twitches, and I can see pride soften his eyes. His arms encircle my waist, and he plants a soft kiss behind my ear and whispers, "You did so well, princess. I'm so proud of you." I fucking *melt*. "I can't wait to reward you."

Our driver pulls into the queue of cars at the hotel hosting the gala—at least this one is for a deserving cause and not to raise money for rich people to get a new golf course. Seeing the cameras flash up ahead sends me straight back to the last time I was at a gala. The scene will play out eerily similar, except this time, I will be walking in with Finn on my arm instead of Hudson.

Finn must notice my accelerated breathing the closer we inch in line. He places a weighty palm on my chest and reminds me to breathe. We are almost to the front when he says, "One last thing..." He pulls out a small black box, and telling me to breathe was pointless because the emerald ring inside is the most beautiful thing I've ever seen. "Can't let you go in there without everyone knowing exactly who you belong to."

"Jesus Christ, Finn, that's the biggest rock I've ever seen."

He slips it on to my finger, a pleased smile playing on his lips. "Guess I'm bigger and better than him in two departments."

The joke, as ill-formed as it is, makes me laugh and helps chase away some of my nerves. I look down at the new ring on my finger and laugh. "I did buy that last one myself."

"I know," he says smugly.

"No, you didn't."

"Spiteful, stubborn and rich enough to pull it off." He gives me a wry smile. "Though, I may not have thought of it if you hadn't given me the idea."

I look at him confused, and he parrots my words back to me, "'You think I bought this for myself just to convince you I'm engaged?'"

"Oh." I bite my cheek.

"It doesn't matter, that ring was never meant to be on your hand. But this..." He holds up my hand and takes in the sparkling emerald. "—would also look great wrapped around my cock."

"*Finneas Fox.*" I slap him in the chest.

He looks proud when he says, "Did I not say that's where this hand belongs no matter whose ring is on it?"

The car stops and seconds later our door opens, I shoot Finn a testing stare. "If you mention anything about your cock near my father, I will saw it off with a rusty blade. Do you hear me?"

He gives me a wolfish grin. "Loud and clear, darling," he says as if accepting a challenge not a threat.

"I'm serious, Finn." I hiss through a smile as he helps me out of the limo.

He places my hand in the crook of his elbow and we begin to glide down the red carpet. "As am I."

The ballroom at the Ritz has been transformed into a luxury casino straight off the sea cliffs of Monte Carlo. Everything is dripping in gold and satin, and I'm reminded how little these events have to do with the actual charity and everything to do with the who's who of June Harbor. We are some of the youngest people here, but that doesn't surprise me. We're only here at the request of my father anyway.

Speaking of Satan himself, I spot him across the room, and he ushers us over, his smile as wide as it is fake. I can feel Finn tense as we approach, and I'm starting to wish there were metal detectors at the door because Finn pulling out a gun at a charity gala feels completely on brand.

"You'll be fine," I whisper and give his arm a squeeze.

"I'm not worried for myself, princess," he says, his voice low and lethal.

"Euphemia, my dear," my mother squawks and flings her arms around me. "I feel like I haven't seen my baby in forever." I try to loosen into her embrace, but I feel like I'm in the jaws of a lion. She finally releases me and turns gushing to Finn. "And my goodness, Finneas, is that really you? So grown up." She grasps his cheek, and now I'm not only worried about my father getting shot but my mother too.

"And wow, look at all those tattoos," she says with mock astonishment as she takes in the ink sprawling out of his neckline and sleeves. My mother is happy to pretend my brothers don't have any tattoos as long as she can't see them.

But to my surprise, Finn turns on a dazzling, panty-melting smile. "Mrs. Luciano, you haven't aged a day in ten years. I see where my wife gets her beauty." He gives me a warm smile, but it radiates with the same type of heat I imagine hell has.

"Yes, how is married life treating you two…" My father pauses to look us up and down with taunting amusement in his eyes, "…lovebirds?" I cringe, my hand balling into a tight fist. *Lovebirds?* He knows exactly how this marriage came to be. Why pretend when we all know the truth.

"Little Ef!" I turn at the nickname only two people call me. "Look at you, all grown up and married, huh?" Renzo strolls up to us with a cocky grin and drink in hand.

"I didn't know you were back?" It shouldn't matter but for some reason my brother's surprise return has me feeling off balance. "Is G here too?"

I don't get a response. Instead he turns to Finn and offers a terse, "Fox."

"Lorenzo." Finn's calm composure gives me an anchor. If anyone should be freaked out by this bombardment of Lucianos, it's him. I watch my father's eyes narrow, scrutinizing the interaction. An unexpected sense of pride wells, seeing Finn so confidently holding his own. Not that I'm surprised.

Two hands land on my shoulders from behind. "Baby sis, look at you, all grown up."

I turn with a sneer to face Gianni. "Did you two rehearse that fucking line or something?"

"Euphemia, *language*," my mother chides. Being treated like a fucking child makes my anxiety rise.

"Please excuse us while we find our seats." Finn's steading palm finds the small of my back, and he pulls me into his side.

"You're at our table, son," my father says, and Finn's jaw ticks. I remember the last time my father called him son and his eyes have the same murderous energy as they did then.

Christ, this is going to be a bloodbath.

Chapter 19:

Amongst the Stars

Finn

Amazingly, I make it through dinner without plunging a fork into either of the Luciano brothers' hands. I've been determined to keep a lid on my burning desire to slit everyone's throat, if only to avoid making this any worse for Effie. Though, I'm starting to think she might thank me if I do. She seems more uncomfortable around her own family than mine, and that says something when she had a full-blown panic attack over fucking cups.

I can't help the territorial hand I keep on her leg the entire time, tapping a soothing rhythm to remind her I'm right here and I'm not leaving.

Except to maybe piss because I've held it all dinner and things are getting urgent. When the final speaker for the night ends, he welcomes the guests to the dance floor and her father asks Effie to dance. I grip her thigh tighter, but she gives my hand a small, reassuring tap and stands.

I figure this is my chance. I excuse myself from the table and make my way to the restroom. The lively chatter of the evening and music fills the room, and stepping into the hallway is a relief to the senses. It's much quieter, which means I instantly notice when the ballroom door opens again.

I spin as casually as I can while also sticking my hand in the pocket with my switchblade. Sure, it could be any number of guests innocently following behind me. But I've seen too much shit to believe in coincidences and someone entering the quiet, empty hallway at the same time as me isn't one.

"Governor," I step toward him. I see him flinch minutely, but he tries to quickly recover.

"You won't get away with this, Fox. I *will* find him."

"Find who exactly?" There's nothing but dryness in my tone, not even fake sympathy.

"Just tell me, is he dead or alive?" he orders, as if he has any fucking right to make demands of me.

"In case you're losing your hearing, I'll say it again: I don't know what you're talking about. Now, I suggest you go right back through that door and enjoy your night." I give him a pointed nod and walk away.

"You have no idea the enemy you've made, boy." His voice shakes with anger.

I turn slowly, straightening my lapels. "What did you hope to accomplish with this little hallway ambush? To intimidate me, threaten me? Because you obviously know who I am and that *this,*" I wave a bored hand, "won't work."

"I won't stop until I find him." He glowers, and I meet his stare eye to eye.

"I sure hope you find whoever you're looking for. Good evening, Governor."

When I return, it doesn't take me long to pick Effie out of the crowd, she's down right show-stopping in that sinful emerald dress. I weave my way through the dance floor of people toward her and her father. They look to be in tense conversation, her forehead is fretted and her eyes are downcast. It takes all the control I have to not storm up and rip her away from him, throw her over my shoulder and take her far away, somewhere we can be just the two of us.

They don't see me coming and I hear the tail end of their conversation. "I don't want excuses. I want results."

"It's taking longer than I thought, but I'm trying, Papa."

Their hushed and suspicious tones make my stomach turn to lead. I tell myself not to over analyze their out of context words. *I trust Effie,* I remind myself. Before I have too long to question what evidence she's given me to trust her, she spots me and waves, relief clear on her face.

I instantly warm from the smile that tugs on her lips, the creases in her brow melting away upon seeing me.

"I'd like to steal my wife for a dance."

"Of course." He inspects me as if searching for signs of tension that would tell him whether or not I heard their conversation.

Effie accepts my hand and I pull her into me. I like the way she sighs as soon as she's firmly in my arms. "I thought you don't dance?"

"I never said that."

She narrows her eyes at me, and my chest expands just having her gaze on me, my bow tie suddenly suffocating. "You had a fit last time I tried to get you to dance."

"I dance now." To prove my point and that my lessons with Stella have paid off, I swing Effie out and then reel her back in, wrapping my arms around her and dipping her low. It's smooth and graceful and just a bit closer to the man she deserves.

But as I pull her back up, I give her plump ass a squeeze, and she gasps in a mix of arousal and pain. She tries to cover it by asking a question. "What's changed?"

"You." I brush a chaste kiss across her pinkening cheeks and whisper in her ear, "Tell me, princess. Are you blushing from this dance or because I just reminded you who owns that perfect ass?"

She gives me a coy smile and looks up at me through her lashes, arching one brow as if to say *wouldn't you like to know.* So I grab a handful of her ass again and she blushes even brighter and buries her face in my chest giving me all the answer I need.

I laugh into the top of her hair, and she only comes back out once her flaming cheeks have cooled. "I haven't seen the governor yet, maybe he didn't come?" There's an excitement in her voice that makes me want to lie just to keep her smiling. *Honesty and loyalty.*

"I ran into him in the hallway."

Her face blanches. "Did he say anything?"

"Only idle threats from a limp dick old man."

"He knows, doesn't he?" Panic leaks into her voice and her eyes flit around the room nervously.

I wrap my hand more tightly around hers and hold it to my chest. "He doesn't know anything. But more importantly, he can't *prove* anything." Her brows pinch together, and I want to kiss the tension away, but I know that won't help.

"How many people do you think I've killed?"

"*What?*" Her attention whips back to me, eyes scrutinizing.

"Well, if I started when I was fifteen and average *at least* one per month—"

"Finn, where the fuck are you going with this?" she whisper-yells, and internally I am celebrating that she now looks infuriated rather than forlorn.

"If we're being conservative, that's more or less a hundred and fifty people—"

"*Finn,*" she hisses again, and I take her by surprise with a spin under my arm.

"As I was saying, it's not a small number. Do you know how many times I've been convicted for murder? Or even arrested?"

"I don't know," she says stubbornly, still peering around at our neighboring dancers.

"Oh, come on, take a guess."

"Jesus, Finn, I don't know…ten?"

"Zero."

She stops in her tracks. "Zero?"

"I've never even been brought in for questioning about a murder or disappearance."

She nibbles on her lip. "You're really that good?"

I chuckle. "Baby, I'm the best."

"Whatever." She rolls her eyes. "Dance with me."

The later into the evening we get, the more into the drink Effie gets. She's on her third martini and I am quickly realizing she is a lusty drunk. She's well in control of her senses, only a touch past tipsy, but her eyes as well as her hands keep roaming.

My blood is on fucking fire with every graze of her fingertips against my thigh or up my arm. My jaw aches from clenching it so tight in restraint. She makes it look like they are accidental touches but the heady look in her eyes after is a dead giveaway.

We're seated at the table, just the two of us. The rest of her family is mingling while everyone waits for the auction to begin. This particular one is infamous for being a battle of the riches. People drop obscene amounts of money on things not nearly worth it, just to be seen doing it. It's a multi-million-dollar dick swinging contest.

She idly plays with poker chips left on the table from a previous game while I drum on the rim of my drink. Her eyes catch on the movement. "You have nice hands."

"Thank you?" I cock a brow at her.

"They would look good around my throat," she says hushed over her glass as she takes another sip.

"Jesus Christ, Ef..." I breathe.

"You've told me plenty of times where my hands would look good. I'm just returning the sentiment." Her pink tongue darts out and wets her lip as she gazes up at me. "Do you not agree?"

"I—"

"She totally got a boob job," Renzo plops down across from me.

"No, she's always had massive tits," says Gianni as he also sits.

"Who are you talking about?" Effie asks her brothers.

"Marcella DeGrossi," they answer at the same time.

She leans back in her chair and smirks. "You're both wrong."

"No, I'm not—

"How do you know—" *Are these fuckers capable of speaking one at a time?*

"She's pregnant. And I know you both have fucked her…" She wiggles her eyebrows and both brothers' jaws fall open. They exchange curious and amused glances, and then Effie bursts out in laughter. "Jesus, you two are so fucking gullible."

The three of them heckle back and forth, and I tune them out, instead watching the light in Effie's face, the brightness of her smile. Being able to witness her like this, without the weight of stress or fear, is a fucking gift.

Their debate on Miss DeGrossi's boobs is cut short when the MC announces the start of the auction. Numbered paddles are distributed along with a pamphlet on the night's items. [20]Effie twirls the toothpick from her olives between her teeth, giving me a look that sends blood straight to my cock. She proceeds to wrap her lips around an olive and pull it off with her teeth. Then has the audacity to pretend she has no idea what she's doing, looks at me innocently, mouthing, "*What?*"

The auction begins, and I'm having trouble focusing on anything other than the rise and fall of her chest against the brilliant green of her dress. Tension crackles between us like we are both waiting for the other to strike. I'm finely attuned to each subtle shift of her seat or tightening of her lips that tell me she is still feeling my gift. I could watch her all fucking night and still find things that mesmerize me.

Strands of her neatly styled hair have fallen loose, and I idly twist one around my finger. I brush my thumb across the tiny scars by her eye. She blinks at me, her eyes rich and moody like whiskey. I bracket my hand

---

20 Insane—Post Malone | SummerOtoole.com/playlists

around the back of her neck and tug her to me, kissing the scars and breathing into her flushed skin. "I can't believe you're my wife."

Her hand drops to my thigh and ghosts over my groin, she looks up at me with a pouty bottom lip and hooded eyes. "To do with as you please…"

I shudder, my skin becoming electrified and my hunger for her claws at me.

A laugh flutters out of her lips and she tries to scoot away, but I keep her locked at my side, hand grasping her thigh. She gets a wicked glint in her eye like she's about to come back with some smartass comment but then the auctioneer announces some random French name and Effie nearly jumps out of her damn seat.

"Oh my god," she says awestruck as helpers bring out an impressionist painting on a canvas the size of a twin bed. I have no idea who the artist is, and quite frankly, don't care. All I care about is her reaction to it.

"We will start the bidding at a half million—"

"Six hundred!" Someone calls out immediately.

Effie's eyes ping-pong around the room as a bidding war quickly drives the price up to five million. Soon it's down to the governor and one other man.

"You want it?" I ask, and her head snaps to me.

"It's too much, no way." She shakes her head and fidgets with her dress.

"Five point one—do I hear five point one—" The auctioneer prattles and the man battling the governor sits down defeated. "Five point one going once going—"

"Do you want it?"

"Fin—"

I stare into her eyes while I raise my paddle. "Five, three."

Effie bounces in her seat and latches onto me giddy. Her petite hands wrap around my forearm draped over her leg while the governor glares at me from across the room. My lip curls into a smirk.

The bid climbs to five and a half million and I lazily raise my paddle, then take a leisurely, warming sip of my whiskey. "Five." I say under my breath for only Effie to hear.

Another bid, another raise. "Four."

Another bid, another raise. "Three."

"What are you counting down to?" She whispers excitedly.

"Until we win."

She rakes her teeth over her bottom lip. "We?"

"You, the painting. Me, the pleasure of my wife sitting on my dick in gratitude." Her mouth hangs open, and I can't help but brush my thumb across her bottom lip.

"We *can't*—"

"You can't deny me what's mine, princess. You should know by now that I always get what I want." I'm barely paying attention to the auction, raising my paddle while my eyes are fixed on the increased pace of her breathing and blushing cheeks.

I only know we've won because Effie starts jumping up and down cheering, and when I look at the governor he is angrier than he was in the hallway. I stand, as the room claps, I'm sure this was the highest bid of the evening. I grab her by the hips and tug her in front of me, my cock already celebrating our victory.

She feels my erection against her back and taunts over her shoulder, "Good luck, getting that anywhere near me in this dress."

She's right, her dress would certainly prevent anything I have in mind. As it is *now*. Luckily, with our table in the corner, our backs face a wall. I whip out my switchblade and hold it to the slit at the back of her dress.

"*Finneas.*" She gapes, looking behind her. "Jesus, control yourself."

I graze my teeth along her ear. "I lost control around you a long time ago." Then I'm cutting the dress straight up to the small of her back. My chest hammers the more I reveal of her perfect body and the need to sink myself inside her is dizzying.

I sit, pulling her down onto my lap and she gasps, no doubt because of the toy being jostled. "Hips up, princess." My breath on the back of her neck makes her shiver, and I want to lick away the goosebumps.

She rises a few inches but never enough that the billowing sides of her dress don't keep her covered. I swiftly undo my pants and cut her panties off. I see the jewel in her ass and my heart feels like it's going to beat out of my chest. Knowing that everyone can see the emerald on her finger, but I'm the only one who gets to see this one makes me impossibly harder.

I pull her hips all the way back at the same time I take my dick out and line her up with the tip. Her fingers grip the table as she lowers herself down, a deep groan threatening to spill from me.

"*Fuck,* you're so tight." Her pussy clenches around me as she takes me to the hilt, the toy in her ass making everything narrower.

"Oh my god," she gasps, and her hands twist into the black tablecloth. "It's so…much." There's an intrigued and excited tinge to her voice and she relaxes back a little.

"Look at you, such a good fucking girl, taking my cock with your ass filled. My princess and my *plaything.*" I nuzzle into the back of her neck, nipping the skin, fighting the urge to sink my teeth deeper. "You feel so fucking good."

Christ, too good. It's taking everything I have not to thrust up into her hot, wet cunt like it's the only place I'm ever meant to be.

"God, Finn, I'm so full." She wiggles a little in my lap, and I bite back a groan as she pulses around me. "I could come just like this."

"Gonna come for me in a room full of people? Naughty wife." I breathe against her neck.

"Still got money in the bank after that for a game of poker?" Gianni says, breaking off from the conversation with his brother. They both turn to us, and Effie's back goes rigid. I give her hip a reassuring squeeze.

I brush off his dig and start stacking my chips together as an answer. After wiping their asses in Blackjack earlier in the night, I'm surprised they are coming back for more. "Hold 'em?"

"You're on," Renzo says, shuffling the cards with ease and dealing out the first hand.

Poker is technically a game of luck, but I have a feeling my princess won't lose tonight. "Good luck," I say and press a quick kiss to her cheek.

I keep one hand on Effie the whole time, drumming on her hip. Any nerves she may have had dissipates and she's left with the glowing thrill of the game and our illicit secret.

As we play several hands, I notice how her hands ball into fists on the table and I find it amusing how she seems to be more emotionally invested in this game than anyone else playing. Her sweet face scrunches up in frustration anytime one of her brothers wins a hand and takes a portion of her winnings.

I give her a small punch of my hips, disguised as repositioning in my seat and she gasps, any traces of irritation melting away. She shoots wide eyes at me, but I look straight ahead, my tongue tracing my bottom lip. Her face morphs into a cocky grin, as if to say *challenge accepted.*

Her luck seems to change after that as she plays the next hand. Renzo deals and Effie glances at her holding cards. I peek over her shoulder and see she's holding pocket aces. As I glance at her, I notice she's trying to hide a smirk. I think she's going to slow play it as she calls the bluff bet Gianni just obviously made. "Pot's right" Renzo says, and as the turn card comes, I see her third ace and know she's won. Everyone lays down their hands and Effie claps and reaches forward to scoop the pot. Her pussy slides up and down my shaft as she clutches the chips to her chest, and it forces me to grind my teeth together to avoid groaning out loud.

When it starts to feel like every inch of my skin is on fire, I dig my fingers into her hips, stilling her, and growl in her ear, "Princess, I swear to God if you don't stop bouncing on my cock, I'm going to bend you over this table and let everyone hear how you sound when you get *truly* fucked by your husband." She sharply inhales and presses her lips closed, a guilty but mischievous look on her face. "Unless that's what you want?"

She looks over her shoulder at me and worries her lip through her teeth, she shakes her head but the love-drunk look in her eyes says otherwise. "Let's finish this game and then I'll take you somewhere I can give you everything you're craving."

Renzo deals the last hand. Effie grabs her cards, peeks at what she has, and fans the cards out in front of her perfect pink lips. As the flop comes, I say low and hushed, "By the end of the night those pretty lips will be wrapped around my cock." Her pussy flutters at my words, and I breathe, strained, my chest tightening.

Once the rounds of betting have occurred and the turn comes, she erupts in cheers, takes the remainder of the chips, and her brothers groan in defeat. She twists in my lap and grabs me by the face for a kiss that knocks all the air out of me. This singular public display of affection is the first time that I've ever felt like I truly belong to her——not even my cock inside her or the ring on her finger has made me feel this way.

She's always been mine, but now I'm hers, too.

Her laughter is bright and fills me with warmth as we run up the stair-well, her hand in mine. My tux jacket is slung over her shoulders to cover the *modifications* I made to her dress. I push open the heavy metal door at the top and drag her onto the hotel roof with me. The air is cold and sharp. A few hundred dollars to the security guard, and we have the rooftop pool deck that's closed for renovations all to ourselves.

Effie drops my hand and wanders ahead of me, neck craning to take in the canvas of stars above us. She faces me with a heated look, and I stalk toward her, ready to burn. She walks backward, a devilish smile playing on her lips as she drops my jacket off her shoulders. She hits the railing and leans back into it, impatience and lust radiating from her. I stop a foot away from her, raking over her body with my gaze. She tilts her head and assesses me right back.

Our stares latch, and I feel the universe looking back at me. Getting lost in her eyes is so easy, and I never want to be found. I undo my pants and take my cock out. "Lift your dress."[21]

Keeping my gaze locked on hers, I drop my hand to her bare pussy. Tracing my fingers over her swollen clit, she moans, and the sound heats me down to my very bones.

I drag my fingers lower and slip them into her. Her mouth falls open and

I can't help but bite her lip, swallowing the sweet sounds spilling out of her, drinking them down as if I can consume her soul through them.

She reaches between us and strokes my cock. "If you don't fuck me the way you've been threatening to all night, I'm gonna lose my goddamn mind, Finneas."

I clutch her chin and kiss and suck under her jaw. "And which way is that, princess?"

"Like you're trying to ruin me." *Fuck.*

I hike her leg around my hip, and she positions me at her entrance as I push my two fingers coated in her arousal between her teeth. I slam into her. "I thought I already ruined you," I grunt as I withdraw and thrust back in, deeper, harder. I slip my fingers from her mouth and collar her throat

"You did. But the only time I feel whole is when you're breaking me apart." Her nails dig into my shoulders, and I give her everything I have. I pour my fucking soul into each thrust, give her my heart with every punch of my hips as if through her, I can claw my way to salvation and out of the darkness before I bring her down with me.

"*God, Finn,*" she mewls, "You feel amazing."

My abs constrict and pressure builds in my balls. "Do you want me to come in your cunt or your ass, princess? Because I'll be having both to-night."

"Stop asking me questions and just take me how you want," she pants, and I recognize the heady need in her eyes. She wants to just let go, give up control and forget about everything but the pleasure I'm giving her, the submission I'm demanding of her.

And I'd rip my own heart out before I deny her that.

"Fucking you is a gift, calling you mine is an honor." I stroke her cheek as I lower her leg and whisper against her lips, "Now get on your knees."

I step back, gliding out of her and giving her space to kneel in front of me. She looks up at me, doe-eyed and supplicant. I tilt her chin up. "Go ahead, princess. Clean up the mess you made."

Her eyes darken and her tongue flicks out to lick her lips. She slides her palms up my thighs and licks me from hilt to head. "Eyes on me. You look away, and you don't get to come."

She desperately latches onto my gaze and my chest expands, filling with the purest form of greed. She languidly drags her hot tongue up and down, swirling around my piercing and making pleasure wind like a tight ball around my spine. "Put your lips on it."

Obeying like a fallen angel, she wraps her pretty lips around my cock and bobs tentatively past the tip. "Now choke on it."

I scrutinize every subtle message she subconsciously sends me with her body. Her eyes widen in excitement with a hint of fear. Her thighs squeeze together, and her breathing deepens. She sinks her mouth further down my cock, and she feels like fucking heaven itself. "That's a good girl. All the way." I encourage her, my fingers only lightly wrapping around her hair. "I love your fire. Christ, it makes me wanna burn alive. But your submission? There's nothing sweeter."

I hit the back of her throat and it constricts around me as she gags. "*Fuuck.*" Even as her eyes well with tears, she doesn't break eye contact. "Do you like tasting yourself on your husband's cock?" She bobs her head yes, and I wipe a fallen tear with my thumb.

"Play with the toy." She reaches behind herself and moans, sending vibrations shooting down my length and my whole body tenses to hold back my climax. I pull her off me. "In my jacket pocket, there's a small bottle. Go get it."

When she stands, I sweep her against me and kiss her long and hard. We pull about, both gasping for air. "And then, I'm gonna take that sweet ass. I don't care if you have to work for it, you're going to love every fucking inch I give you." She swallows hungrily and then scampers away.

Mere seconds later, she's back and hands me the small bottle of lube. She sets it in my palm. Then she turns around and grabs the railing. The jeweled base glints, and my handprints turning light purple on her ass are a work of art. She pushes her hips back as I spread lube up and down my shaft. I squirt some more at the top of her cheeks and spread it around the base of the plug. I give it a small wiggle. She whimpers, and it makes a dark part of me light up.

I gently begin to pull it out. "Has another man ever had you like this—" I stop myself, "Doesn't matter, I'm erasing all those memories tonight."

She hisses as I pull it all the way out. I apply more lube to her ass and nudge the tight hole with my tip. "Say sunflower if it's too much. Other than that, don't make a sound until I give you permission. Nod that you understand."

She bobs her head and I stroke her back, encouraging her to relax as I slowly push my hips further. "*Fuck, so good—*" A groan engulfs my words. Her tight ass feeling like a hit of the strongest drug. I want to be gentle, I do. But fuck, the feel of her, the sight of her, shimmering emerald dress cut and splayed at her sides, it's driving me insane. I close my eyes and drop into the rhythm of my index finger tapping a beat while my other fingers' grip turns bruising.

Her head drops forward and bites her wrist, and I realize I've picked up pace and force, fucking her with strong and powerful thrusts. I brush her loose hair out of her face. "I tried to be gentle, but you make me fucking crazy. Taking my cock like this, every inch without a sound.

"You've been so good, princess. It's time for your reward." I slide my hand to her front and find her clit. Her teeth dig into her skin deeper, and her brows pinch together when I stroke her clit, my fingers slick with lube and her own juices. "*Christ*, you look so beautiful like this. Amongst the stars with my cock buried deep inside your ass, covered with my handprint."

She grinds into my hand and her body tenses around me, strained sounds coming from her. "It's hard to hold back, isn't it? Hard to stay quiet when all you want to do is fuck me until you're screaming and crying my name?" She looks at me, a crease tugging between her brows, teeth digging rivets into her lip and desperately nods her head.

"Then do it, princess. Fuck yourself on my cock." I give her an arrogant smirk I know will make her mad. "I won't tell anyone how much you like your pretty ass fucked. *"*

Her first sounds are pained moans like she'd been close to death holding them back. She begins to pump her hips back, eagerly taking every inch of my dick. "Oh god," she cries into the night. "Oh, god, Finn. Keep playing with my clit. I'm gonna come. *F—f—fuck!"*

"That's it, princess," I groan, her tight ass stripping my cock, making pleasure build and build. "Scream. Moan. Cry. I don't care as long as you remember it's your husband making you feel this good."

"Finger my pussy," she begs, and I shift my hand to plunge two fingers in her dripping cunt and circle her clit with my thumb. *Fuck*, through her pussy, I can feel my fingers drag against my piercing with every stroke.

"*Yes—Jesus—Oh god!"* Each nonsensical word she spews is like kerosene on a fire, igniting the monster inside me that wants nothing more than to hear her shatter.

"Give it to me, Effie. Come for me, my perfect plaything—" I thrust into her, pouring every good and kind part of me into her. Gifting them to her so she can keep them safe. After all, maybe she's the only good part of me.

"*Finn, fuck—"* She cries as her body shakes and her pussy squeezes my fingers, her clit throbbing. Even her ass clenches down hard around me, pulling my release from me. I spill into her with a rumbly groan.

I carefully and gently pull out of her, taking a handkerchief out and cleaning up my cum spilling out of her. She sighs softly and contented, blissed out and beautiful. I envelop her in my arms, holding her back tight to my chest, and release a sigh of my own.

"I wish I could live in this moment forever," she says, sinking back against me.

"Then forever it is, princess. You and me, *forever.*"

Chapter 20:

Juicy Tracksuits and Star Wars DVDs

We spent another night in the city after the gala but then came back to Bartlett Farms. While I know we are technically here for safety, it's starting to become much more than just a hide out. Before moving in with Les Arnaqueuses, I stayed with my parents. I wasn't permitted to live on my own for "security" purposes, and I certainly wasn't allowed to live with any boyfriend before marriage.

For years on end, I was never able to fully let my guard down. I always felt like I was walking on eggshells, waiting for the next shoe to drop. It was exhausting, chipped away at everything that made me, *me*. Things that Finn has embraced and even encouraged—like this sweet little painting set up I'm at right now.

There's something comforting about knowing that anyone who wants to reach me has to drive over an hour to get here, and I can guarantee no one in my family cares enough about me to do that. I like the simplicity of the barn apartment too. There's nothing fake, unlike the home I was raised in, there's no need for something garish to distract from an ugly core.

It's been four days since the gala, and the conversation with my father has been weighing on me. The stress has been getting to me, so I've been painting my life away. I need to reach out to Linnie again soon and map out our next moves.

I nibble on the end of my paint brush in thought. I get a swooping feeling in my stomach like I'm going to be sick. There's so much on the line and so many things that can go wrong. And last time things went wrong, I was nearly killed.

But falling for Finneas Fox? That was certainly never part of the plan and makes it even more crucial that things are executed sooner rather than later. The further things go with Finn, the greater the potential for hurt.

I peer out the window and my chest squeezes seeing Finn working on his truck. He's messing with something on the engine, his forearm leaning against the propped open hood. Since we got back from the city, he's been working on it nearly all day every day. It tugs on my heart strings to see him back at it after so many years.

He steps back, wiping his grease covered hands on a rag. I look down at my own hands, covered in paint, and in some way I can't explain…it feels like healing.

When I look back up he's waving at me and I go over the window, pulling it open. "I have to run to the auto shop for a part, shouldn't be longer than twenty minutes. You good?"

"Yep, see you soon."

"Okay," he smiles softly and heads to his operable car. I go back to my stool and listen to the engine rev and drive off.

It feels like mere seconds have passed when I hear the sound of crunching gravel again. I pop my head out the window, "What did you forget—"

My heart slams into my sternum when I see my father's car creeping down the drive.

Finn

I'm probably driving faster than I should on these winding country roads, but I'm chomping at the bit to flush out the last few corroded lines. Leaving a truck in a barn for a decade tends to leave things eroded and rusted. But if I'm right, this should be the last obstacle to getting her started up and running. I can't wait to hear that rumbly groan of her engine again.

I zoom past a whir of yellow. Realizing, it's the patch of sunflowers I passed last week, I pull a quick U-turn. I get out of the car and cut down three big flowers, being extra careful setting them in the passenger seat where they won't get ruined like last time. But just in case, that's why I got three.

I speed over the gravel drive and whip behind the big house, slamming on the brakes and skidding when another car is in my usual spot.

My pulse dive bombs, and my heart nearly stutters to a stop. *Fear.* That's what floods my veins. A rare and disturbing emotion that propels me out of my seat and has me sprinting to the barn. I know whoever I find won't be a friendly. No one would come without a heads up unless they wanted to get shot on arrival.

I draw my gun before throwing open the door. The scene before me is enough to make my stomach churn. Some burly fucker I recognize, whose name I can't remember in my fear, has Effie's hands held behind her back as her father plows a fist into her stomach. Her legs lift off the floor, and all the air is pushed out of her lungs in a pained groan. At the sound of my entrance, Luciano spins around, stepping aside and her head is hung limply, giving me a straight shot.

Blood sprays as the bullet enters and exits the burly fucker's head. Effie collapses without his hold, and I fight the instinct to run to her, turning my gun on Luciano. His hand is reaching behind him, and I growl, "Drop it or I won't hesitate to put a bullet between your eyes too."

He plucks his piece from his waistband, dangling it with his hands raised as he sets it on the ground, kicking it over to me. I pick it up and stick it in my pants. My blood is pumping and my hand shakes trying to control my trigger finger because every ounce of me is screaming to kill the man who hurt my wife.

"Finn." Her voice is the softest velvet as she places a hand on my arm and lowers my gun. Air struggles to leave my lungs as I can barely contain my rage—rage doesn't feel like nearly a strong enough word.

"Get the duct tape out of the top drawer, Effie." My eyes never leave him. A slick, disgusting smirk grinning back at me. I imagine my fist knocking his fucking teeth out before I cut out his tongue.

Effie hands me the roll of tape, and I gesture for him to sit in one of the dining chairs. He only chuckles mockingly as I quickly tape him to the chair. As soon as he's immobilized, I am going to Effie and wrapping her in my arms so tightly it would take a fucking titan to pull us apart.

I loosen my hold just enough to look her in the eyes. "Fuck, I'm so sorry." I scan her face for any other signs of injury and don't find any. "Are you hurt anywhere?"[22]

She ignores my question. Her voice is soft and airy. "You killed for me."

I cup her cheeks, brushing the sweaty strands of hair out her face. "Baby, I'd *die* for you."

She closes her eyes with a heavy sigh, and it hurts that she ever doubted that. "Now to deal with this piece of shit." I pull away and face Luciano. "What to do with you?"

"Well wasn't that a sweet moment," he sneers.

"I don't care if you're her father or God reincarnate, no one hurts my wife and walks away scot-free."

"I don't know if it's honorable or embarrassing," he muses.

"What is?" I'm already sick of these games.

"You playing white knight for a snitch." He cocks his head to the side, his mouth curling into a smug taunt. My jaw shifts, my fingers tightening around my gun as I process his words. I clench my other hand into a fist.

"Do you want to tell him or should I?" He looks past me to Effie, and I get a sinking feeling like my entire world is about to implode. "Ach, I'll just go for it: I know about the fallout shelter. It's only a matter of time before we figure out how to get in."

"Is this true?" I flick my gaze to Effie, and she breaks eye contact right away, staring at her feet. That one small movement is enough to shred my heart like it's nothing but a piece of paper. Effie's always been able to look me in the eye, even when I held a gun to her head she didn't waver.

That one glance tells me all I need to know but I still storm over to her. "*Tell. Me.*" I can't conceal the hurt in my voice, it's ripped from me the same way my tattered heart is ripped from my chest.

"Yes, but—"

There is no *but.* "Leave."

"Fi—"

"If you don't walk out that door right now, you'll be leaving in a body bag.*"* My voice is stripped of emotion, cold and detached because if I lean into what I'm feeling I'll burn this fucking place to the ground, and I won't care who's inside.

I cut Luciano out of the tape next. "The only reason you're still living is because I haven't decided how I want to kill you yet," I say with deadly intent.

He gets up, acting like he doesn't have an ounce of fear in him, but I see the sweat stain down his back and the heavy exhale he releases. Effie is still standing at the same place I left her. "Euphemia, let's go," he says gruffly, not waiting for her before disappearing out the door.

She gives me one last teary-eyed look before following him. I react without thinking and pull her back by her hand. There's a flicker of hope on her face before I speak, crushing every speck of light in her painfully beautiful eyes.

"This is the last time. If you ever betray me again, it won't matter how sweet your pussy is or how I once felt for you, I'll just fuck you one last time before slitting your throat."

[23]Then I let her leave. I let her leave so she doesn't see me crumble.

Her words from the gala dance through my mind, soft and pleading: *I wish I could live in this moment forever.*

What I thought was the start of forever, was just a spoonful of sugar before the poison. I realize now, she wanted to stay in that moment because she knew *this* moment would follow. I close my eyes, willing my brain to push down those sweet memories plaguing me so I can think about my next moves.

I've never had trouble shutting off my emotions. It was like flicking a switch, if the lights were even on to begin with. I came to prefer operating in the dark. Easier, cleaner, and hell of a lot less painful. But right now, it's like trying to stop a flood with paper walls. *Useless.*

Well, I can start by getting rid of the dead body on my floor. But I can't be in here any longer, I feel like I'm drowning in memories of her. I call my cleaning crew while walking to my car, it's a ten-second conversation.

I get in, sliding behind the steering wheel and slamming my head back on the headrest, not feeling any less like I'm drowning. I glance to my right and see the sunflowers I never grabbed in my haste to save her.

It's like the sunshine yellow of their petals is laughing at me. *What a love-blind fool.*

I stare at the flowers a little longer, are they laughing at me or screaming at me to open my fucking eyes? Or maybe I'm just losing my goddamn mind if plants are talking…

I'm trying to think through the torrent of emotions battering my insides. I force myself to focus, drumming my fingers in thought.

If Effie was working with her father behind my back, why was he beating her? I wouldn't put it past the son of a bitch to hit her over a small slight, real or imagined. But I've conducted enough interrogations to recognize one. Fuckhead holding her arms while her father took swings…yeah, they were after information that she clearly wasn't giving them.

I hop out, slamming the door behind me. Effie was up to something, but I don't think it was betraying me…at least not intentionally.

Or maybe I'm letting my emotions cloud my judgment. I think back to the conversation I overheard at the gala. Her father was again trying to get something out of her, but was she participating?

It's too damn hard to be objective when the person I've grown to treasure most in this fucked-up world is being accused of breaking the one thing I asked of her: honesty and loyalty. My mind and heart are tied up in a crippling knot, and there's only one way to untangle this mess: Find out what she was planning.

Storming back into the barn, I check the downstairs first before coming up empty. I try her studio next, finding exactly what I was looking for in the drawer with her materials. I pull out her phone, my chest cracking open when I read the painted message on the back.

Inbox

I <3 u

I navigate directly to her messages and open the top chat. The number isn't a saved contact, but the most recent interaction was an outgoing text:

Finn is going to call, tell him everything. Juicy tracksuits and Star Wars DVDs.

I read the damn thing ten times. I have no idea what the second half means, but the first part is pretty fucking clear. I call the number, my heart waiting in my throat while it rings.

The line connects. "It's Finn."

"Ah, the great Finneas Fox." There's something familiar about the feminine voice, but I can't place it. "We need to meet. I'll text you an address, get there as soon as you can."

Chapter 21:

Transgressions and Penance

Finn

Three women who were once my enemies are sitting across from me in a diner booth. The buzzing neon Open sign on the window next to me is giving me a headache and washing us in red like hellions. I certainly feel like I'm in hell.

"How soon can you execute?" I ask.

"Thank you." Linnie smiles at the waitress refilling our coffee mugs before turning back to me. "We can do it as soon as tomorrow. We just need the art." They've spent the last forty-five minutes walking me through every step of the plan they'd been working toward with Effie.

I scribble a number on a napkin and slide it over to her. "This will get you to Roman who will get you to Cash. I'll fill him in and make sure he will get you whatever you need. But we can't do anything until my wife is safely back to me."

"Understood."

I slump back in the long booth, trying to figure out why I still feel like I've been sucker punched. Even after finding out Effie hadn't purposefully betrayed me. "What's in it for you guys?"

"Is helping out a friend not reason enough?" Hadis poses.

"No. Not in our world."

Marguerite pushes her ketchup-soaked hashbrowns around her plate—I've never understood breakfast for dinner, and she's not making it seem very appealing. She looks to Linnie to answer for them.

"We fucked up," Linnie says honestly. "Not as much as you, but we weren't there for Effie. We let her loose on you without any proper training. We tried to use your blackmail plot to our benefit instead of trying to eliminate it. And we were off licking our wounds when Hudson showed up at our door."

"You're saying you owe her?" All three nod and I realize that's not what was bothering me. I know exactly what is. "Why didn't she tell me what she was planning?"

If she had told me, I wouldn't have reacted so cruelly. I could have helped her. But what hurts the most is that, even after everything we've gone through, she still didn't trust me enough.

Linnie looks at me thoughtfully. "When no one else was there for her, you were. She called and you came—"

"I fucking put her in that situation." I slam my palms on the table, the saltshaker tips over and the utensils rattle. Three unimpressed faces stare back at me.

"Yes, you did and honestly, fuck you." Marguerite shoves a bite of soggy hashbrowns in her mouth and waves her empty fork at me. "She's a better person than me, because I wouldn't have forgiven you, let alone felt like I *owed* you."

I swallow stiffly. My transgressions are piling up, but Effie is the one being punished.

I have to get her back.

My wife belongs at my side, and I belong at her feet.

[24]The drive from the diner to the Luciano mansion is the most excruciating twenty minutes of my life. My lungs feel splintered, my skin too tight, my heart one beat away from giving out.

I shudder to think what will happen if she doesn't give her father what he wants, or worse, if he finds out what she was planning behind his back. I've made a lot of mistakes in my life, but if something happens to her at the hands of that monster, not hearing her out will be my biggest one. I slam on the gas and shift gears, blazing through the residential streets at dangerous speeds.

I roll down my window as I approach the gate to their drive, one hand on the stick shift, the other on my gun pointed at the guard. "Open the gate."

"No—" I shoot him in the foot, and he screams, hopping back on one foot.

"Open it or the next one goes in your knee, Hoppy."

He curses amid groans, but all I care about is the gate hinging open in front of me. *Has it always been this goddamn slow?* I consider blowing through it partially open to save time as it lazily yawns open.

I race down the driveway lined with hedges and column statues topped with lions. I round the last turn of the winding driveway, a grand colonial revival estate home coming into view. Porsches and Ferraris are lined up outside despite the four-car garage.

I guess my friend at the gate must have been able to alert my arrival because I'm greeted by six armed men, guns raised and pointed at my car. Every single one of them has the same slicked back hair, like they are on set for a hair commercial rather than defending the Don.

"This seems like overkill," I say, getting out of the car, ignoring all the barrels trained on me. I recognize Renzo among the men, looking obnoxious and arrogant as ever. "Bring her to me now, Luciano"

"Who?" He cocks his head to the side with a snide grin.

"My. Wife." My fingers flex around the gun at my side. "If something happened to her…" My growl is predatory, ready to tear anyone limb to limb who stands between us.

"Oh, my sister? No, she's fine." His lip curls. "But she's not your wife anymore."

"The fuck she isn't—" The front door opens, and her father steps through. All my attention is directed to him when I demand, "Where is she?"

"You're too late, boy." He clasps his hands in front of him. "Euphemia is getting married."

"*She's. Married. To. Me.*" I slap my chest punctuating each word.

"Not for much longer," He straightens his lapels like this conversation is wrapping up, but it's only getting started.

"I won't fucking sign." I shove my gun into my waistband and step up to him, face to face on the cobblestone porch.

"Come on, you're smarter than that. We don't need you to sign anything. Hell, we didn't even need you to sign the marriage license." He scoffs and my blood curdles. "We paid to get your phony marriage on the books, and we'll pay to get it annulled. With or without you."

Venom laces my words as I tower over him. "That will never fucking happen. Now, where is she?" I shout while fisting the collar of his shirt. Multiple pairs of hands grab my arms, dragging me off, but I never stop yelling, my heart raging. "Where is *my wife?!*"

A sharp sting hits my neck and my hand flies up to the spot. My vision instantly blurs and my equilibrium shakes. I look over my shoulder and get a flashing glance of Gianni holding a syringe before my knees give out and I slam into the pavement.

My head spins, like it's stuck in a whirlpool. Everything in my sight becomes fluid, bending and flowing as my surroundings fade into a black current.

I don't know how long I'm out for, but when I wake up, the sky is a hazy pink. I can see the rising rays of sun through the small square window of the...*where the hell am I?*

I smell gasoline and dirt and as I wriggle in my bindings, rough unfinished wood scratches against my cheek on the floor. My head feels like it was stuffed full of kerosene-soaked cotton balls and then lit on fire. Even opening my eyes to the darkness sends blinding pain through my forehead. My muscles are stiff and sore like I've been in the same position on the hard surface for hours.

My feet, bound at the ankles, kick out and hit long poles of some sort. They clatter loudly to the ground. One of them falls in front of my face, the dirty head of a shovel, and the pieces come together: I'm in a gardening shed. I laugh out loud in the dark space. Effie's idiot brothers must have been in charge of my captivity because a shed full of tools doesn't make the most secure location.

In addition to my ankles, my wrists are tied behind my back. Judging by the scratchy feel against my skin, the rope is crude fiber. Sawing through the ties with the edge of a spade won't be quick, but it's not impossible.

I flop around like a goddamn fish out of water until I'm positioned where I need to be and get to work. I drag my bound wrists against the blunt edge of the spade until my wrists are raw, my back is cramping but I'm finally free.

As soon as my hands are unbound, I am ferociously ripping at the ropes around my legs. My fingers feel like I'm fisting ice made of broken glass as circulation returns to my hands. Each tug at the ropes is a sharp pain, but I don't care about any of it. Don't care about anything other than stopping that fucking wedding.

My insides are like an inferno as my thoughts fill with her wearing a ring from another man, warming another man's bed. But what shatters me most is knowing that she's facing all this alone, thinking I hate her.

I won't even entertain the option that I won't get to her in time. I need her to know that I fucked up, I judged her too quickly. I didn't give up on us. I *haven't* given up on us. I'm going to fight until she's by my side or I'm six feet under.

I stagger to my feet, my head spinning with the lingering effects of the drug. I reach for the knob, but even though it turns, the door doesn't open. I try again and again until I come to the conclusion that something must be blocking it from the outside.

I take to ramming my shoulder against the door, throwing all my weight into the cheap wood with so much force I'm surprised I don't dislocate the joint. At last, I hear the sound of splintering planks and know I am almost there. A few more slams and the boards that were nailed over the door snap in half and I'm stumbling into the cool, early morning air.

I try to get my bearings, scanning the manicured lawn and rose bushes in front of me. I could still be at the Luciano's, but I can't be sure, I never spent much time here. I could circle back and if I haven't left their property, I might be able to get to my car. That poses a larger risk of being seen, my only advantage right now is they don't know I've escaped. And while her brothers are not the brightest, I doubt even they would be stupid enough to leave the keys in the ignition for me.

I creep further out into the lawn and away from the shed until I can get a better view of the house and confirm it is the Luciano's. Which means that the fence across the grass should border the road. I sprint across the lawn, praying there aren't motion sensor lights or that I get another dizzy spell that sends me eating shit.

I make it to the iron fence, my shoes soaked by morning dew. I climb over and onto the street below. Of course, in this rich as fuck neighborhood there are no beater cars parked on the street. Nothing I can hotwire and get the hell out of here, so I continue on foot.

No phone, no weapon, no plan—yet—but despite all that, my end goal is crystal clear: I am getting my wife back.

Chapter 22:

Née Luciano

Effie

[25]My father took me directly to one of his safe houses from the farm and threw me in this room. The deadbolt in the door turns, snapping me from my riveting game of counting bricks on the wall. It's a newly installed deadbolt, I assume to be able to lock me in from the outside. One of his soldiers was outfitting the door and another was removing everything from the room except for the mattress I'm sitting on.

Either they are exceptionally confident in my lock-picking skills, or they know what they have planned is at risk of making me suicidal. Honestly, it could be both.

My father enters the room and looks down on me on the bare mattress with disgust, as if he wasn't the one who put me here. "You're getting married."

My first reaction is to laugh. "I feel like we've done this before," I say.

"Don't be cute, Euphemia. You have continued to fuck up every opportunity I've given you. This is your last chance. You'll be marrying the youngest Campbell son—"

I shoot to my feet. "Are you trying to get me killed? Hudson almost murdered me for being seen with another man—and we weren't even engaged! They'll finish the job he started if they find out what really happened." I feel like a roasted pig offered up with an apple in my mouth.

My father doesn't even flinch. "Then you better ensure they never find out. The governor only suspects Fox, make sure it stays that way."

The mention of Finn is like being doused with ice cold water. "What's going to happen to him?" I knew my father had sway with powerful people, but I never realized that he could make my marriage to Finn disappear in the blink of an eye. Will the Campbells compel me to testify against Finn without the protection of spousal privilege? The thought makes my stomach churn.

"What do you care?" He squints at me. "Don't tell me you fell for the Irish bastard? I guess you did spend a lot of time together out in that ramshackle hut. I thought he'd never leave." He tuts, and I try to piece together his words.

"You were waiting until he left to confront me at the farm?"

He scoffs. "Wasted fucking hours just for him to kick you to the curb anyway. I don't know why I bothered, you're as goddamn useless as ever. At least now you won't be able to fuck anything up as long as you're locked up 'til the wedding."

I can feel him slamming the door by the violent vibrations in my ribcage.

And just like that, as if the last few weeks never happened, the game continues. My father is vying for more power and connections, and using my hand in marriage to do it. I wonder if he'll ever realize his own greed keeps getting us into these situations.

The only reason my father decided to threaten the decade-long truce with the Fox family was due to his own greed. When he orchestrated my marriage to Finn, he wasn't satisfied with being connected to one of the most powerful crime families. No, he made it clear that despite the marriage, our objective hadn't changed. We were still going after the cache.

I was so mad at Finn, so livid at myself, so exhausted and traumatized by everything, that I went along with my father's plot. I saw the photograph of the shelter and sent it to my father, saying it was a potential to explore.

When Finn took me to the cache, I realized what a bomb that one photo would end up being. I knew at that moment that I would eventually break his heart. I never guessed that moment of curiosity in the hallway would become this liability for our relationship. He asked for my loyalty and honesty, and selfishly, I promised him something I'd never be able to give.

That small mistake became like a neglected hangnail that festered into a deadly infection. I knew I'd messed up beyond repair with Finn. But I thought I'd try, even if it was a fool's errand.

The governor was the biggest threat to our future. Spousal privilege or not, as long as he was trying to solve his son's murder, Finn and I were never going to be safe. A corrupt politician with criminal connections is a formidable opponent and he was ready to knock down our door.

When I killed Hudson, I put a target on his back. I owed it to him—to *us*—to fix this. We were being hunted from both sides. The governor trying to find his son, and my father still intent on destroying our decade-long truce to get to the cache. I thought I could hold my father off for the time being but knew moves had to be made to eliminate the governor and the constant threat he posed.

I lay back on the mattress and trace the cracks in the ceiling with my gaze. I am both exhausted to the bone and humming with uncontainable energy. I can't stop thinking about my phone and the message I left for Finn.

Did he find it? Did *Les Arnaqueuses* fill him in on our plan? Are they going to finish the new plan we put into motion?

Does any of it even matter when I'm marrying the brother of the man I killed?

The turning deadbolt startles me, and I sit up, on constant alert. One of my father's soldiers enters. He sets a bowl of minestrone in front of me on the floor. No silverware. Not even a spoon. *Do they really think I'm going to be able to get out of a room four-stories up with nothing but a spoon?*

"Have they picked a date?" I ask.

He nods. "In four days."

²⁶Four days later, I'm staring at my reflection dressed in white. I feel and look hollow. My usually full cheeks that now look slack from nothing but soup for five days. The bags under my eyes are dark and pronounced despite my mother's best effort. She loops a string of pearls around my neck and clasps it in the back. It feels like the noose of a condemned man.

She prods me in between my shoulder blades. "Stand up straight, you don't want to look like a hunchback in all your wedding photos, now do you?"

"Does he really not know? Or does he just not care?" I ask, my stomach churning.

"About what?"

"That I killed—" She claps her hand over my mouth.

"Men will forgive almost anything in the name of power. And you'll be wise to remember just how powerful these men are. When it comes to the governor's son, you know nothing. Do you understand me, Euphemia?" Her eyes that look just like mine implore me to fall in line through the mirror.

"Which one? My first fiancé or my second husband?" My head whips to the side, my cheek burning from her slap.

She purses her lips. "If you want to survive in this world, be sweet, smile, and when the time comes, spread your legs." Why she bothers telling me this, I don't know. I've already been here before, face down, ass up as Finn made me his wife. As transactional as that night was, it seems like a blessing compared to what I'm about to face.

She pats my shoulders and fluffs my veil, a sickly-sweet change in her voice. "You look beautiful, dear."

I struggle to find my mask again. The meek compliance I used to wear so often it became a second skin is now difficult to summon. Finn saw me. Heard me. Maybe even loved me without it. And now, trying to shove it back down, my true self feels like carving myself in half. Before my mask was a comfort, a security. Now it's just treachery.

"Take a minute. But not too long, everyone's ready downstairs." My mother gives my shoulder a squeeze and leaves the room.

I try not to let my mind wander to the message I left for Finn on my phone for the hundredth time in the last four days. Surely by now he must have found it. Which means if he found it, it wasn't enough to make up for what I did. Or maybe he couldn't get in touch with *Les Arnaqueuses* or— *No*, what's done is done.

There's a church full of people downstairs. Who are they? Does it matter? This wedding is happening, and innocuous details won't change that.

I was a survivor long before I was a wife. I still am. The battle has changed, but I'm just as strong.

I take one long look in the mirror then head downstairs to the church foyer where my father is waiting. His black hair is slicked back, and his eyes are dark as coal. He offers me his elbow. "You look beautiful, *principessa*." He calls me princess and painful images flood my mind of lazy mornings, soft sunlight and the warmth of Finn's body wrapped around mine.

I wrap my arm around his, but I don't give a fake smile. I'll do my duty, but I won't pretend my prison is a castle.

The organ music begins as we push through the double doors to the sanctuary. It's a song that's supposed to make your heart swell with romance and joy, and instead it feels like I'm leading my own funeral procession.

Seeing William at the end of the aisle makes my lungs collapse. It feels as if my head is being held under water. My pulse races at the similarities between him and Hudson until I'm dizzy. My body screams at me to retreat, my throat grows tight as if Hudson's brutish hands are still clutching it. My father squeezes my hand on his arm to keep my stalling feet moving, to drag me toward a marriage I don't want.

The people in the pews are faceless blurs. I don't even recognize the priest. It feels like walking onto a staged movie set, cold, impersonal, a farce. The only real things are the bouquets of white roses at the end of each row, and somehow even those feel like part of a con.

My father unceremoniously passes me off to William, and his hands are just as sweaty as mine. His blue eyes bore into me with a dutiful chill. They may have been handsome if I didn't have to fight for my life staring into an identical pair. A sour taste spills down my throat as the priest begins the ceremony, his words nothing but dry droning.

When it comes time to exchange rings, there is no ring bearer. He pulls them out of his coat pocket and my hand goes numb as he grasps mine in his. Cold bitterness slides over my shoulders and down my back. The priest begins mumbling the most bland, simplified vows and William parrots his words sentence by sentence. There's nothing personal about them. Why even bother when all the promises tying this marriage together are inked in a contract by power-hungry, callous men. Not the two people standing at the altar.

Surprisingly, my hand doesn't shake, but his does when he lifts mine and holds the ring at the tip of my finger. Perhaps my hand is steady because in this brief moment I'm no longer in this church, I'm in a limo with Finn and he's telling me how proud he is of me.

William begins to slide the ring up my finger and someone screams. At first, I question if it was me, if I was finally snapping, but then more follow and commotion stirs.

The priest is yanked back and a sharp, silver blade presses against his throat, and Cash Fox's wild grinning face appears over his shoulder. "Nobody moves or Father here gets a VIP meet and greet with that God he's so fond of." He looks to me with a wicked smile and quick wink. "Good afternoon, Mrs. Fox."

The double doors at the back of the sanctuary swing open. "Did we already get to the '*speak now or forever hold your peace*' part? Because I object on account that Euphemia *Fox* is already married. To me."

Chapter 23:

Run

Finn

[27]The past four days were the longest of my life. My lungs had to relearn how to breathe without her. My blood had to acclimate to constant boiling temperatures. And my rage, my blood thirst, has never had to wait so long to be sated. It took two days to finalize our plans and then two days of doing nothing but stewing, seething, dreaming of the ways I would like to torture everyone involved in making this wedding happen.

Finding out she was getting married was like being hit by buckshot, the pellets tearing multiple tracks through my muscles and flesh. Waiting was agony, but it had to be done. Holding off until the wedding was the best way for us to get to Effie and hit the governor at the same time.

I've been posted on a bench in the park across from the governor's city residence for the better part of an hour. The Campbells own a large estate elsewhere, but the governor keeps this luxury townhouse in June Harbor for intown business. I stand up when I see the first black armored vehicle arrive.

More SUVs with government plates start lining up around the block. A deep sense of satisfaction takes shape in my gut, the kind you can only get when a plan comes together perfectly. While Effie is somewhere getting ready to marry his son, her plan to take down the governor is in full swing. Despite the fact that the thought of her preparing for the wedding feels like a hundred arrows to the chest, I am incredibly proud of what she started with *Les Arnaqueuses*.

The men in tactical gear lining up outside the townhouse will soon break down the door to find rare, stolen masterpieces from our cache that we planted early this morning.

The crew meticulously planned every detail to ensure that there will be no way he can wiggle out of the charges or get them brushed under the rug. They leaked small details about a potential raid of long-lost art in press circles and circulated information through sources in the police to get the FBI looking at the governor.

It only takes a few more minutes before I start seeing the satellites of news vans arrive around the block. Eagerness bites at me and I wish I could stay longer, but I have a wedding to crash and a wife to take home. I would have loved to see the FBI march out the lost masterpieces to a hoard of news cameras. Every second of the bust will be publicized, the people will demand accountability and scream corruption.

But as much as I want to see Governor Campbell's demise unfold before my very eyes, nothing compares to my desire to have Effie back in my arms.

I leave the park and hop on my motorcycle to race back to Cash's place.

"How did it go?" Hadis asks me as I take off my helmet in the underground garage.

"SWAT and news are flooding the street. Everything went according to plan." She smiles, satisfied, and I turn my attention to my brothers who are loading our soldiers into SUVs. Roan is barking instructions, divvying up the men appropriately, while Lochlan straps more magazines of ammo to his belt.

I wait to walk up to Cash until he is done having a goodbye kiss with Harlow, like he's going to fucking war. "Remember to go straight for the priest. It will be our best point of leverage. Luciano will sacrifice just about anyone else in that church." The Mafia's hypocrisy when it comes to religion always amused me. They will treat clergy like living saints then turn around and make a living off sin.

"I know she's your girl, but I swear to God, Finneas, if you remind me one more time about the priest I'm going to blow your fucking brains out."

I roll my eyes. "Then don't fucking forget."

I'm last to roll up to the church. A decoy call has already been dispatched to the governor's security posted in the front of the church, so there's no one to stop me from walking straight up the steps and inside. Now, I'm in the foyer and the object of all my thoughts, desire, my will to fucking live is behind those doors about to marry a stranger. I spark like a livewire as soon as I hear the first screams, my signal to move.

I use both hands to swing the sanctuary doors wide and step into the aisle. My brothers have the governor's son and the priest at gun or knifepoint. Effie looks heart-wrenchingly beautiful in white, eyes round and full of surprise. *Didn't she know I was coming for her?*

"Did we already get to the '*speak now or forever hold your peace*' part? Because I object on account that Euphemia *Fox* is already married. To me.*"* I stride down the aisle at a cool pace, plucking my leather gloves off and tossing them into the pews with smug indifference to the people sitting there. At Cash's orders, everyone in the pews is on kneelers and placing their hands on top of their heads.

I drink her in with every step I take toward the altar. Her chestnut hair swept up and off her neck. Angelic body covered in satin and lace that I can't wait to rip off. Amber eyes igniting with deviant flames.

I reach the bottom of the steps of the altar and extend my hand. She bites her lip, holding back a shocked smile. "You came…" she stutters and places her hand in mine, and for the first time in days, there's solid ground under my feet.

She hikes her dress off the ground and looks at me with a shy grin. She looks ready to run, but instead I swoop her up and carry her down the aisle and straight out the door. I never got to walk out of the church with my wife the first time, and even if this isn't quite the same, there's an unrivaled satisfaction, holding her in my arms.

There's a limo parked in front of the church, streamers and cans tied to the back, *just married* painted on the windows. Alfie is tugging the driver out of the front. "You wanna die for this car? You know how many people have probably had sex in this thing? Gross. You should be thanking us for taking it off your hands. Now, Jesus Christ, get out of the fucking car before I shoot ya!"

Alfie sees us running down the steps and shrugs. "Ope, time's up." He shoots the driver in the knee and then shoves his crippled frame out of the car. I open the passenger door, and Effie hops in. I slide in behind her and bark at Alfie to raise the partition.

We pull away, cans jingling, just as rows of police cars, sirens blaring turn down the street behind us. The blue and red of their lights is so bright, it breaks through the tinted limo windows and dances across Effie's scared features. "Your brothers," she gasps.

"They're not coming for them." I lean back in the deep seat, unable to take my eyes off her.

"Then who?"

"This morning, the FBI found certain Van Gogh and Renoir paintings at the home of one Thomas Campbell," I wrap my hand around her wrist, my fingers brushing against her hammering pulse.

"You found the phone." Her eyes crinkle at the corners in a soft smile.

"I did, and I lov—" My words are swallowed whole when Alfie slams on the brakes and we fly forward in the back of the limo, my arms leaping out to catch her and pull her back to me.

"Oy, back to the nursing home if you don't know how to use a crosswalk!" he hollers.

She looks up at me, cradled in my arms, with heavy eyes. "When I told my father, I didn't know—"

"It doesn't matter." I cut her off.

"I want you to know—"

"I know all I need to know, Ef. I know I hurt you, and you still gave me a second, third—*Christ*, a fucking tenth chance. I know that I was brash and cruel, yet you never gave up on me." Her bottom lip quivers, and I rest my thumb on it. She kisses the pad of my thumb, and I wrap her in my arms, back where she's meant to be.

[28]The sun is setting when I begin to wake Effie a few miles from Bartlett Farms after she fell asleep in my lap. The sun breaks the horizon into bold rays of copper and rust. The setting sun bathes the black cattle in pastures along the road in a warm light, turning their backs the color of whiskey.

"We're almost home." I stroke her hair, plucking the veil from it, a caustic taste hitting the back of my throat as I realize she is still fully in her wedding garb.

"Home?"

"Yes, princess, *home.*" She nuzzles into my hand as she rouses, and my chest constricts at the sweet, mindless movement.

I carefully sit her upright as I sweep out from under her and kneel on the limo floor. I lift one of her heeled feet onto my thigh and unbuckle the clasp around her ankle as she blinks the sleep fully from her eyes. "You make a breathtaking bride, but no way in God's green earth am I bringing you into my home in another man's wedding dress." I remove her second heel, dangling it from the ankle straps before dropping it and taking out my switchblade.

Her eyes widen then darken as I flick the blade open. I suck my lip between my teeth and my gut swirls with heat at the dangerous desire behind her gaze.

I slice into the hem of her satin gown. My eyes burn into hers as I begin to tear a slit up the center, exposing her silky thighs. Little breaths slip between her lips the higher I go, and my body responds with a sharp pulse. Halfway to the bodice, the fabric snags. I raise her ankle onto my shoulder, ghosting my lips up her calf and inner thigh, until I reach the snag. I flip the blade and plunge it into the floorboard.

I lock my gaze with hers as I take hold of the dress between my teeth and tear past the resistance. Her breath gets stuck in her throat and her pupils blow wide as I am left with unfettered access to her lace-covered pussy. My heart beats erratically as I indulge in her untethering scent, dragging my nose over her hot core, feeling her legs tremble on either side of my head.

I nip at the fabric, pinching her skin, and growl, "*Mine.*"

"Yours," she agrees breathlessly as I free my knife from where it's staked. I grab the top of her bodice, pull it harshly away from her body and slice down the middle while staring her straight in the eyes.

Heat crackles down my back as I flip her around onto her hands and knees on the seat. A blackness swirls in my gut as I rip the rest of the dress off her revealing a white lace bodysuit. I bring my hand down hard and hot over her ass. I lick up her spine before tugging her hair out of its pinned confines. It falls in heavy locks down her shoulders as I flip her back over to sit upright.

I clasp her jaw tightly in my fist. I roughly pull her chin to the side to devour her neck, shoving my face into her cascading curls and suck bruisingly into her skin. "*Mine.*" I bite, carving my claim into her with my teeth.

My voice is raw and rumbly as I promise, "I may not have been the man intended to see you in this, but with the devil as my witness, I will be the man to ruin you in it." She sucks in an agreeing breath and arches her back to push her breasts out into my greedy palms. "*Fuck,* I want to tear you apart piece by piece, break you down bit by bit, so that I can rebuild you as mine and only mine."

I know we've arrived when the limo turns and begins to crawl over the rocky gravel. I groan into her supple flesh. She tugs my head up, her fingers knotted in my hair, until we are nose to nose. "Finneas Fox, I've never been anything but yours. But I'll still let you try…"

She pulls me onto the seat next to her and spins to straddle me, my hands latching onto her thick hips. The car comes to a stop, and she clutches my face between her hands. Her honeyed eyes fix on mine as if words evade her. In the time that we stay like this wordlessly pouring our souls and apologies to each other, I hear Alfie exit and drive away in the car he left here.

With her thumb, she traces under my eye, down my cheek and over my chin. Her touch is gentle and sincere. It makes me feel bare and seen. "I've never apologized for my role—"

I stop her, "You don't have to."

"I *want* to." She places a hand over my heart. "I'm sorry for playing you. Betraying you. Hurting you. But I'm not sorry I'm your wife."

My breath lodges in my throat, my heart stuttering. "Say that again."

She arches a brow. "I'm not sorry I'm your wife."

A pleased rumble escapes my lips, and I tighten my arms around her waist, gliding her over my growing cock. "We never had a proper wedding night."

A devious smile plays across her lips. "This could be our wedding night. One we both will love."

"Oh yeah? And what would that be?"

"Letting my husband do whatever he wants. Knowing I want it too." She slides off my lap to kneel at my feet, dragging her palms down the length of my thighs as she does.

A dark amusement drips through me when I ask, "You wanna play, little wife?"

Her delicate pink tongue flicks across her teeth as she tucks her chin and nods, looking up at me through hooded lashes. "Anything I want?" She nods again, and fire licks up my spine.

I jerk my head at the door. As she exits the limo, I get a peek at the inky sky, sun fading and stars just beginning to emerge. The perfect backdrop for all the ways I want to ruin her.

I follow behind her, my darkest urges igniting. She faces me, and I see the same need for depravity staring back at me. "What do you want me to do?"

I look behind her into the dark of the woods. There's only one thing I want of her.

"*Run.*"

Chapter 24:

Can't Hide

Finn

I watch her chest rise and stay as she holds her breath as she takes in my one wish. Slowly she lets out an exhale through slightly parted lips before a dash of mischievousness flits across her face and she tries to run.[29] I catch her wrist, and she looks down at my tattooed knuckles and shivers. I wait until she looks back in my eyes to say, "And when I catch you, I want you to fight." Then I release her.

With a squeal, she spins on her heels and runs deeper into the woods. She's playing with fire and loves the way it burns.

I already feel my cock stiffening watching her hair fly loose and wild over her shoulders. Her bare feet patter into mulchy earth.

"Better run, princess," I call after her, my blood already heating. "'Cause when I catch you, there'll be no mercy." I whisper into the night.

My inner predator narrows in on the bright white of her lingerie like a torch in the dark.

---

29 E-GIRLS ARE RUINING MY LIFE—CORPSE, Savage Ga$p | SummerOtoole.com/play-lists

I want her. I need her. She's mine, and I'll have her.

I pick up my pace, but don't run in pursuit... yet. I enter the woods she disappeared into and laugh to myself as I can hear her giggling and breathing heavily as she scampers. My pretty prey is making this too easy.

The moon is full, sending silver beams through the trees. I catch sight of Effie behind a trunk, her back to me. I'm light on my feet. She doesn't hear me approach until I'm right behind her. Her sweet scent goes straight to my cock. She spins at the last second and her scream of surprise is snatched with a kiss as I easily pick her up and slam us up against the tree.

"You found me," she purrs.

"There's no hiding from me." I can feel her heart beating in her chest and my fingers itch to wrap around her throat and bury my cock into her heat.

I grind into her. "You feel what you do to me? How hard I get for just a taste of you." I devour her with a bruising kiss, bending her to my will, needing her to be as hungry for my soul as I am for hers.

I've survived dozens of fights I shouldn't have because I know how to read the smallest changes in a person's muscles, their face, the quick flick of an eye. So when I dip my head to lavish her neck, I'm not surprised when her fingers twist into my hair and she yanks my head back.

What I don't expect is the slap across my face that follows. I drop her and she gives me a devilish smile over her shoulder as she runs deeper into the forest. *Naughty, little plaything.*

"Next time you catch me, you better not wait to fuck me," she calls, and every muscle in my body burns at her taunt.

I stalk after her like a monster in the dark. I wonder if she knows what she's doing to me. If she knows the way her dark hair shimmering in the moonlight makes me want to wrap it around my fist and fuck her so hard she'll feel me for days. If she knows the sound of snapping twigs under feet makes me want to throw her down among them and eat her perfect cunt until she's dripping and begging for my cock.

I wonder all this, but of course, she knows. Because she knows me just as I know her.

I know her pulse is hammering with anticipation right now, that she's equally thrilled about eluding capture as she is by the prospect of being caught.

She looks back at me, eyes wide and round with excitement, but the quick distraction causes her to trip and stumble to the ground. I take the opportunity to close the distance in a few quick strides. She flips over and scuttles back on her bottom, but she's too slow. I'm right there.

She stares up at me, desperately scooting away as I undo my belt without ever breaking eye contact. I drop to my knees and grab hold of her legs with both hands, yanking them down. She tries to wriggle in my vice grip, and while she puts up a convincing fight, I can smell her arousal. My naughty little plaything—no, my naughty *wife* is soaked for me.

I rip down my fly and fist her lingerie, yanking it roughly to the side as I pull my cock out, hard and throbbing, ready to plunge inside her. She freezes as I tease her slick entrance. "This what you want? Me to fuck your needy cunt until you scream for mercy?" She bites her lip as I ease an inch into her. I close my eyes at the overwhelming feeling of sinking slowly into her. "Christ, Ef, you're so wet for me."

"Mercy, my ass," she spits and kicks me in the chest. I growl at the loss of her as she scrambles onto hands and knees. I let her make it a few feet— loving the view of her on her knees—before grabbing her hips with a grip she won't be able to break and press her into the ground. I twist my fist in the sides of her bodysuit, my cock jumping at the sound of it tearing.

She looks over her shoulder at me, and for a split moment, I expect to see terror and pain written all over her face. But instead, she looks my monster in the eyes and smiles.

"No mercy it is then," I growl with promise. I shove my fingers into the mesh of the lace covering her pussy and rip it open, slamming into her. She moans, and the sound is so sweet, I pull out halfway and thrust in harder to hear it again louder. Her sounds of pleasure only bring me closer and closer to my true monstrous self. Her hands sprawl out, clawing at the ground.

I move my hand from her hip to pin the back of her neck and her cunt clenches around me. I can't contain the guttural groan that escapes me. *God*, she feels too fucking good.

"*Finn*," she mewls, and my heart threatens to shatter my sternum.

Effie

[30]"You can scream as loud as you want. No one's gonna hear you." His voice is drenched with dominance and the thrill of the hunt. I feel it scratch against my skin like a physical thing.

He wraps my hair around his fist like a leash and sparks skitter across my skin as he gives it a sharp tug.

"*Harder*," I beg, my voice thick with insatiable hunger even as I continue to claw at the earth to escape. He yanks my hips into the air and fucks me harder, deeper. I want it all and more, but I'm also not ready to give in. I want to make him earn my submission.

The next time he plunges into me, I flatten myself to the ground making him fall on top of me. Catching him by surprise, I'm able to flip over and drive my elbow into his nose. Immediately, his hand shoots out and latches around my throat, and I dig my head back into the earth trying to get away.

He uses his other hand to wipe at the blood dripping from his nose, and I use both of mine to push against him unsuccessfully as he drags his hand across my chest, smearing me with his blood. My lungs struggle to fill between his weight crushing on top of me and the corset bra I'm wearing. I groan in frustration as my thrashing gets me nowhere.

"Aw, poor little wife." His fake sympathy makes me angry and hot, and I push harder but his hand at my throat just squeezes tighter. The fire in his eyes matches the fire burning in my core and *good god*, I'm incinerating.

He drags his hard cock over my slit, and I writhe and hiss, the grazing pressure over my clit not nearly enough. "Always so needy," he tuts and moves fast as lightning, releasing my throat to pin my hands above my head with both of his. He thrusts again, sliding over my pussy and I whine in

---

30 Chills – Dark Version—Mickey Valen, Joey Myron

frustration.

"Will you beg? Go ahead. Beg me for more," he orders with a dark chuckle, and I bite my tongue.

"When hell freezes over," I snarl, but internally I am pleading for him to fill me the way only he can.

"You don't like being teased?" He grinds harder and my toes curl. "I don't care. Not when it makes your husband feel so fucking good." He gets a wicked glint in his eyes and my heart skips a beat for whatever idea just floated into his twisted head. "How about a taste?" He pulls my hands down by my sides and slides up my body until his dick is inches from my face.

"Taste how much your body wants me." He pushes his cock over my lips, and I try to turn my head away but there's nowhere to go. Heat coils like a burning rope in my core as I give in and lick a wide hot path up his length. "God, that wicked mouth," he groans as his eyes roll back.

I see an opportunity for one last fight. I suck his cock into my mouth, swirling my tongue over his piercing until he loses himself in the feel and his grip on my wrists slacken. Ripping my hands free I roll onto my stomach and make a desperate attempt to crawl away.

He laughs darkly and the sound is like cool water dripping down my spine, giving me chills. He grasps for my lingerie, and it continues to shred in our tussle. I feel his hands clamp down on my calves. "You won't get away again. Whose pussy is this now, Effie?"

My body lights up, and I yelp as he tugs me back by what's left of my bodysuit and slaps my ass so hard it takes a few seconds for the burn to fully set in. He wraps my hair around one fist, tugging my head back while the other hand wrenches my arms behind my back.

"Go ahead" he taunts as he slots his dick at my entrance. "Make all the noise you want. No one could ever stop me from taking what's mine." And then he slams in, burying himself to the hilt and my back arches at the deepness.

"*Oh god,*" I cry out. He drives his hips forward and back, taking my breath away with every full stroke. "I need it, fuck, I *need it.*" I plead for more.

He bites my shoulder, and the pain only adds to the pleasure. "More, Finn, *more.*" He answers by pulling me onto my knees so my wrist is pinned between my back and his stomach. The tantalizing feel of his piercing is enhanced with the new angle, making me see stars, and I can't help but bounce back on his cock. Especially when he wraps a hand around the front of my throat and my walls clench around him.

"*Fuck,* your pussy loves it when I choke you," he grits out on a strained breath.

I slip my hand between my thighs to play with my clit, whimpers spilling uninhibited from my lips. He matches me with deep groans and crude words as we rut like animals on the forest floor.

Time and space begin to collapse, I become lost in the joining of our souls. His heart is so sure in the way he possesses me that I feel what he promised earlier, to break me down bit by bit, tear me apart piece by piece. The closer I get to my climax and the harder he fucks me, the more I feel my old self crumbling away and a new, stronger, version of who I was always meant to be emerges in its place.

My mouth hangs open as my release dangles in front of me. He knows my body and pleasure as well as his own, so he gives me a finger to bite down on as my orgasm threatens to overwhelm me. "Come right now," he demands. I scream around his finger, biting down so hard I feel the skin break, and with a roar, he shoots his cum deep inside me.

I go limp in his arms and can feel his own exhausted muscles tremble to keep us from collapsing. Panting and dizzy with ecstasy, he holds me, all of me. All my broken, burned and ruined pieces that now have new life breathed into them.

He gently lays down, bringing me with him to lay on his chest. We stay there, listening to the chorus of night sounds, bathed in silver moonlight until our breathing slows and the chill catches up to us. He clutches me tight when I shiver, and as if reading my mind, he whispers with nothing but devotion, "You make me so fucking whole, Effie."

Chapter 25:

Water Lilies

Finn

[31]I wake to Effie tracing my chest tattoo. She lightly follows the winding lines of the Celtic knot, and I pretend I am still asleep. I don't know why. Maybe because I don't want this moment to end. Her soft breasts push against my side with every steady breath she takes. My arm is wrapped around her back and her silky hair drapes over it. The birds are heralding a new day outside the window, and even with my eyes closed, I can picture the morning sun coloring the loft a hazy gold.

"Good morning." Her voice is husky and sweet, thick with sleep.

"I'm asleep," I mumble with a small teasing smile.

"You're drumming on my hip," she laughs, and I squeeze my hand on her naked hip, unaware I was tapping, but not surprised. "Have you noticed how often you do that? It's like you're trying to communicate in morse code or something."

I open my eyes and look down at her face. Her dark eyelashes rim her

---

honeyed brown eyes and a touch of pink from sleep colors her cheeks. "It's because I am."

She tilts her head and rolls onto her elbow at my side. "You are what?"

I tuck a loose lock behind her ear and fight the urge to keep my secret a little longer. The words are loose on my tongue, ready to spill but still my throat goes dry. I meet her gaze and swallow the last of my resistance. "Using morse code."

She perks up, her interest piqued. "Really? What does it mean?" She looks at me with a love I can't even begin to comprehend, but at the same time, understand inherently. My love for her is woven into the very fibers of my being, and I want her to know how deeply she has touched me.

"Water lilies." Her mouth opens on a silent gasp. My throat ties itself in knots feeling so exposed. But now that I've started, I want to claw apart anything left unsaid between us, so I continue. "It was the first and last time I ever felt true peace. That night with you. Since I didn't have you, tapping became my calm."

"Stop." Her lips tug in an unsure smile, her eyes well with tears and I don't have to ask, I know they are the sunflower type.

"I can't." I roll us over and hold myself above her. "I can't stop loving you. I don't think I ever did." She clutches my face and pulls my mouth down to hers. I fall into our kiss, trying to make up for ten years. My nose drags over her tear-streaked cheeks, and I can't control the overwhelming feeling exploding in my chest.

It's beyond happiness, beyond lust, beyond this fucking life. She's mine in this lifetime and the next. Suddenly I'm questioning what's ten years when we have forever?

I can hardly let her go when she pulls us apart, breathing heavy and eyes welling with emotion. "I love you, Finneas Fox." My lungs somehow find a way to breathe, despite the weight of her words slamming into me with the force of a thousand comets.

My jaw clenches painfully and my throat tightens into a tight ball. I can't look away from her, my entire world between the palms of my hands. She reaches out and brushes her thumb across my cheek. "I hope those are sunflower tears."

I sniff and swallow the knot in my throat, falling forward and burying myself in the crook of her neck. "Fuck, I love you so much." I feel like I'm breaking apart, my ribs cracking open and my heart floating out to hers.

She wraps her arms around my head and shoulders, hugging me tight to her. But fuck, it's not close enough. I kiss her neck, a burst of salty sweat from last night on my tongue. And I want more. I inhale the scent of her hair and kiss a path across her collarbone, licking over my blood, and suck on her nipple.

She arches into me and threads her fingers through my hair. "Show me," she says on a breathy moan and reaches between our bodies to encircle my cock, directing it to her cunt.

My broad head slots against her pussy, and I grab her face, kissing her deeply as I sink into her, swallowing her moans like they are air itself. There's nothing hurried or rough about the way I slowly rock into her.

She clings to my shoulders, biting down hard on my lip when I hit the sweet spot inside her. Our breathless pants fill the space between our lips as tender pleasure skates up and down my spine.

If last night was a wildfire, this morning is the warmth from a hearth. The foundation of a home. A home that we have found with and in each other.

Her pussy flutters around me and her kisses become pleading as her pleasure spirals. I keep my strokes passionate and intentional, her body pulling my own release forward. Our breathing becomes choppy as if we share one set of lungs, our desire and euphoria cresting together. Sparks ignite behind my eyes as I come, but I can't look away from the rapture dancing across her face. Watching her brows pinch together and her mouth falls slack on a silent cry as she comes with me is a beauty that would rival the northern lights.

My limbs become liquid, and I melt into her, falling to the side and pulling her into me. My hands wrap around her soft belly as her ass snuggles into the crook of my hips. I catch my breath, slowly running my fingers through her tangled hair. My hand snags on something and I huff a laugh as I pull a twig out of her hair.

"I think I owe you a long hot shower." I hold out the twig in front of her to see.

She twists around in my arms to face me. "I'd say so. You have mud on your cheek. But I don't really care..." She raises her brows with a proud smile. "About that or the mud on the sheets."

Steam fills the shower, and I rinse the shampoo out as Effie wrings her hair, already done bathing. "By the way, what does Juicy tracksuits and *Star Wars* DVDs mean?"

She looks at me and laughs, a cute drop of water sliding down her nose. "It had to do with a story Hadis told me. I needed to prove the text was genuinely coming from me."

"I'd like to hear it sometime. The story."

"Okay." She smiles and gives me a quick peck as she pulls the shower curtain back. I slap her ass on her way out. "Hey!"

"Spousal privilege." I shrug smugly and step back under the hot stream of water.

I'm finishing toweling off in the bathroom and just stepping into my jeans when the sound of Effie's scream from the other room makes my blood go cold. My heart leaps out of my goddamn rib cage as I rush out of the bathroom to see William Campbell pinning Effie to the wall with his fucking hand wrapped around her throat. His other hand holds a gun to her temple, and I see red. A yell rips from my throat, "*I'll fucking kill you.*"

I race across the loft, ripping him off her. My fist latches onto his gun hand, and we fall to the floor as I try to wrestle it from his grip. My blood is pumping harder than it ever has, nothing but white-hot rage coursing through me. "Effie, the truck!" I holler and he manages to roll on top of me in the struggle. "The keys...under the mat...I got it started—*Oof!*" I'm too distracted trying to track Effie and make sure she gets out safely that the bastard is able to knee me in the ribs with all his weight. I've had enough broken ribs to know I just got one as my lungs gasp for air and pain radiates my side.

"*Finn!*" Effie screams, and I can't afford to look at her right now, my fist making contact with Campbell's jaw, but he still has the upper hand.

"Go. Now!" I yell, trying to flip us over with a leg lock. The fucker must have had some wrestling training because he skillfully blocks, and I barely manage to knock the gun from his grip.

It skitters across the floor, and we both scramble after it. He lands a foot in my face and my head is whipped back, giving him just enough advantage to reach the gun before me. He grabs it and leaps to his feet. Both his hands shake, but he trains the weapon on me as I'm sprawled on the floor.

I slowly sit up with my hands raised, needing to see if Effie made it out. The fist around my lungs loosens realizing she isn't in the barn and I'm able to bring my attention to the gun to my head. I lazily turn my gaze on the washed-up frat bro in front of me, feeling much calmer now that I know she is safe.

"Rough night?" I look him up and down with fake pity. He's still in his tux from the wedding, his bow tie loose around his neck and his shirt untucked. His hair is disheveled and not just from our fight. His eyes have the glossy look of someone who's been up all night drinking.

"*You—*" His voice trembles with anger and adrenaline. "You've taken everything from me."

I leisurely wipe the blood from my nose with the back of my hand, inspecting it with an unimpressed shrug before turning back up to him, "You're gonna have to be more specific."

He roars in frustration and lunges forward, pressing the barrel to my forehead. "Where should I start? You killed my brother—"

"Um," I hold up my finger and interrupt, "I thought he was still missing?"

"You goddamn know he isn't still alive," he growls, and pistol whips me across the face.

I flex my jaw back and forth, then yawn, his eyes glow red at my indifference. "Sorry, you were saying?"

"You killed my brother—I don't care what the police say, I don't care there's no body, I know it. You framed my father, destroyed our reputation, and stole my wife."

"I'm gonna have to stop you there, technically you stole *my wife.*"

"You arrogant bastard, I'm going to kill you!" He jams the muzzle firmer into my skull and—

"Not before I blow your head off." My eyes shoot behind him to see Effie dwarfed by the giant shotgun she has pointed right at her erstwhile groom.

Chapter 26:

Euphemia Fox

I escape the loft with the sounds of Finn and William's fight echoing. Hearing each grunt and punch feels like wind knocked from my lungs. I run to the garage, my torn-up feet from last night splitting over the scraggly gravel.

I don't even consider getting in the truck. I just got him back, there's no fucking way I'm leaving him now. Not when he's fought for me again and again. Not when he's finally given me something I've always craved: safety.

My family blew up his world ten years ago. I won't let him become another casualty in my family's continued struggle for power.

I tear open every drawer and cabinet in the garage, knowing there has to be a weapon somewhere in all this rubble. There's not a single room in my parent's house that doesn't have a stashed gun, and I'm certain Finn will be the same.

Fucking hell, there has to be. And if not—fuck it, I will go in there swinging with a goddamn socket wrench.

I hear a loud boom from up above that sounds distinctly like a body hitting the ground and my heart races. I throw open the door of a tall, free-standing cabinet, telling myself if this one comes up empty, I'm going with the wrench.

I nearly scream with relief when I find an old shotgun with a tarnished barrel and wood handle tucked into the corner. I frantically search for cartridges, fumbling to get them in the barrel. I take off manically sprinting again, hoping I'm not too late.

I creep back to the loft. I hear Finn taunting William and can tell in the way his voice shakes in response that he's one more insult away from firing. My hands are slick with sweat and my heart pounds in my ears as I round the top of the stairs.

William jabs his gun against Finn's forehead and my legs almost give out, terror like I've never known poisoning my blood stream. "You arrogant bastard, I'm going to kill you!"

I slot the shotgun under my armpit and raise the barrel, willing my hands to remain steady. "Not before I blow your head off."

Both sets of eyes spin to me, and I feel an eerie sense of calm as I straighten my aim on William's chest. "Step the fuck back from my husband."

His eyes narrow in disbelief and his mouth falls open and closed with a lost response. His stunned silence is all Finn needs to leap up and knock the gun from his hand. Their arms tangle with each other as they grapple, elbows and knees flying. My mind is racing a mile a minute trying to figure out how to help but knowing I don't have time to sit and think.

I just act, my need to see Finn safe loud and blaring, driving my movements. I close the distance and spin the rifle around to wail him in the back of the head with the butt. He goes limp, collapsing to the side like dead weight.

Finn scuttles over to the pistol on the floor before dashing to me and yanking the shotgun from my hands. He checks the chamber, discarding two cartridges before pocketing them and throwing the empty weapon on the bed. He rounds on me, tucking the pistol in his waistband and clutching my face between his hands.

"Jesus Christ, Ef, do you even know how to use that thing?"

"No." I exhale shakily. "Thank god I didn't have to."

He releases a laugh mingled with a sigh and tucks my head into his chest, "Fucking mad woman."

We work together to tie William to one of our wood dining chairs. He wakes up halfway through, and I get the pleasure of holding his own gun to his head—sans bullets after Finn insisted I wouldn't be touching a loaded weapon until he teaches me how to "not fucking kill myself with one." William scowls bitterly but stopped spewing obscenities once Finn threatened to cut his tongue out.

"I'll be right back." Finn gives my shoulder a reassuring squeeze before walking out the door, returning shortly with a hunting knife.

William's eyes widen as Finn sits down on the couch next to the chair, toying with the tip of the blade with his finger. "Which hand was it?" Finn slowly raises his head to level me with his stony stare. "Which hand did he have around your neck?" My stomach drops with his line of questioning, but I can't deny the sick thrill that races up my spine too.

"That one," I say when he points the blade at his left hand.

"Very well." He stands and pulls out his switchblade from his pocket. My mouth waters remembering that the last time I saw it was when he used it to cut off my wedding dress before chasing and thoroughly fucking me like a wild beast in the forest. William's wrist is tied to the arm of the chair, and Finn pushes the handle of the hunting knife into his palm so his fingers splay open on the wood.

I watch his breathing deepen as he looks on, frightened, both of us in suspense to what Finn is going to do next. Finn stabs the switchblade through William's middle finger and into the wood, like a viper sinking in his fangs, with a blood curdling scream from him. I clutch my hand to my mouth and bile crawls up my throat at the same time sparks of vengeful intrigue shock my system.

"I don't like anyone laying their hands on my wife, Campbell." His voice drops to a low and dark timber. "I don't like it at all."

Finn notches the hunting knife at his wrist, and he begins to scream, plead, wail. My shoulders roll down my back and I set my jaw, preparing to watch a man be relieved of his hand.

As Finn slowly cuts into his flesh, I think he's purposely dragging it out. But then, to sounds of agony, Finn begins to work the tip of the blade under the slit at his wrist and lifts the skin from his palm.

Completely undisturbed by the ear-shattering screams being torn from William's throat, Finn continues his bloody craft. Methodically, he flays every inch of skin, peeling it away from the muscle on his palm and every finger until it dangles like a fleshy glove around the switchblade still staked through his finger.

Finn straightens back up after hunching over his work and rolls his neck as if stretching from a nap. Wordlessly, he saunters over to the kitchenette and begins washing his hand, along with the blade.

My feet remain glued to the floorboards, and I can't seem to tear my eyes away from the raw, meaty lump dripping blood over the chair arm and onto the floor. William is slumped in the chair, sweaty and pale. His eyelids flutter, and his breathing is an odd mix between heavy and shallow. His similarities to Hudson are exceptionally striking at this moment. I can't help but wonder if Hudson's hand would look just like this skinned.

I hear the faucet shut off and watch Finn walk casually back over to me, drying his hands on a white towel before looking up. The darkness in his eyes slams into me but it doesn't scare me. It compels me because I know its depths. Like the serenity and wonder that accompanies the terrifying chill you get looking into the black of the deepest ocean. The deeper the darkness the fiercer the love.

He pulls the handgun from his waistband and holds it out to me, handle first. "I know I said you weren't touching a gun until I taught you how to use one, but if you want it, the kill is yours."

I look at the gun, then at the bleeding mess of a man in the chair. I turn back to Finn, letting a small smile peeking through. "I have a better idea."

[32]It's Sunday, ten a.m. Which means my father will be having espresso and playing chess at Nonna Rosa's after mass. When we arrive, the front door is unlocked as restaurant staff are still coming and going with morning deliveries before opening in a few hours. We barge in, Finn keeping William moving with a gun between his shoulder blades as he shuffles holding his bandaged hand.

I used to love coming here as a kid. It felt like family, the waiters and cooks spending time at our table and always bringing out my favorite pasta without ever having to order. For dessert, when my parents got espresso, us kids got vanilla ice cream in the cutest glass cups in small, melon-ball scoops. I used to like stacking the little globes into a snowman while my brothers would try to fit them all in their mouths at one time.

But as I grew up and realized the insidious underbelly of the place, it lost its charm. Men would disappear into the walk-in and come out hours later beaten and bloody. There were always groups of young soldiers who'd look at me with lecherous eyes and crude remarks as if somehow that would get them their boss's daughter. This is a sanctuary for bad men, but it's never been for me.

Today, I don't feel any of that trepidation or unease of the hunted. Instead, I walk in like the hunter. I head straight for the walk-in freezer and am not surprised to see a fresh-faced recruit standing in the back.

I look him in the eyes and order, "Open it." His gaze bounces between me and the men behind me with a concerned and indecisive look. So I give him a little help deciding, I grab William's wrist and he groans in pain as I wave his bandaged hand at the guard. "Open the fucking hatch or you'll be my husband's next craft project."

"M—Ma'am," he sputters and hurriedly gets to lifting the floor panel.

32 you should see me in a crown—Billie Eilish | SummerOtoole.com/playlists

I've never been one to make a scene, constantly shrinking myself to fit neatly in the background. But being the center of Finneas Fox's world has made me no longer content to stay in the shadows. So I'll make a scene... and a fucking entrance. I push William to the top of the steps and kick him in the back of the knees to send him tumbling down.

There's chaotic shouting down below as he crumbles to the floor of the speakeasy. I walk down unhurriedly behind him. My resolve hardens as I hear my father curse roughly in Italian. I step onto the floor as my father and his associates are all in various phases of reaching for their weapons at the unexpected arrival. Cigar smoke thickens the air and mingles sourly with the smell of fresh coffee.

"Father." His eyes meet mine and for the first time in my life, I think I see the look of utter surprise on his face. I don't have to look behind me to know Finn's got my back. His presence and strength permeate the room.

"*Euphemia,*" he gasps and contorts his face with a sneer.

"I always knew you weren't a good man. Or honest or loyal. But if there was ever anything I respected about you, it was that you always did your own dirty work." He narrows his eyes in a silent threat. A gesture that used to make me cower, now looks like a fragile and desperate attempt to intimidate.

"So imagine my surprise, when William here—" I kick his huddled form still on the ground and he moans. "—said that he knew where to find me because *you* told him. Not only that, but you also suggested he 'go get what he's owed.'"

He opens his mouth, but I hold out my hand. "Hudson Campbell is dead. Governor Campbell is going to prison for the rest of his miserable life. And William here," I look down at him in disgust, "isn't even worth my goddamn time—"

"You're nothing but a whore—"

"*I'm speaking.*" I hold his stare, daring him to interrupt me again. "The only reason I bothered returning your trash is to tell you this is the last time. This is the last time you meddle with my life, with my marriage."

"Euphem—"

"Try again and I will put you down like a rabid dog."

His mouth opens and closes like a fucking fish, red and steam raising on his face. He snarls, spittle flying. "You're no daughter of mine."

His hands ball into fists at his sides, and I know with confidence those fists will never hurt me again. "You're right. I'm not a Luciano. *I'm a Fox.*"

Epilogue

Effie

The door to my newly built studio opens and Stella pops her head in. "You ready, babe?"

"Yeah, almost. Can you help me with this?" I hold up a gold chain necklace.

"Course." She comes in, pausing to look at the canvases on the wall. The setting sun washes the studio in a warm golden light and Stella looks at the masterpieces in awe. "Wow."

I tilt my head, still finding new things to appreciate in the painting Finn bought at the gala. The colors are so vibrant and layered, the brush strokes crude in places and seamless in others.

Stella's nimble fingers clasps my necklace around my neck, then she gives me a once over. "Just gorgeous." Her smile is warm and infectious as she offers me her arm. I loop mine around her elbow.

[33]We built the studio on the farm just a short walk from the lake. String lights hung in the trees light our path, and my stomach is awash with excited butterflies. I opted to go barefoot, something about it just felt right. The forest floor is cool under my feet and fireflies flickering between the trunks breathes a whimsical feel into the air.

"Are you nervous?" she asks me as we get closer to the dock, and I have to laugh.

"No, I feel like I've done this a hundred times already."

Though as we round a small bend in the path and the dock comes into view, I'm not sure that's honest. My heart beats faster as I make out Finn's frame at the end. Harlow is the only one bringing a pop of color to the group in a slick, red dress. All the boys are dressed in black like it's a funeral rather than a wedding. Well everyone except Alfie who, when he turns around to watch us approach, is wearing a pink striped tie with his navy suit.

My eyes lock with Finn's, and my breath is snatched from my lungs. Even in the dimming daylight, I can see the vibrant jade of his eyes and his jaw clenches when he takes in my white, flowing dress. We step onto the dock, our footsteps making a hollow thump, and he drags his hand over his mouth with a slight shake of his head.

I can't believe you're my wife.

His words from the gala echo in my head, and my chest feels light realizing that after tonight, I finally will be, with no strings attached. Just me and him, forever. The way it was always meant to be.

Cash stands at the end of the dock next to Finn, his hands clasped in front of him.

My eyes get misty as Stella walks me down the aisle—if I can even call it that, with it being so short. She hands me off to Finn after a quick hug and squeeze.

I look down at the water and my first tear falls at what I see. Candles floating in the pond in between the lilies, lighting up the water, with glowing reflections dancing on the ripples. My bottom lip trembles, and he reaches out to brush his thumb against it as if we are the only two people here. He

---

33 Dandelions – slowed + reverb—Ruth B., slater | <u>SummerOtoole.com/playlists</u>

tips my chin up with one hand while the other taps a gentle tattoo on my palm: water lily.

"Well," Cash begins, "Let's hope this is the last time we have to do this." I snicker, but Finn cuts his brother a glare. "Alright, let's get to it."

To start the handfasting ceremony, Cash pulls out a green twisted cord and instructs us to take hold of each other's right forearms. He has Finn hold one end of the cord and wraps the rest around our hands twice before handing me the other end. The entire process, Finn continues to rub light circles on the inside of my wrist.

"Finneas." Cash nods to him, and he takes a wedding band from his pocket with his free left hand. My heart skips a beat as I hold out my left hand and he slides the ring to my first knuckle.

Finn licks his bottom lip and meets my eyes. "I've made a lot of mistakes but loving you was never one of them. I may not be a gentleman, but you are worthy of gentle love, and I vow to give you all you deserve and more."

As he slips the ring down my finger, I struggle to see all the ugliness of our past as anything but gifts because they carved the path to this moment.

"I never wanted a gentleman. I only wanted you." I give his forearm a squeeze, and the taut muscles flex under my hand as he squeezes me back.

My throat constricts and warmth blooms in my chest as Cash passes me Finn's ring. As he holds out his left hand for me, my eyes dance over the fresh water lily tattoo now covering the back of it. I find our story to be much like the plant itself: incredibly resilient, still able to bloom even after the coldest winters.

My tongue twists around the emotion trapped in my throat, and I will my sunflower tears to wait until after my vows. "You've shown me the beauty in darkness, the strength in myself, and the perfection in ruin."

As I glide the ring to the base of his finger, Cash pronounces, "By the power vested in me by Instant-Online-Ordination-dot-com, I now pronounce you husband and wife, *again*."

Our friends and family clap, and Finn quietly clears his throat, giving Cash a nudging look. "Oh, right...you may kiss the bride!" Heat floods my cheeks as Finn dives a hand behind my neck and through my hair before dipping me low with a kiss that burns through my entire body.

Everyone roars in applause and cheers, and he pulls me back up but is in no rush to end it. I lean into him, feeling every layer of heartache, pain, trials, and tribulations it took to get here melt away.

In the time since we first stepped on this dock eleven years ago, we've spent so much time trying to find the razor fine line between love and hate, too stubborn and afraid to choose a side. When in reality, the line never existed. I've always been his and he's always been mine.

Dear reader,

Hey, thanks for reading to the end! Finn and Effie hold a special place in my heart and hope they stay in yours too. If you enjoyed it, it would mean the world to me if you could take a minute to review this book on Amazon. Even a one-sentence review helps! Reviews are truly the best way to support indie authors, and I appreciate every single one. I know other readers do too. Effie and Finn continue to make Bartlett Farms home...To read this extended spicy epilogue, visit SummerOtoole.com/hatemeextra and get a sneak peek at who the next Fox brother to find love might be.

Feel free to reach out to share with me your theories, reactions or anything else you liked (or didn't) about this book on Instagram @SummerOtoole and TikTok @SummerOtoole. Or we can go old school and shoot me an email at hello@summerotoole.com.

Wanna talk book boyfriends with often questionable morals? Join me weekly on The HEA Book Club, available wherever you listen to podcasts. Or join Little Teaser's (Hot n Ready): A Facebook Community for Smut Lovers at Facebook.com/groups/LittleTeasers

Acknowledgments

I don't even know where to begin thanking you, my readers, for all your support and love for this crazy family. *Make Me*, book 1 in the Fox Family Crime Syndicate series hit number one best seller in several categories and made it further up the charts than I ever dreamed of. Your excitement for the next book was so meaningful and kept me going, pushing to make this story the best it could be. I hope I did it justice.

As always a huge thank you to my entire team of alpha readers: Jess, Val, Angie, Naomi, Shani, Alexandra, Malika, Muftiat, Bonnie, Suz, Meghan and Kimiya.

Naomi, thank you for being my author twin and always helping me get out of my spirals. Your talent is so raw and impressive, I feel so lucky to be able to watch your journey and have you be a part of mine.

Kristie, thank you for taking my random criteria and whipping it into something hot and fun.

Meghan and DJ, thank you for your insight and assistance. I hope you get your own backpack of wonder one day.

Shani, I can't put into words how amazing you are and how much I relied on your friendship and brilliant brain.

Val for keeping my life together. You're not only an incredible friend but a terrific PA and I literally couldn't do this without you.

I'd like to recognize the bravery of Iranian women. Hadis, one of the characters *in Les Arnaqueuses,* was inspired by one of the protestors who lost her life fighting for women's rights in Iran. While her story is fictional, the threads of her life woven into the story are inspired by the complicated lives of Iranian women and their immense bravery, strength and selflessness.

Kimiya, thank you for helping me bring Hadis's character to life. May she forever be alive and happy in fiction.

Kelsey, I don't know what I would do without you. Thanks for being my best friend.

To my FHH, you all are the absolute best. Thank you Haylee for the crooner tunes, Angie for the excited screeches, and Mary for the outfit descriptions and endless facts. I turned to you guys so many times and you were always there for me. Your support is unfathomable, and I consider myself so lucky. To my Gabby, my forever valentine.

Also by Summer O'Toole

The Fox Family Crime Syndicate Series
Make Me
Hate Me
Keep Me (coming June 2023)

The Taken Series: Dark Historical Romances with lethal heroes and fearless heroines.
(Interconnected Stand-alones)
Stolen at Sea*
Stolen to Fight
Stolen Secrets

All content warnings can be found at SummerOtoole.com/content
*read for free at SummerOtoole.com/freebook